# HIS SEED

AN ARBORETUM OF EROTICA

EDITED BY
STEVE
BERMAN

UNZIPPED

Published by UNZIPPED BOOKS,
An imprint of LETHE PRESS
118 Heritage Ave, Maple Shade, NJ 08052
lethepressbooks.com

ISBN: 9781590213063

*

'Audrey Jr. 2017'
by MICHAEL BUKOWSKI

Cover and interior design
by INKSPIRAL DESIGN

# CONTENTS

# INTRODUCTION

I REMEMBER A SPRING AFTERNOON when I was in elementary school and the sweatiest boy in class, out of breath from his endless running around the yard during recess, plucked one of the countless buttercup flowers. His fingers looked dirty, as if he had to unearth the bright yellow flower rather than snap its tiny neck. He dashed over to me. He shook as he gasped breath. He asked if I wanted to know whether I liked butter (*who didn't*? I thought at the time and still do) and, when I nodded, he brought the flower to my chin, tickling my skin. He bent down so he could see if there was a reflection, proving I did like creamy butter, and, in doing so, took one misstep. He bumbled into me, I fumbled backward, and we both tumbled to the ground. His limbs covered my own, his sweat-streaked face, pressed against mine, and...

I never wanted the other boy to get off me. I remember this happy accident but not his name. The color of the flower but not the color of his eyes.

A book of vegetation-themed gay erotica might seem a bit...well, queer, but when was the last time you went for a stroll at a botanical garden? I happen to enjoy such walks and am always amazed at how homoerotic shoots and stalks and pistons can be. I'll admit imagination is really to blame.

A dare is to blame for this book. A dare with Matthew Bright, the designer of both the cover and the interior. Puns in gay titles have a long and august tradition dating back to 1855 and *Leaves of Grass* by Walt Whitman (honest; consult Jerome Loving's biography of Whitman; though I accept guilt for being meta in this introduction). A number of authors share my giddy game of inventing titles for erotica books that would elicit groans. And so when I suggested *His Seed* to Mr. Bright, I only anticipated a chuckle, not a very lovely work of cover art. I felt as if he had called my bluff. How could I not see if I had a green thumb?

(Actually, I don't. Mother does. She moves potted plants from room to room based on the angle of sunlight and the appetite of her cat. And that's all I'll ever say about my mother and her cat in an anthology of gay erotica.)

Thankfully, in this, the Era of Kale, we've grown to admire, desire, and readily consume Nature. The stories that follow range from the whimsical to the weird, chilling to thrilling.

I hope these tales quicken your pulse, perhaps to the same rushed beat that happens when a boy finds a flower pressed to his chin, then finds a another boy atop him, and wonders what is growing inside both their jeans.

STEVE BERMAN

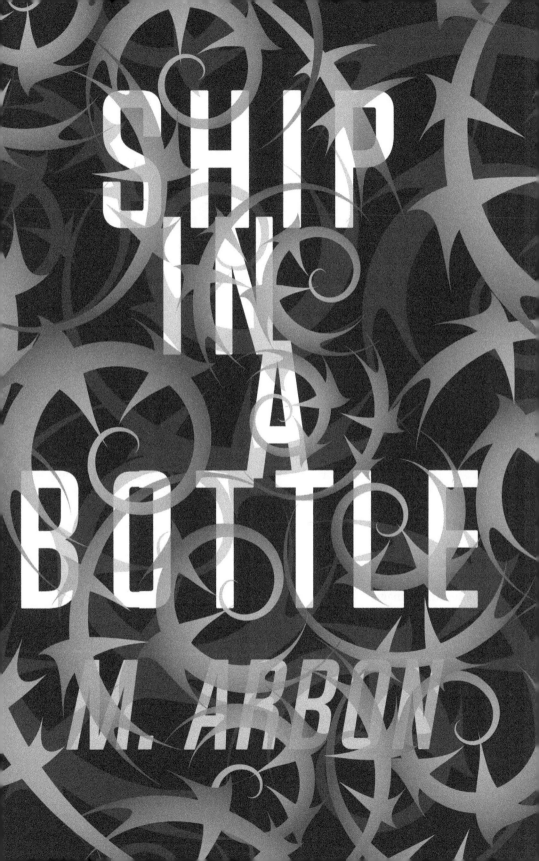

## 1888

"LOOK, EDGERTON LEFT HIS COAT," said one clerk, pulling it from the hook in the convenient modern closet the new building's architects had included in the office.

The other snorted. "I doubt he'll be coming back for it, after that exit."

"It's good enough cloth." The first rubbed the dense boiled wool between thumb and fingers.

"To hear him tell it, he could buy a hundred coats tomorrow and never feel a dent."

"Hmm. It'll never fit me." The clerk glanced over. "It'll never fit you."

"Yes, yes, I *am* short, thank you for reminding me. Why is Edgerton's abandoned coat any concern of yours?"

"We binned thirty years of flotsam and jetsam when we moved. Why do we have to immediately start cluttering the new place up?" The clerk stretched out a long arm and dropped the coat on the farthest hook at the back of the closet. "If it's still here in the spring, I'll bundle it up for the church rummage sale. Don't let me forget."

## 1916

"THAT'S NOT MINE. MINE HAS a velvet collar."

"Flash," muttered his friend, putting the coat back on its hook. "I think this is Jenkins's, isn't it?"

"Is it? I don't remember him in it. It looks a little old-fashioned, don't you think?"

"Jenkins wasn't a natty dresser. Isn't, I mean. And when he comes back, he'll want it."

They were both silent for a moment, thinking about those who would never be coming back.

"You're right, best leave it," the first said. "This yours?"

"Finally. Come on. It's chop night, and I don't want to be late; it's the only recognizable dinner my landlady serves all week."

### 1954

"IT MUST BE MR. SIMPSON'S," she said. "It's about his size."

"Freddy? Aww, he'd never wear an old sack like that."

"You're going to be in such trouble if he ever hears you call him that. Anyway, I meant his father." She ran her palm down the thick black sleeve.

"Mustn't throw it out, then. I'm sure we've cleared enough space. Let's get one of the boys to move the boxes in. I'm dying for a cigarette."

### 1976

"SHHH."

She giggled. "*You* shhhh."

He pressed her against soft cloth. "Would you like it," he whispered, "if we did it right here? Against Mr. Arnold Get-Me-Some-Coffee-Hon Dane's good winter coat?"

"*Oh*," she said, and reached for him in the darkness.

### Now

ALEX STAGGERED FORWARD AND GRATEFULLY dropped the box onto the surface of the desk.

"What's in that one?" Cheryl asked.

He flipped open a flap of the lid. "Some kind of paper." It had green and white stripes, and holes in the sides.

Cheryl clicked her tongue. "Blue box it. How much more to go?"

"I think that was about it." Alex ducked back into the closet. Oh, right, that coat. He lifted it off its hook. It felt good and solid over his arm, a weight equal to any Toronto winter. He backed out of the closet door. "Do you know whose this is?"

She shrugged, tossing an unopened box of Sharpies into her tote bag. "Probably left behind by some hipster douchebag consultant."

He laid it out over the back of one of their twelve-hundred-dollar ergonomic chairs. Dark, straight-cut, classic, the kind of coat that made him think of black-and-white movies, silk scarves and leather gloves. Judging by the shoulders, it might actually fit him. "Is it okay if I take it?"

A handful of cello-wrapped Post-its followed the Sharpies. "Take anything that isn't nailed down, I couldn't care less. In fact, if you see something you like that is nailed down, go get a goddamn pry bar. It's all going to be condos in a year anyway."

Cheryl was bitter. Cheryl'd been banking on stock options and early retirement, and what she'd gotten was two weeks' notice and a bagful of stolen office supplies.

That was what came of having *expectations*.

Alex slid the coat on and stretched his arms out. The sleeves were a little long, but it felt good. Substantial.

"Okay, that's it for me," Cheryl said, hefting the bag over her shoulder. The phone on her desk rang. She gave it an incredulous eye. "See you in the unemployment line."

"Yeah, take care."

The coat was a little heavy for September, even if they were having the fall's first cold snap, but wearing it would be less trouble than carrying it. Alex gathered his windbreaker and bag.

At the door to the offices he paused and looked over the bags of trash, the denuded cubicle walls, the shredder with a few festive curls of paper hanging over its edge. There hadn't actually been much to the job, making it the best eighteen months of his working life—ordering sushi for catered meetings and pigging out on the leftovers, flirting madly with hot graphic designer Matthew, taking two hours in the afternoons to pick up his boss's dry cleaning, dicking around on the Internet. He'd always known it wouldn't last.

Well, it was back to the coffee-shop mines for him.

But he was walking away with a well-padded bank account, eligibility for EI for the first time in his life, a backpack full of Moleskine rip-offs customized with the company's exceedingly cool logo, and a pretty decent winter coat. Best of all, Cheryl aside, there had been almost no drama: no firing, no quitting, just the quiet sale and gutting of an internet startup that had been barely more than imaginary to begin with. He could have done way worse.


THE WAY THE COAT BRUSHED against his calves made him swagger a little as he walked, and he stuck his hands into the side pockets on pure movie-montage-fuelled instinct. They were deep enough that his hands didn't fill them. That made him wonder whether there might be something at the bottom of those pockets, say, some forgotten wallet or a lost iPhone with a reward attached, and he broke his stride to pat himself down. Nothing in the side pockets. Nothing in the right-hand breast pocket; nothing in the left.

He almost missed the last pocket, a little slit in the lining, just the size for a key or, he supposed, a pocket watch. He poked one finger inside, and his fingertip met cool, smooth glass.

He stepped off the sidewalk and stopped entirely to tease it out. It was a small, clear bottle, the length of his palm. There was a cork stuck fast in the neck, and a tightly rolled, age-browned scrap of paper inside.

Cool.

Somewhere in his cutlery drawer there was a corkscrew that had followed him home from some waitstaff job or other. The instant he kicked his door shut, he threw the coat and his bag over the back of the couch with one hand and rummaged in the drawer with the other, a maneuver made possible by the fact that his kitchen was two Masonite cupboards, a sink, and about six inches' worth of countertop glued against one wall of his bachelor apartment. The cork wasn't thick, and he ended up pretty much destroying it getting it out of the way.

He upended the bottle and shook the paper out into his hand.

It wasn't a roll of paper after all. It was...a twig?

Something happened.

He blinked. The world shivered and dipped, like when he'd had that weird reaction to that tropical nut trail mix that one time.

Something...dropped? Landed? Appeared, on the scuffed parquet of his floor. A man. On hands and knees, breathing hard. Naked.

The man's hands tightened into fists. "Ten years!" he gasped. "You fool, did I not say but *ten*—"

He flung his head up. Under its cherrywood hue, his skin had a sallow tinge. His eyes were frantic, black pupils nearly eclipsing irises like backlit spring maple leaves.

"Have you any idea what you," he panted, "you nearly—I nearly—"

He took a long, shuddering breath, and seemed to see Alex for the first time. "You...are not he," he said uncertainly.

"I'm guessing not," Alex said.

The man sat back on his heels. "Is this the year of your lord eighteen hundred and ninety-eight?"

"Nope."

The man rubbed his arms as if to comfort himself and looked around the shabby apartment. "Well," he said, and wearily pushed cinnamon hair out of his eyes, "fuck me green."

ALEX DUMPED VEGETARIAN CHILI OUT of the can into the smaller of his two pots and set it on his hotplate.

"This fastening is baffling," the man said, frowning down at the zipper on the hoodie Alex had given him.

"Okay, just a sec." Alex gave the chili a stir, and walked the three steps over to where the man sat on the arm of the couch. He demonstrated, zipping the hoodie up over the *Keep calm and chill out* T-shirt he'd gotten for volunteering at that meditation thing in the park last summer.

"We do not fashion from metal on my world," the man said, rather defensively, Alex thought. His accent, though mild, was precise and faintly clipped, like Oxbridge through Stuttgart with a detour via Delhi.

"No big deal," Alex said. He went back to stir the chili again, because the hotplate didn't offer much of a middle ground between "lukewarm" and "carbonized."

The man followed him and sniffed over the pot. "Do you eat beasts on your world?" he asked.

"Well, *I* don't."

"At least you are a civilized people." That was under his breath. "However, I fear that your dead foodstuffs will not fully restore me."

Alex looked at the chili, which wasn't an aesthetic dish in any event and now looked markedly less appetizing for having been described as *dead*. "So when you said you needed sustenance, what did you mean?"

The man went to the larger window and peered upwards through the grimy glass. "Does your sun's light reach this abode?"

"Sure. For about twelve minutes, about half an hour ago."

He shook his head. "After so much time, my reserves are gravely depleted. How close is the nearest nourishing ground?"

"That depends. What does one look like?"

"What does—oh. Yes. I forgot that animals cannot nourish themselves directly. It must be such an inconvenience."

"You looked like you needed something fast," Alex said, letting the man's slightly patronizing tone pass.

"Yes. I thank you." The man looked abashed, and gave him a strained half-smile. "It will be a green place where all are welcome."

Alex turned the dial on the hotplate to Off. "Let's go."

THE BLUE TITANIUM WALL OF Frank Gehry's art gallery addition loomed above them like a stage set of a summer sky. Alex had begun to lead the man into the park proper, but his guest had stopped on the western edge, in a patch of orange-tinted sunlight, and begun pulling off his socks and shoes. "This will suffice. We have little time before your sun sets."

"If you're going barefoot you might want to watch where you step," Alex said.

The man looked down at the cool grass. "Do hooligans despoil your public nourishing grounds?"

"...Yes," Alex said, considering and discarding a long explanation about syringes and broken bottles and inconsiderate dog owners and the lack of public washrooms downtown.

He clicked his tongue. "People are everywhere the same. Very well, I will remain in this spot." Foregoing the zipper, he took hold of the hem of the hoodie and pulled it over his head. His hands, Alex noticed, were shaking. Then he grabbed the bottom of the T-shirt and divested himself of it as well. He pushed both articles of clothing towards Alex, who took them by reflex, and his hands fell to the drawstring of his baggy yoga pants.

"*Whoa*," Alex said. "Okay, stop there."

The man looked at him curiously. "I have said I will remain here."

"Yeah, better remain in your pants, too."

"But—" The man made a face. "Very well. It is not ideal, but I will have what I can now." He dug his toes into the grass and lifted his reddish-brown arms to the fading sunlight. His eyes closed.

Alex glanced around. On the tail end of rush hour on a cool late September weeknight, there were still people walking home through the park, or heading down to Queen Street to grab dinner. On the other hand, this was downtown Toronto; a reasonably attractive shirtless guy could jump up and down and shoot a rainbow laser show from the top of his head, and most people would shrug and walk on past.

Not being "most people" himself, Alex turned back for a discreet eyeful and—

*Wait, what?*

He stared until the sun dropped below the line of buildings across the street. His visitor sighed, lowered his arms, and opened his eyes.

"Was that what you needed?" asked Alex.

"It was but a tidbit," the man said, "and your soil is packed hard and laced with unpleasant contaminants, but there is nothing for it but to wait until your sun rises again."

Alex handed him his clothes. "So, about you turning green..."

The man's head popped through the neck of the T-shirt. "Receptors are tender. We have evolved—you understand evolution, I take it?—to protect them when not collecting nourishment."

Alex thought about that for a second, and decided to just keep rolling with this thing.

They crossed the street. Alex stopped at the line of newspaper boxes to pick up a copy of the city's free lefty weekly. It often had ads for medical study participants; a few years ago he'd scored a month's rent in one admittedly dismal weekend by not sleeping for thirty-nine hours straight.

"You have much green in your city," the man said, looking up and smiling faintly as they passed under century-old ash and chestnut trees on the way back to Alex's apartment.

"Yeah, it's not too bad," Alex said. "Look, what's your name? I'm Alex, by the way."

"It is a pleasure to make your acquaintance, most generous Alex. You may call me..." He gazed into the overhead branches. "Names are complex to translate. To those I work with, I am...Instinctual Middle Redleaf? Is that acceptable in your tongue?"

"How about just Redleaf?" Which sounded like someone's World of Warcraft name, but elf, alien, whatever.

"That will do."

Mrs. Yeung, who had the first-floor apartment in the house, was sitting out under the porch light with her Sing Tao Daily and her post-dinner cup of "tea." Alex waved to her as they went in, and she raised an arthritis-stiff hand at him in return.

"I thought perhaps you had the responsibility for this abode. But do you live communally?" Redleaf asked as they mounted the creaking stairs.

"In this city? I'm never going to afford to own," Alex said. "But it's cool. I don't need the hassle."

"I admit I have always hoped to be the caretaker of my own grant of grounds," Redleaf said wistfully. "But the pursuit of scientific knowledge is not as lucrative as it would be in a better world."

In the apartment, Alex filled his small kettle with water and plugged it in. Long discussions always went better with a pot of tea.

When he turned around, Redleaf was yawning. "I must rest. Where shall I sleep?"

"Sleep? It's not even eight o'clock."

"Ah, I see. You are nocturnal?"

"No, I—okay. You can have the couch. Tomorrow, I'd like to ask you some things."

"Of course." Redleaf put a hand on Alex's arm. His fingers were room temperature. "I am grateful to you, Alex. An unexpected thing has happened, and without you it might have gone much worse for me. I will be happy to satisfy your curiosity when I have recovered."

"It's cool. It's not the first time someone's surfed my couch," Alex said, and went to get his spare blanket out of the apartment's single closet.


HE WOKE WITH A SPARKING surge of adrenaline to a pounding on his door.

"Alex! Friend Alex, are you awake?"

"Nnnnrrg," Alex said to the empty apartment, and rolled off his futon to shuffle to the door in his boxers and turn the knob.

"Your door closed behind me, and I lack the cellular pattern to open it." Redleaf pushed into the apartment. "Come greet this glorious morning!"

Alex blinked at him. Redleaf's skin was a deeper cerise shade than it had been, and had lost its dullness; he looked sleek, almost polished. His eyes had darkened to the green of orchid leaves.

"So I guess you got breakfast?" Alex said, yawning.

"It was marvellous! Your sun is strong, and your generous neighbour of the name of Ho granted me access to his grounds. He is a most gifted steward. It was a feast! I feel I am myself again."

Mr. Ho had been supplying the neighbourhood with bitter melon, pak choy, and tomatoes from his corner lot for a quarter of a century, and the soil in his garden was like crumbled chocolate cake. On occasion it had made *Alex's* mouth water.

Alex refilled the kettle and fumbled with tea leaves and strainer. "I guess you don't drink tea?"

"Water would be welcome."

Alex scratched his scalp. One of the many benefits of not having to go to work was not having to wake up in time to go to work, but it looked like the universe had alternate plans for him today. "I'm going to take a shower. Don't touch that thing, it'll turn off on its own."

Hot water and peppermint soap worked together to bring him fully awake, and through long if reluctant practice, he was back in the kitchen just as the water was coming to a rolling boil. Four minutes later, he was sitting on the couch with a mug of lavishly honeyed tea and a bowl of dry Cheerios. He put his feet up on the low coffee table, tipping a half-knit chemo cap and a book on making vegan cheese over onto the floor to make room. Redleaf sat on the other end, cross-legged to face him, his hands wrapped around a mug of plain warm water.

"So," Alex said.

"I was injured after my ship ran aground on your world's gravity, which was stronger than I had expected it to be. I paid one of your people gold to guard me while I healed in a pocket dimension, but he betrayed and abandoned me and I nearly perished there," Redleaf said.

"...Huh," Alex said.

"My poor, brave ship did not survive, but I planted another from her seed. She must be well past maturity now, and I must harvest and shape her in order to return to my world."

"Well, okay, then." Alex turned a Cheerio on its side and broke it between his molars. "Okay. Interesting."

"Do you have further questions?"

"I can think of a few, yeah." Alex took a slurp of hot tea, and looked at Redleaf's glossy hands against the blue Starry Night mug. "First thing, why aren't you, like, an octopus or a nasturtium or a cloud of glitter or something? Why are you a *guy*?"

Redleaf let out a snicker. "A nasturtium?"

"You know what I mean."

"I do. As it happens, wherever in the universe there are sentient species, this is the shape we take. Even on worlds where it seems anomalous, which are many. It is one of the great mysteries." His lips twitched. "Nasturtium!"

Which brought Alex to his second question. "How can we understand each other? Did you study English before you came?"

"Your tongue? No, no. I grafted a translation bud long since." He paused, the mug cradled in front of him. "Is our communication unclear?"

"It's...a little idiosyncratic. Nothing to worry about," Alex reassured him. "Did you actually say you were in another dimension?"

"Of a sort. I created a pocket in which to heal while I waited for my ship's new generation to grow."

"So, uh, why were you naked?"

Redleaf stiffened a little. "I had more than enough to do transporting only myself and could take nothing with me. As I say, my ship was injured. *Plenty* of travellers cannot do the calculations manually."

"Relax, no judgement here." He regarded Redleaf's new glow. "But you were there longer than you planned?"

"Much longer. I fear I was pushing the limits of my endurance. It was supposed to last a mere ten of your years. I left the token that brought me back to you in the hands of a Trust." He pressed his lips together. "Never would I have imagined that he would break faith with me. A *Trust*!"

"What's a Trust?"

Redleaf stared at him. "Has the tradition died out? Become degraded? That would at least go some way to explaining the situation."

"I've never heard of anything like that."

Redleaf tilted his head at Alex. "How did you come into possession of my token?"

"It was in this old coat someone left at my—wait. Wait." Alex squeezed his eyes shut and envisioned the antique wood panelling and frosted-glass doors of his soon-to-be-condo-ized former workplace. The chipped gold curve painted on the main office entrance, words passed so often they had become invisible to him: *Simpson Trust Co. Ltd.* "It was a trust company?"

"Yes, as I have said, a Trust."

"*Really* different thing, I'm guessing. So you just walked in and...gave the first guy you saw a bottle and a handful of gold?"

"*Trust* was written on the door!" Redleaf said. "I explained my need to the young man behind the barrier. He seemed sober and accommodating. Who would dare impersonate a Trust? There is no reason I should not have relied on him!"

"Yeah, exactly how much gold did you give him?"

"It is always difficult to judge the local markets, and I was short on time. Perhaps five hundred grams?"

Alex crunched a Cheerio contemplatively. Yeah, he could see it: Crazy guy with a twig in a bottle and a bagful of gold, check. Random low-level employee, check. Somebody making a quick decision and skipping town with the proceeds, check.

Redleaf's mug clattered against the coffee table as he set it down. His hand was over his mouth. "He *did* abandon me."

"Looks like it," Alex said apologetically.

"He abandoned me to my death." His complexion had gone dull.

"Not to your death. Hey. You're safe. Totally safe. *Breathe*," Alex ordered as Redleaf swayed where he sat.

"I-I knew the journey to your world would be perilous, but—" Redleaf swallowed. "To have come so close to death due to another's negligence..." His jaw tightened. "That perfidious wretch."

"There's always gotta be one," Alex agreed.

Redleaf stood. "I am sorry, Alex, I will answer any more questions you have later, but now I must go to my ship. I must see her."

"Yeah, no problem. So did you...bury it or something?"

"I planted her, yes."

Alex rubbed the back of his neck. "Um, yeah. So, you buried something, what, a hundred and twenty-five years ago... I don't want to freak you out, but Toronto's changed kind of a lot in that time. How are you even going to find, um, her?" *If it still exists.* There wasn't a lot of downtown that hadn't been excavated deeply for highrises since the fifties. On the other hand, if anyone had ever found an alien spaceship buried under the city, he was pretty sure he would have heard about it.

"Ah, now this I am certain of. I planted her near a landmark I knew would endure, your highest institution of learning. "

What year had he said, eighteen-ninety-something? U of T had to be that old, right? "Okay, I think I know where that is."

"Is it near?"

"Yeah, we can walk there."

"Very good! Let us go at once."

Standing up, Alex crammed the last handful of Cheerios into his mouth, and chased them with a cooling swig of tea.

"I am not keeping you from your employment, am I?" asked Redleaf, as if it had just occurred to him.

"Me? Nah, my last gig just ended yesterday. I've got time."

Redleaf watched him shove his bare feet into laceless Keds. "What work do you do?"

"For money, you mean? A bit of everything. Barista, cater waiter, messenger. Office temp when I can stand it. To tell the truth, when it comes to work, I'm pretty much a slacker. I've got other stuff to do, you know?"

Alex turned from locking the door behind him to find Redleaf looking at him with interest.

"A slaker?" he said in that curious, crisp accent. "You slake? Interesting. I did not know they had such people here. That is a happy chance." He turned and barrelled down the stairs. "Come, Alex, I am anxious to meet her!"

They had slackers in space, or alternate universes, or wherever? People really *were* the same all over, Alex marvelled, and followed him down.

They headed up Beverley Street, Redleaf's urgency pulling Alex along in its wake. The only times he stopped were to lean over fences and step onto lawns to put both hands flat against the trunks of some of the taller trees.

"They breathe shallowly," he said distractedly, not looking at Alex. "The water parches them with its—salt? How can that be? We are not on the ocean here. Their roots are boxed in by stone on all sides. I planted her where I could find her again in a strange city. Perhaps it was too near the buildings. Is she confined? Is she undernourished? Will she be able to speak to me?"

Alex traced a finger down a valley between rough plates of bark. "Are the trees actually telling you those things?"

"No, no, they are not awakened. But—I can sense what they feel."

"They're not...in pain or anything, are they?"

"They do not know anything better," Redleaf said, and let his hand fall.

At College Street, Alex turned them east, towards the older buildings on campus. As they passed the pillars that marked the university's official entrance, Redleaf looked up and grabbed Alex's arm. "That is it!"

Straight down the brick-paved road and across the lawn of King's College Circle, the central tower of University College pointed to the sky like the vanishing point in a perfect perspective drawing.

By the time they were halfway across the field, Redleaf was jogging, and when they neared the building he was running full out. He dashed across the road with complete obliviousness to traffic. Alex had to stop to let a Beemer hybrid and a couple of irate cyclists go by, and when he caught sight of Redleaf again he knew it was bad news even before he reached his side.

Redleaf was hunched with his arms folded over his stomach, pacing around and around in a tight circle, looking up at the building, then down at the ground, then up again as if there were something he might have overlooked on the previous dozen passes.

Alex looked at the trees that shaded the building's age-dark stones. Tall, but he'd bet none of them was anywhere near a hundred and ten-odd years old.

"She's not here?" he asked softly.

Redleaf flapped a hand at the corner of the building. "She would be right where I stand. This many paces from that arched window." He made another circuit. "I see no mark of roots, no swell where she was left to feed the soil." He turned again. Alex suspected he wasn't even aware he was doing it. "She has been gone for years. Decades, even." He took a hoarse breath. "Did she live near her full years? Was she felled young by lightning or disease? She would never had been awakened. She would never have known—" He bent over as if in pain.

"I'm sorry," Alex said.

"I left her," Redleaf whispered. "I should have stayed. I should have tended her."

"You said you were injured...."

"I should have found some way." His voice shook. "My ship's line is ended, her daughter is gone, and it is my fault. My greed, my pride." He ran a hand over his face. "And I pay, though not as dearly as they. They are lost to me, and I can never go home."

Redleaf knelt, and pressed his palms against the grass. When he rose again he pulled his hood over his head, shadowing his face. "Take me away from this place, Alex. Please."

When they got back to the apartment, Redleaf crawled onto the couch and lay in a tight knot, knees bent up to his chin. Alex spent the afternoon half-heartedly surfing job sites on his laptop, sending off a few emails to temp agencies he'd used before, chasing obscure hashtags through Twitter, and scoring low on Bejewelled. At lunch, and again at dinner, he left his futon and went over to the couch to ask Redleaf if he needed anything. Redleaf shook his head and said nothing.

The next morning, Redleaf hadn't moved. Alex left a mug of warm water on the coffee table for him and went out for some literal and figurative air. He dropped by Dustin's juice bar and vegan eatery to shoot the breeze and see if he was hiring (no). He browsed the new magazines at his local library branch and treated himself to a two-dollar bahn mi at the corner store. He stopped into his favourite bike shop to see if there were any jobs open (no). On the way home he ran into the ex of a party planner he'd been waitstaff for. She had just started her own catering business, and he came away with the possibility of work once things picked up for the holidays, if his EI benefits had run out by then.

Redleaf was still on the couch.

The mug was half-empty, though. Alex replenished it, grazed on salsa and chips for dinner, soaked in a hot bath to read a few dozen pages of the battered copy of *Infinite Jest* he'd been trying to get through for the past year, and made it an early night.

The sound of his door closing woke him.

The windows were grey in the dimness. Rain thrummed on the roof.

Something—instinct or just curiosity—prodded him. Alex switched on the lamp on the floor beside his futon. He rolled out of the bed alcove and pulled yesterday's cargo pants and sweatshirt on over his T-shirt and boxers. He dropped his keys and i.d. into a pocket, slipped his feet into sandals, and grabbed his jacket and umbrella from the hook on the back of the door.

Morning traffic drove and cycled past, headlights bright against the rain-thick dimness. Alex shook the umbrella open as he scanned the street. Movement caught his eye: a woman dashing past in business suit and red rubber boots, the piercingly orange vest of the crossing guard two corners down. Would Redleaf have gone left, towards the park, or right, towards Mr. Ho's, or...

A shape detached itself from the bough-shadowed trunk of the pine tree across the street. Redleaf slogged across a front yard of patio stones streaming with runoff, and put his hands against the ancient elm that dominated the next yard. By the time Alex had reached the sidewalk, he had moved on to another tree a few doors down, reaching over the low iron fence that edged the lot to press his palms on it like a faith healer awaiting a miracle.

Alex caught up to him at the chestnut on the corner. "Hey, Redleaf," he said. "What's up?"

The man's eyes were closed. "Alex?"

"Yeah. What are you doing?"

"I must find one. There must be one."

"What are you looking for?"

Redleaf pulled his hands back from the tree, and looked at them. "One I can awaken. One I can shape, and slake. One who will take me back home."

His hair was slicked to his scalp and the sides of his face. His hoodie was sodden and dripping. Alex angled the umbrella, futilely, to shelter Redleaf's face. "You couldn't have waited until it wasn't raining?"

"Your season is darkening. Already they are withdrawing and thinking of sleep. I have little time."

Alex sighed. "You can't touch every tree in Toronto."

Redleaf turned evergreen-dark eyes on him. "If I must."

Cold water seeped through the backs of Alex's pants. "Fine. Let me help."

"You have not the knowledge for this." Redleaf pushed by him and rounded the corner to encircle a sapling with his hands.

"But you must have criteria, right? Where you come from, you don't just talk to every tree until you find the right one, do you?"

Redleaf blinked water out of his eyes. "We grow them from established lines." He was silent for a moment. "But yes, when we seek new stock, there are qualities we look for, that is true."

"So come inside and tell me what they are," Alex said. "Or draw me some pictures. We can narrow down probable locations online. Or at least I can Google some photos of parks. Don't just go wandering around an unfamiliar city in the rain fondling trees. You'll get arrested for trespassing or hit by a minivan or something."

Tilting his head, Redleaf said, "This online...is it like the tangle?"

"Is that what you call the place where you keep all the information and blogs and porn and illegal movie downloads?"

"The knowledge and the stories, yes."

"Close enough." Alex changed hands on the umbrella, and stuck the freed one, cramped with cold, into his jacket pocket. The storm front must have dropped the temperature a good ten degrees between yesterday and today.

"Compatibility is not a matter of *knowledge*," Redleaf said. "Can you fall in love by brushing someone's node in the tangle? It is *feeling*."

He moved as if to step past Alex on the sidewalk, but Alex stopped him with a hand against the clammy cotton of his sweatshirt.

"You won't make the right choice as long as you're panicking," he said.

Redleaf bristled and began to say something. Alex overrode him firmly. "There are better ways to do this. And honestly, you're freaking me out a little. Just come upstairs and we'll work it out, okay?"

Redleaf glared at him for a moment, then looked away.

"Very well," he said stiffly. They were both silent as they squelched back across the street and up the stairs. Alex unlocked his door with chill-clumsy fingers. Redleaf sat down on the couch, back rigid.

Alex reached into the bathroom and snagged two towels from the shelf. He tossed one in Redleaf's direction. "Go throw those clothes into the bathtub. I'll get you something dry."

Redleaf went. Alex peeled off his own pants, which were wet to the thighs, towelled himself down, and changed quickly into thick sweats and a woollen sweater. He looked at the increasingly faded and worn offerings on his closet shelves—a laundromat and possibly a visit to Value Village needed to be in his near future—and grabbed a change of clothes. He bent his arm around the half-open bathroom door and dropped them on the floor.

The kettle had boiled and he was sitting on the couch with his hands wrapped around a mug of tea and an afghan over his feet when Redleaf emerged from the bathroom.

"Show me the—" he said, and paused. "Alex? Are you ill?"

"No, I'm *cold*," Alex said. "Aren't you cold?"

"No, of course not. My kind are not afflicted by temperature in the way that animals are." Redleaf's eyes widened. "Oh. You believed that I was uncomfortable in the rain."

"Well, yeah."

Redleaf's shoulders drooped. "You are a better friend than I could even have wished for, had I chosen one for my stay here." He grimaced. "You were quite correct. I was panicking. And I have been known to become... fervent when pursuing an idea."

"Not a problem," Alex said, recognizing the spirit of an apology when he saw it. "You've had a rough few days." He leaned forward and tapped the trackpad of his laptop. The screen bloomed into brightness.

Redleaf sat down beside Alex. He put out a hand and traced a finger along the rounded corner of the screen.

"It is so odd to me," he said, "that you fashion things rather than growing them."

"You grow computers?"

"Is that what you call them? Yes, our nodes are the portals to the tangle." He made a circular motion with his finger against the screen. "How do you communicate with it?"

Alex demonstrated the trackpad and the keyboard, making the cursor trace the curves of the mandala on his desktop.

Redleaf shook his head in fascination. "Perhaps one day I may return at my leisure and spend some time learning your world's ways."

Alex thought back to their earlier conversation, and the questions he hadn't had a chance to ask. "You said you crash-landed. What were you coming here for in the first place?"

Redleaf stared with an air of absorption at the screen.

"You're not a smuggler or something, are you? Or a pirate? Are you a pirate?"

"I beg your pardon, I am a man of science! And it's *perfectly legal*," Redleaf snapped. "Just..." He cleared his throat. "Just somewhat inadvisable."

"What is?"

Redleaf sighed. "Very well." He braced his elbows on his knees as he sat forward. "I have said that we raise our ships, and our other technologies, from established lines. There are also those of us who work with experimental strains. We incorporate new materials, with their unique forms and energies, found on different worlds. The amount we can learn and improve is endless! These materials are additions to, not replacements for, the traditional lines, and to think that we must choose one or the other is— Er. That is a discussion for another time.

"But in my generation, the exploration for such new materials has slowed. Branches other than mine have staked claims on materials from the easily reachable worlds. All they have left us is dregs and salvage. For those of us not long from saplings, prospects are scarce.

"Except! There are worlds that have barely been explored and that are mysteries to us. Anyone who succeeded in travelling to such a new land and bringing back viable samples for breeding and study would be welcomed into any branch he chose. He might even earn enough to establish his own branch.

"Your world is one such. The passage to it is, as I have said, perilous and arcane. I was warned against it, but still, its ferocity surprised me." He looked down at his hands. "At the time, it seemed worth the risk."

Alex hovered his fingers over the keyboard. "What kind of samples are you looking for? A particular kind of plant?"

"Oh, yes. Several."

"Okay. Give me an example."

Redleaf pursed his lips. "I am working through a schematic for an improved communication node, and I lack the perfect element. The stems must be straight, the energies long and silken, the flowers imperfect so they yearn towards another, and orange pink dawn as through the ether they stitch round silver together in braids." He looked at the laptop, and then at Alex. "Why are you not doing your computer? Was that not clear enough?"

Alex leaned back against the couch. "What do you think you just said?"

"I described the characteristics of a plant I seek." He tilted his head. "Does your world use a different taxonomy?"

"Pretty much completely different, yeah." Alex scratched his nose. "Those were all actual words, but I have no idea what that meant."

Redleaf titled his head. "If I say to you that my ship was deep golden seeing and polished to the heart...?"

Alex shook his head.

"Interesting. It seems the translation bud has its limitations."

Alex extended his hands over the keyboard again. "Let's start with the basics. What does it look like?"

"What does what look like?"

"The plant you're looking for. The...long silk silver dawn one."

"Why would its appearance matter?"

They stared at one another.

"Okay, new plan," Alex said.


THEY STEPPED DOWN, AND THE streetcar creaked away at speed.

As they waited for the light to change, Redleaf looked up with interest at the tree-dense hillside on the other side of the Queensway. "You say this is a sanctuary of plants?"

"Yeah, the website says there's a couple of different kinds of woodlands, and marshy habitat near the pond, and there's cultivated species in the flower beds and allotment gardens. It's the largest park close to downtown." The light winked to green, and he stepped off the curb. "But there are others, and they're not impossible to get to, so don't freak out if you don't find what you need today, okay?"

Redleaf had sped up ahead of him, and was already closing his hands around the gnarled branches of a lichen-covered tree beside the park path.

Alex shrugged. At least he'd been able to persuade Redleaf that they should wait until the rain actually stopped.

Three hours later, he had a picture in his mind of a High Park so different from the one he knew that he felt as if he were seeing in entirely new colours.

The weeping willows that dotted the eastern edge of Grenadier Pond were in fine health, but "truthfully, for artists," Redleaf said, with a roll of his eyes. The bulrushes made him wrinkle his nose and look past them up the path. When they passed a stand of the park's famous Sakura cherry trees, Redleaf smiled at them sidelong and dipped his chin, but when the path took them along a row of forsythia, he went yellow under the gloss of his skin, and pulled Alex by the elbow until the embankment blocked them from view. He wouldn't explain why.

He spent a long time with the chrysanthemums in the flower beds that made up the maple-leaf-shaped central garden, stroking their thickly clustered petals, looking from orange to purple to rust.

"Maybe, I think—this could—I would have to twine—" he muttered, and left them with a frown of speculation.

They were cutting across the lawn when he gasped and dropped to his knees.

"These. You have *these*?" He cradled a golden blossom against his cupped hand.

"Is that rare?" Alex asked.

"Rare, and treasured." Redleaf brushed a thumb over feathery petals. "I would not so far forget myself as to rob a sanctuary, but—friend Alex, I know many who would pay dearly for such as these."

"For those," Alex said, looking down at the cluster of late dandelions in the damp grass.

"If you could only feel how their lustre pulls at me! And this one in particular has a sustained harmony of which I have never seen the like. An I am able to return to your world a second time, I would trade you much gold for even a few specimens."

Alex pursed his lips. "I...might be able to get you a good deal on some."

Redleaf looked up at him. "Within the bounds of the law?"

"One hundred percent," Alex reassured him.

In the restored black oak savannah, Redleaf embraced trunk after trunk, while Alex surfed a few disappointing job sites on his phone.

"They are so *aged*," Redleaf said as they climbed the trail up to the park road. "Even the youngest among them is well at the end of their shaping years. There are perhaps two I might call to me—though whether they might awaken at all..."

"It's not the only park in the city," Alex reminded him.

Redleaf shook his head. "I understand. Yet it is frustrating. Everything is so *muted*. On my world, their qualities would sing to me the way your birds call, but here, I must be near atop them before I can feel their colours. What if I pass steps from my best match, and never hear?"

They followed the road as it sloped back south to the streetcar tracks. The sun, lowering towards the west, speared out from under of a glower of grey clouds, and a mosaic of greens glowed to life around them.

"We haven't even touched the east side of the park," Alex said. "Tomorrow, why don't we—"

"Those are not so old," Redleaf said, and veered off onto a path that led up railway-tie steps and through trees and knee-high undergrowth. Alex, with a brief struggle to accept the moment and not think instead of dry socks and a cup of tea, followed.

Redleaf wove through the young trees as if through a crowd of friends, putting his palms against them, letting the whip-thin ends of branches drag through the curl of his fingers. He checked himself at one, closed his eyes, patted it, and moved on. He smiled at another, but kept walking.

Then he stopped in front of a sugar maple. He looked up at its summer-burnt leaves, and laughed with relief in his voice. He put his hands on both sides of the trunk—they went perhaps halfway around—and rested his forehead against the grey striations of its bark.

"This one. Oh, friend Alex, this one may have me."

Alex rested his hand against the tree. The bark was rough under his skin, and damp from the rain. "What do you do now?"

"We will see if she will let us inside her. The calculations—fortunately these I know well—but hush, let me—"

Alex waited, while Redleaf whispered under his breath, nodded and shook his head, and finally pulled away and opened his eyes.

"She is awake." His smile glowed. "Give me your hand."

Alex put his hand in Redleaf's outstretched one. Redleaf's skin was smooth, and no warmer than the air, and—

The world staggered.

Alex squeezed his eyes shut and opened them again.

He wasn't sure where the light was coming from, but he could see the wall beside him clearly, an undulation of polished wood curving up into leafy shadows above his head. Across a space that didn't feel quite like a room, he saw...vines? Moss? A sensation of both coziness and openness, a softness to the air, an anticipatory stillness.

"Are we...inside the tree?"

"After a fashion," Redleaf said. "I have drawn out a pocket of its heart spirit, thought it golden with longing, rooted it to the physical plane and pulling with the leys brought it young and sap running to house us."

Alex lifted a hand and held it an inch from the sleek wall. "Is it all right if I touch it? It won't be hurt or offended or anything?"

"Of course you may touch her. After all, now comes your part."

"My part?"

"You said you were a slaker, yes?"

Gingerly, Alex brushed his fingertips along the wall. He didn't feel tingling, or a heartbeat, or any kind of movement. At the same time, it didn't feel like furniture. More like something large and slow, sleeping.

"I'm happy to help, but I'm not actually sure what you want me to do," he said.

"It is, of course, slaker's choice," Redleaf said. "I am hoping that we alone will be enough. I found one other sufficient before, but each ship is different. I know a pilot who required four." His lips twitched. "He was so exhausted he delayed the virgin flight for days. But I know of no one who has ever shaped a ship from your world, so we are embarking into the unknown. That is not necessarily to our disadvantage. I have been thinking; it seems possible to me that she may hold an affinity for her home, and perhaps that will enable me to more safely run the passage back to your world. If I am able to return regularly, the resources your world may offer to my funding and my research—" He caught himself, and shook his head sheepishly. "But let us deal with first things first."

"How did your first, uh, slaker like to do it?" Coming right out and saying *No* to a new experience wasn't really Alex's style, and he generally found learning by doing preferable to formal instruction, but he was kind of at sea here.

"We decided upon the oldest way. Many pilots have found that the most rewarding. Gratification at the beginning of one's awakening seems to have a sustaining influence."

"Okay, let's do that, then."

Redleaf smiled at him. "I confess, friend Alex, I am not unhappy that that is the method you have chosen."

He put a hand on Alex's shoulder, and the other on his arm, and leaned in to kiss him.

*Huh,* Alex thought. This week was just *full* of unexpected personal growth opportunities.

Redleaf's lips were cool. This close, he smelled faintly of something herbaceous, freshly pruned branches or shoots of new grass. His mouth tasted like maple sap straight from the tree, slightly sweet.

Redleaf stroked a hand down the side of Alex's neck and trailed his fingers over his throat. His thumb inched under the neckline of Alex's T-shirt and sweater, moved slowly along his clavicle.

Alex heard himself make a sound into Redleaf's mouth. Redleaf cupped the back of Alex's head. Firm fingertips massaged a circle at the base of Alex's skull. Redleaf's hands warmed with Alex's body heat. Alex curved his arms around Redleaf's back and pulled him closer.

After a time, Redleaf's mouth left his, brushed along his cheek. Teeth closed gently over his earlobe.

Alex gasped. His hips twitched forward.

Redleaf hummed. "Is that something you enjoy, friend Alex?" Delicate moisture traced the curve of his ear.

Alex shuffled backwards, pulling Redleaf with him, until they shored up at the wall. He could tell he was going to need something to lean on before long.

Redleaf's mouth travelled down Alex's neck. Alex titled his chin to the side. His right hand, curving around the bottom of Redleaf's ribs, met a gap at the edge of his T-shirt. He wormed his fingers in, pulled the cloth free. When he ran his fingers up firm torso and flattened his palm over a hard nipple, Redleaf's breath hitched.

Alex put his other hand on Redleaf's tailbone and pressed him forward. Redleaf's hips angled as his feet moved, one thigh between Alex's, just exactly where Alex needed it. He rotated his hips, not really thrusting, just experimenting with the stimulation, half relief, half tease.

Redleaf's hand dropped to Alex's waist, slid back and down to cup the underside of his ass, fingertips brushing the junction between buttock and thigh, and okay, *now* Alex thrust against Redleaf's hip.

"You must warn me when you are nearing the climax of your pleasure," Redleaf said breathlessly against Alex's shoulder.

Something about that ridiculous, precise phrasing sent a thrill through Alex. "Yeah, getting there," he gasped, with another thrust, aware that if he was supposed to be the representative of all human males he was giving a pretty pathetic showing; they hadn't even gotten their pants open—

Redleaf pulled back from him and stood breathing hard at arm's length.

"Um. What the," Alex managed, gulping in air.

"We must have the self-mastery to make her strong," Redleaf said. He swallowed. "The build, the sustain, the ebb and surge of our need bring her flush to her slaking—"

"Nrgh, *stop talking*," Alex said desperately. *Polar Bear Swim, uncooked steak, uh, practising piano scales, uh... Breathing, concentrate on your breathing.* Noticing that he was panting gave him the ability to slow it down, smooth it out, ignore his body's urgency until he backed away a bit from the brink.

He rested the back of his head against the wall and eyed Redleaf. "Okay. You're on. Just tell me I get to come at some point today."

The look Redleaf gave him sent a jolt straight down through his core. "Oh, yes, most assuredly, friend Alex. I vow it."

The third time Redleaf brought him to the edge and abandoned him there, Alex's knees turned to water. "Gotta lie down," he said hoarsely, and without waiting for a response he pitched forward in a semi-controlled hunch and rolled with immense gratitude onto his back. The sides of his unzipped fly settled against his thighs.

Redleaf, who was already on his knees, sat back on his heels. He looked as ragged as Alex felt, hair pointing in all directions and wet lips parted as he breathed heavily. At some point he had discarded his T-shirt, and his chinos pooled around his knees. Alex wanted to grab him and *don't think of it, think of anything but that, uh, job hunting, filling out forms...*

Redleaf opened a hand against the floor. "I believe—we may be—this feels as if it is vigorous enough for her," he said.

"Yeah?"

"Yes. Now we may continue to our release."

"That...is the hottest thing anyone's ever said to me." Alex rolled his head to the side and grinned giddily. "Come on over here."

Redleaf crawled the few feet to Alex, kicking his pants off behind him as he moved. Alex, unsure he could even prop himself up on an elbow, pulled Redleaf's leg over his and nudged his arms into position, until Redleaf was braced over him on hands and knees. Alex took a moment to relish the view, then wrapped both hands around Redleaf's erection and stroked. Redleaf murmured and began to rock his hips, thrusting into Alex's hold.

Alex felt a tingle go through him with each push. His hips, touching nothing, moved in time with Redleaf's. The second Redleaf touched him, he knew, he would—

"I—oh—haaaa*aaaaa*hhhhh." Redleaf spattered pale green liquid all over Alex's rucked-up T-shirt. Alex, briefly distracted, watched in fascination as Redleaf's arms and chest whirled through sunrise yellow, pale yellow, spring green, acid green, deep forest green, and back to brown, like a kaleidoscope under his skin.

Redleaf staggered down onto his elbows. "Ah—oh—Alex—" His voice vibrated against Alex's ear.

That tiny stimulation went from Alex's ear to his cock as though there were a single nerve stretched between them. He felt the hot rush begin, inexorable; he blindly seized Redleaf's hips, dragged down, shoved up. His body arched against Redleaf's weight. For an agonizing moment he couldn't breathe, speak, move. Then the pleasure burst through the tension. It took him in long waves, hard and shaking, and he heard himself cry out over and over into the waiting space as the rhythm wrung him empty in the best possible way.

He felt Redleaf move off him and slide to the floor. There was smugness in Redleaf's voice as he said, "Yes, she is well satisfied."

"Yay us," Alex mumbled, and closed his eyes.

He must have dozed off, because when he opened them again, Redleaf was fully clothed and standing with his back to Alex, his hands stroking the wall in long sweeps. Alex sat up, feeling both sore and wonderfully relaxed. He gave up his T-shirt as beyond hope and used it to clean himself up, then got into his sweatshirt and sweater and pants.

He watched Redleaf for a few minutes, not sure whether he should interrupt, enjoying the grace and confidence of Redleaf in his element. Then Redleaf glanced over at him and let his arms fall.

"I am coaxing the manifestation of the controls," he explained. "She is eager to take flight."

"So you think you'll be able to make it home?"

Redleaf's expression warmed. "She is a fine, strong ship. I feel certain I shall." He stepped closer. "Friend Alex, I owe you much. Without your luck in liberating me from my own error and your generosity in guiding me through your world—not to mention your fine skill at slaking—I would be in a hard place indeed."

"Well, think of me the next time you help someone else out," Alex said.

"May I find you again if I return?"

"Yeah, absolutely." He wondered how long interstellar, or interdimensional, or whatever-it-was travel took.

"Thank you. You will see me the day after tomorrow, if I am able to come at all."

"Seriously? You can make it back that fast?"

Redleaf looked puzzled. "No, the journey is far, but—ah. I see your confusion. Once I have completed the configurations, my ship will have the facility to navigate the fourth dimension along with all the others."

It took Alex a moment to parse that out. "This ship is a *time machine*?"

Redleaf pursed his lips. "In layman's terms, yes, I suppose you could say that."

Alex felt himself start to grin. The borders of the universe, already porous, began to blow outwards with possibility. "Your *spaceship* is a *time machine*."

"Yes. Is this another point of mistranslation? Were my words imprecise?"

"And you want to pay me gold for dandelions."

"That is what you call those lustrous flowers we encountered earlier? Yes, if you are able to procure some."

Alex brushed the glossy wall with the backs of his fingers. "Do you ever take passengers on your ship?"

"Passengers?" Redleaf blinked at him. "Not heretofore. I have never been asked." He looked down at his hands. "I confess, a partner in my expeditions would not be unwelcome."

"Would your ship mind?"

"I do not believe so. You are linked to her now. In fact," and he gazed at the wall with apparent absorption, "there are some who theorize that slaking done habitually keeps a ship balanced and nimble. I would not be averse to testing that hypothesis. In the pursuit of science. If you are willing."

Alex looked up into the leafy shadows of the ship's ceiling, and smiled at whatever was up there that he couldn't see. "I'll see you the day after tomorrow, then."

"I greatly anticipate it, friend Alex."

*Later*

THE DINNER CROWD HAD CLAIMED most of the tables. Alex waved to Dustin, and wove between rickety two-tops and a long communal table to the back of the restaurant, where he slid into the coveted semi-circular booth that hunkered between the kitchen proper and the juice bar.

"Hey, man," Eric said. "How's it going?"

"Great." He peeled out of his winter coat, and grinned at his friends. "I missed you guys."

Shelley took a skewer of grilled tofu from a plate and bit off the end. "Since, like, the day before yesterday?"

Right. It had been more than that for Alex. "It's been a long two days."

"That new job making you actually work for a living?" Micah smirked at him and took a swig of kombucha.

"Oh, hey, did you find a new job?" Marla waved black-nailed hands to get his attention. "Because I was going to tell you, Shirley's looking for a back-up receptionist while hers goes on mat leave."

He wasn't sure he had enough tattoos to work at Shirley's. "Actually, no, I've got a couple of things going on."

"Another web startup?"

"No, it's...I guess you could call it a scientific study. And I've been doing some, uh, import-export consulting."

Shelley poked him with the end of the skewer. "Is that a fancy way of saying you got a job at Ikea?"

"No, it's mostly working with plants. With some bonus travel."

Eric gave him a sharp look. "Tell me you are not doing anything stupid."

"What? No, seriously, nothing like that. I'm kind of...a native guide to a botanist who's not from around here. I can't talk about it, for, um, confidential business reasons, but it's totally interesting and the pay's good."

Marla shook lilac curls in envy. "You find the best jobs."

"Pays well, you say? When are you going to let me sell you some decent clothing?" asked Micah, who got on this hobbyhorse at least once a month. "I can tell that that shirt has been previously enjoyed. And that coat? Like something my grandfather would wear. And not in a good way."

"Hands off! This coat has sentimental value." Alex raised a hand at Annie, who was waiting tables tonight. "Anyway, I have better things to spend my money on. I hope you guys are hungry," he said, and ordered every dish on the menu that he hadn't tried yet.

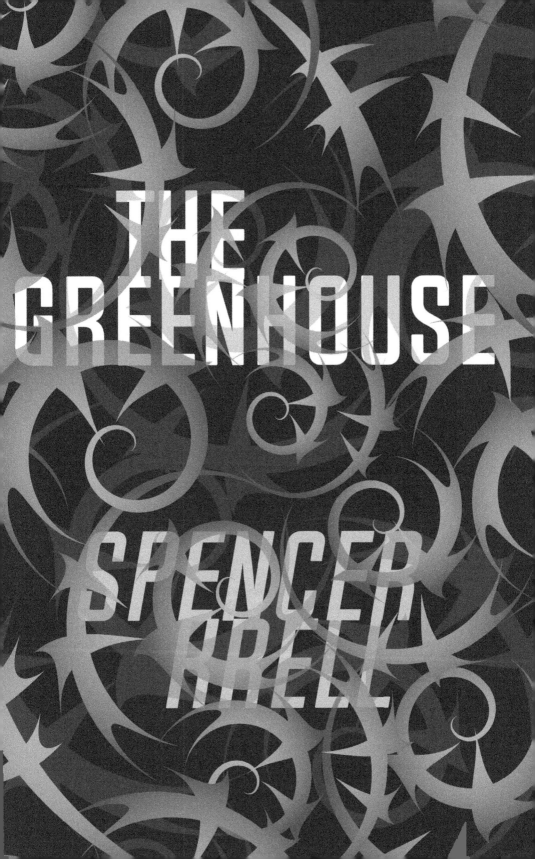

# THE GREENHOUSE

SPENCER REEL

THE GREENHOUSE WAS THICK WITH warmth; Aaron felt like the very air itself was caressing his skin. Outside the leaves were turning brown and falling from their branches; soon there would be snow on the ground and the greenhouse would serve as an even more welcome refuge against the long winter months.

It wasn't yet cold enough to warrant the heat being turned all the way up, not that the pumpkins he'd spent over a hundred days growing would mind it. Like him, they thrived in the heat. He smiled to himself at the sight of the round, orange gourds nestled against their deep green leaves, tendrils curling outward like beckoning hands.

As a child he hadn't understood his father's love of gardening—all those hours spent kneeling in soil, planting and pulling weeds and muttering about early frosts ruining crops. It had always been nice to have a plethora of pumpkins to choose from when Halloween came around, but beyond that, he hadn't really seen the use for it and to his childish palate, homegrown vegetables had tasted just as bad as store bought.

By the time he'd grown older, he'd realized the benefits. It was far cheaper to grow your own vegetables than to buy them from the store, and fresh herbs were an easy way to lend taste to a meal. Once he'd bought his own house, he kept a modest garden plot in his backyard and even went so far as to consider canning to make the vegetables he grew last into the winter.

Though he considered himself quite the gardener, pumpkins had never been something he planned to grow. They took too long and needed too much space. Not to mention, who would want to spend their whole winter cooking pumpkin into foods when they could just buy a pumpkin version of nearly every food under the sun at the grocery store already?

He chuckled to himself at the thought. The previous autumn he'd seen everything from pumpkin-spice pancakes to pumpkin-spice soda. He couldn't say he really understood the craze himself. Pumpkins were all right to eat and nice to look at when carved, but putting the effort into growing his own had seemed absurd.

Until, suddenly, it didn't. Aaron was a geneticist by trade and while writing a grant for a study involving stem cells, he'd started thinking—what if their changeable properties were applied to food? Mixed with known agents to cause supersized growth, could the produce not only be larger in size but also have its very taste changed?

What would it be like to live in a world where a slice of raw pumpkin tasted of pumpkin pie? What if pumpkins could grow at double—even *triple*—the speed they usually took, so crops could be harvested again and again during the same season, yielding more produce than ever?

Once the ideas took hold of him, he found them difficult to shake. He'd constructed the greenhouse for his purposes, having needed a place where he could control the temperature and amount of light the pumpkins got each day. If he were to run this experiment properly, he'd need to control as many variables as possible. It was important to ensure healthy growing conditions, so the genes he'd mutated in the gourds could work their magic.

Alongside the altered pumpkins, he grew an untouched batch, to serve as a control to the experiment. After their long growing period, those were nearly ready to harvest. The rind was cool to the touch and a deep orange color, like a setting sun.

Aaron knelt in the soil, sliding his hands over the smooth skin of them before slicing through the thick vine with a knife. He wiped his blade on the leg of his jeans and then moved on to the next one. As he worked, a bead of sweat rolled down his temple. The heat of the greenhouse had started to become oppressive and he set the knife down to grasp the back of his shirt, pulling it over his head. He balled up the fabric and tossed it out of the way of the soil, before getting back to work.

After cutting another two pumpkins free from their vines, he stretched, raising his arms above his head and arching his back. The movement highlighted his abdominal muscles; his skin still lightly tanned from hours spent outdoors in the warmer months.

He'd been about to get back to work once more when he felt a slight tickle against his ankle. Before coming out to the greenhouse, he'd slipped on a pair of beat-up tennis shoes without bothering with socks and figured a leaf or stick from the soil was brushing against his skin. Without looking behind himself, he twitched his foot, shaking it off and taking the pumpkin knife in hand again.

After finishing with the fourth pumpkin, he moved onto the fifth. That one was smaller than the others and after a cursory glance at its pale orange-yellow color he decided to leave it. It could use another few weeks of ripening before it'd be ready to cut. That done, he stood, reaching down to dust soil from the knees of his jeans, when he felt a more definitive tug on his ankle.

Looking down, he saw the source of the feeling. A fat, green vine had somehow wound its way around his ankle from the line of genetically modified pumpkins he'd had his feet facing as he'd knelt to work on the control batch.

"How in the world?" he murmured aloud, brows furrowing slightly in confusion. His fingers brushed over the vine, starting to ease its hold on him so he could step out of it. He couldn't imagine how he'd managed to get so tangled up in it in the first place.

When he'd planted the pumpkins, he'd made sure there was a clear line of demarcation separating the control group and those which had been modified. Of course as both lines had grown they'd spread out somewhat, pumpkins and vines going where they pleased. He hadn't been aware they were *that* close to touching, though.

After he collected the control pumpkins, he decided he really should prune some of the vines and leaves from each side, so they wouldn't be in danger of mixing. Though as soon as the thought arose, he felt another insistent brush against him—it was on his other leg now, much higher up.

He watched in awe as one of the vines seemed to move of its own accord, sliding across the soil with deliberate intent. It snaked up his leg to curl around his upper thigh, giving a very definite tug backward.

"Is this some sort of trick?" he asked aloud. He heard nothing in response.

There were no wires or strings controlling the vine's movement that he could see, nor was there anywhere someone could hide who might be pulling a prank on him. The greenhouse had only been built large enough for the pumpkin crop—besides the two rows of pumpkins it contained nothing but a wheelbarrow and a small wooden work-top. The walls were clear glass, giving him a good view of his gravel driveway and the house it led to.

A handful of trees dotted the land on either side of the driveway, though they weren't thick enough for anyone to successfully hide behind.

He was truly alone, save for the dark green vine that gave another, very *decisive*, tug.

A smile spread on his face; taste-modified, fast-growing pumpkins were nothing. With a couple of tweaks, he'd managed to make them *sentient*. He let the vines tug him closer to the pumpkin patch and then knelt down in the soil to inspect the plants themselves. The vines stayed coiled around his legs, though they loosened once he'd knelt, as if they'd achieved their goal.

The pumpkin patch looked the same as always. He leaned closer, reaching out curiously to lay his hand on the pumpkin nestled in the soil nearest to him. The rind was smooth and cool, no different than the pumpkins from the control group.

Unsatisfied, he trailed his fingers up to the thick stem at the top; it felt exactly as it should. It was all so strikingly *normal* that had the vines not still been curled loosely around his legs, he'd have wondered if he didn't imagine the whole thing.

After a few more moments of tactile exploration, he realized, belatedly, that he was still holding his vine-cutting knife in the other hand. It felt almost insane to contemplate such a thing, but if this plant really were sentient, would cutting through the vines to harvest the pumpkins cause it to feel pain?

The shine of the silver blade suddenly looked very sinister when Aaron considered that possibility and he shook his head, reaching into his back pocket for its sheath. The genetically modified pumpkins hadn't been growing as long as the control group because of the rapidity of growth wired into their genes and though they were already full-sized, they could be given a few more days to ripen while Aaron puzzled out what exactly he was going to do with them in light of these recent discoveries.

As he slipped the sheathed knife into his back pocket once more, he saw one of the smaller corkscrew curls near the pumpkin's stem move slightly. His rational mind wanted to believe it was just the result of a draft of air, but he slowly raised his hand out towards it all the same. It pulled back in response, nestling closer to the pumpkin's stem. Aaron shook a lock of dark blond hair from his eyes as he made a soft shushing sound.

"It's all right. I'm not going to hurt you."

The vine seemed to hesitate, shaking slightly as it wavered, before stretching out to touch his fingertip. He moved his hand closer, cupping it so the corkscrew vine could curl itself back into its former shape and rest in the bed he'd made of his palm.

"You're a cute little thing, aren't you?" he murmured to it, still feeling somewhat foolish for speaking aloud to a plant, though it wasn't like talking to one was completely unheard of. He'd heard stories of other gardeners going so far as to even play music to their plants to encourage them to grow, but he'd never been one to give into what he'd generally regarded as a largely foolish and scientifically useless practice.

Now, however, he might be forced to change his stance on it, at least for these special plants. It was a shame there was no way for it to answer his questions, because the scientist in him would very much like to understand just what level of consciousness the plant actually had and how it viewed the world.

Still focused on the curl of vine in his palm, he reached out a hand to lightly brush it as though he were petting a small animal. The vines around his legs that had been still while he'd explored loosened and retreated from his thigh. Once free of him, one moved forward again to slide up his side. It reached out, its green leaves brushing against his arm in the same motion he'd used on the vine. By petting the plant, he'd taught it to pet him in response.

Aaron laughed aloud in sheer disbelief. The sound was rich and deep, filling up the space around them with pleasure. "Are you going to mimic everything I do?" he asked.

Wondering how he could test it further, his lips curled into a smirk as he got an idea. He gently let the corkscrew of vine down and then leaned closer to the pumpkin and pressed a firm kiss to its rind. It was cool against his lips and tasted of minerals from having been grown in soil.

The kiss wasn't long. It lasted a few seconds at most, and when he pulled back from the rind with a smack of his lips it sounded almost obscenely loud in the silence of the greenhouse.

"Mimic that," he encouraged, aware of the slight undercurrent of a challenge in his tone.

Again, he felt the vine at his side move up further; tickling the bare skin of his arm with its leaves as it purposefully slid up his neck toward his face. A broad leaf pressed against his lips with surprising firmness, like the kiss of a lover.

That, too, lasted only moments, though the vine's questing movements didn't cease after it had finished mimicking Aaron's. With a feather-light touch, it traced his lips with the edge of its leaf and moved higher, to the strong slope of his nose to outline that as well. As it brushed across his cheek, the soft flat of the leaf slid against the stubble on his cheeks, tickling him enough to bring another smile to his face.

Aaron's eyes slipped shut while the plant continued its explorations.

He could almost imagine the vine and leaves as fingers trying to memorize the contours of his face by touch alone. After mapping out his nose, it pressed even higher, tracing his eyebrows and then slipping into his hair to work its way through the floppy strands.

Without warning, the vine gave a sharp tug in his hair. A soft moan issued from his lips as his eyes flew open in surprise. Had he really just *moaned* at the ministrations of a plant?

He cleared his throat and shifted in the soil, realizing that sometime during the plant's exploration, he'd started to get hard. His erection tented his jeans now, obvious and embarrassing.

Twin feelings of shame and lust battled in his gut as the vine retreated from his hair to give his face another gentle caress. If he shut his eyes, he could imagine the touch was from fingers to make the whole thing seem less strange. Besides, he was entirely alone. If he allowed things to progress, no one else need know about it.

He shut his eyes once more, banishing any uncertainties from his mind. He was going to see this through, wherever it took him. The vine retreated, slipping down his neck and chest. One of the leaves brushed his nipple on its way, sending an electric current of pleasure through him that caused him to suck in a lungful of air.

Seemingly aware of the impact it had on him, the leaf brushed against him again, feeling as soft as velvet as it ran over the hardened bud of his nipple. At the sensation, all of his uncertainties were expelled on an exhale of breath.

He reached for the button of his jeans, undoing it with lust-clumsy fingers. After tugging down the zip, he shuffled the denim down his thighs along with the boxer briefs he wore underneath, and then spread his legs further; he'd let the vines do as they liked with him.

Despite the relative chasteness of its earlier ministrations, the vine seemed to get the message. It ran finger-like leaves down his chest and then wrapped around his jutting cock, giving it a cursory stroke from base to tip. The sensation was unlike anything Aaron had ever felt before. Though the grip of the leaf was sure, there was no weight to it like that from an actual hand, or the roughness of callused fingers that he'd become used to from most of the men he'd been with.

A shiver of pleasure slid down his spine and he opened his eyes once more to look down at the leaf that had curled around him. It continued its slow, measured glide up and down his cock and he spat into his hand before reaching down to slick himself with it.

The saliva helped the glide and his breath caught in his throat when another tendril of the vine reached up to circle the head of his cock ever so lightly. Between the leaf around him and the vine toying with him, it felt like being touched by a thousand fingers at once and he couldn't help but buck into it, needing more.

*"Harder,"* he urged. His arms fell to his thighs, unsure of what to do with them in the absence of another man's body to hold. Convulsively his hands opened and closed before balling into fists as the leaf obeyed and wrapped itself more tightly around him.

Now that there was some might behind it, he could almost mistake it for a human hand. As the tendrils of the vine continued to toy with him, the leaf alternated its strokes from soft to hard and back again, catching him off guard with its finesse.

He wasn't anywhere near the right frame of mind to be thinking in scientific terms as to *why* such a thing was possible and instead just enjoyed the feeling gave. By the time a second vine began to stroke his balls, he was audibly panting.

The vine angled itself so a leaf could cup them, rolling them gently in their sack. A moan ripped itself from his chest, the sound echoing in the small greenhouse. He reached out for the vines then, needing something to hold as a curl of heat unfurled itself in his belly.

He'd never admit this to another living soul, but Aaron wasn't sure that he'd ever been harder in his life than he was at this moment. Not wanting to hinder the vines' progress, he blindly reached out, clasping one that lay still on the ground. He gave it a squeeze that mirrored one the leaf stroking him had just given. His hand started to move up and down the vine like it was another man's member—or his own, though his masturbation sessions were never this good, or this surreal.

"Fuck—I need—I need *more*," he panted. Despite the change in grip, the leaf continued to stroke him at a pace that was too languid for him to get off to no matter how many vines were on him, exploring his body.

For a few moments the leaf continued its slow slide and he wondered if he'd need to teach it what he wanted, before it gave another squeeze and then started to speed up for a few strokes before then slowing down once more.

His mouth opened into a wordless "o" of surprise as it repeated the motion. The plant was not only self-aware but it had apparently learned enough to know how to tease him. He barked out a laugh he barely had enough oxygen for and rocked his hips more insistently into its touch.

*"Please."* The word was exhaled on a breath; no more than a whisper of sound heavy with all the desire he could fill it with.

In answer, the leaf picked up its rhythm. It continued to alternate its grip as it slid along his cock, no longer exploratory or teasing, but touching him in earnest now. Lust poured hotly into the pit of his belly like wood stoking up a fire. Sweat beaded his brow and hairline, a drop of it rolled down his spine.

He panted openly, the sound peppered with moans, and once, a soft gasp when the tip of the vine brushed the slit in the head of his cock. His hand on the stem of the vine tightened, no longer stroking but just holding on for dear life as his body tensed up.

He felt like a rubber band pulled to the snapping point. Any second now the lust kindling inside of him would flare up and consume him, he was sure of it. He sucked in another lungful of air, just willing it to happen.

The very moment he felt about to be pushed over the edge, everything stopped. The vines and leaves pulled back, relinquishing their hold on him as he fell forward on hands and knees, still trying to catch his breath. The arch of his spine was tight, his body caught on a knife's edge of pleasure without the impetus to be pushed over into the abyss beyond.

His head snapped up, looking at the pumpkin patch in shock and he shook the vine in his hand. "Don't stop now. You *can't*." His words were as desperate as he felt and he didn't wait for the vines to make a move.

Immediately, he let go of it to suck two fingers into his mouth, coating them liberally with saliva. Once they were sodden enough to serve his purposes, he reached behind himself and pressed them slowly inside.

It wasn't often he used spit in lieu of lube. The initial intrusion of his fingers stretched him enough to burn slightly, tamping down on the desperate need to come that he'd felt seconds before. Carefully, he pulled his fingers out before pressing them in again, grunting with effort and the awkwardness of the angle, his jeans still bunched around his knees.

He was so fixated on the feel of his fingers inside himself that he didn't notice the vines moving again until he felt the brush of a leaf against his forearm as the vine coiled itself loosely around his arm. Without stopping, it slid toward his hand as if it wanted to feel for itself what he was doing to his body.

"Are you going to do this to me, too?" he asked it aloud, his voice having lost some of its breathlessly desperate edge.

In response, he felt the tip of the vine nudge against his entrance questioningly.

"Not yet," he cautioned. "You need something to slick you up first." He gently pulled his fingers out and brought his hand to his mouth once more, this time not sucking on his fingers but on the tip of the vine that still coiled around his arm like a lazy snake.

It didn't taste like much of anything in particular; the movement of it against his clothes and skin had brushed it free of any soil that might have been otherwise clinging to it. It was only earthy and the slightest bit sour like a blade of grass. Aaron laved his tongue over it, hollowing his cheeks to suck more of it in.

Once he'd gotten it as damp as he imagined it'd get, he pulled it from his mouth and reached behind himself once more. Consciously relaxing his muscles, he pressed his fingers in again.

The end of the vine nudged against them where they disappeared into his body, pressing in between them. It felt hard, and almost as thick as a finger in its own right. The vine began to mirror the movements of his fingers in and out of his body as it loosened the coil on his arm; growing slack enough for him to ease his fingers out and unwind his hand from it.

He braced his free hand flat against the soil again and let out a shuddery breath as his body adjusted to the movement of the vine inside him. It was odd at first, but soon there was something deliciously exciting about the way it moved. It undulated as it thrust into him, touching more parts of him at once than he'd ever had touched before.

By the first brush of it against his prostate, he was actively fucking himself back on it, his cock openly weeping pre-come into the soil. The fire inside him that had almost been doused was now stoked to full brightness. He felt fevered with it. Having been so close to the edge once already left him nearly delirious with the urge to come.

Needing something to tip him over the edge, Aaron reached for his ignored cock but before he could make contact with his heated skin the vines moved once more. Another took up where the other had left off, slithering across the greenhouse floor to wrap its leaf around him, stroking him in counterpoint to the one fucking itself into him.

With the added friction, he was caught between rocking back and bucking his hips forward; his body nearly vibrating apart with the aggressive sparks of pleasure, leaving him feeling as though all of his nerve endings had suddenly turned to live wires.

Panting open mouthed, his hand felt back to the ground, fingers scrabbling fruitlessly against the soil as his eyes shut tight. "Please—I need...*please*..." he gasped, a string of desperate, nearly inaudible words falling from his lips, ending on a high whine with every press of the vine against his prostate.

A third vine moved toward him; this one brushed his chin and then pressed its tip into his mouth, muffling his lust-babbled words. He closed his lips around it on reflex, almost gagging in surprise when it nudged the back of his throat. Then, he realized what it wanted.

He began to suck. His head bobbed up and down and his cheeks hollowed with effort, treating it like a cock. There was something unspeakably erotic about every one of his orifices being filled, owned, *fucked*.

It was the last thing he'd needed to hurl himself headlong into orgasm. He groaned deep in his throat as though the pleasure were being wrung out of him and his hips snapped forward of their own volition, bucking into the touch of the leaf as he spurted hotly onto the soil underneath.

A rush of blood roared in his ears as he continued to rock into the touch with increasingly smaller rolls of his hips until he was completely wrung dry. The vine in his mouth slipped out of his arms' way and he flopped down, exhausted, into the soil.

As he lay there, chest heaving for breath, he felt the vines and leaves start their slow retreat, pulling away and out of him. They fell to the soil, as immobile as they'd begun.

Once he no longer had to fight for air and the white-out of pleasure had receded from his vision, he took mental stock of himself: his muscles were as sore as if he'd run a marathon, and he could feel the increasingly unpleasant sensation of cooling come sticking soil to his thighs. He desperately needed a shower.

He also needed to figure out just what had actually happened between himself and the pumpkin patch. On shaking arms, he pushed himself up again, grimacing as he did his best to brush soil off him before pulling his briefs and jeans back up again.

Aaron surveyed the pumpkin patch again; beyond the body-shaped marks in the soil near the modified ones, there was nothing else differentiating them from the control group. All was still and silent in the greenhouse, save for his slight huff of breath.

He poked at the soil with the tip of his shoe until his hand and knee prints were obscured from view and then continued his task of loading the control pumpkins into the wheelbarrow.

In fiddling with the pumpkin's DNA, he'd given them the ability to mimic—and even *anticipate*—human needs. It had a much further reach than just growing harvestable pumpkins in half the usual ripening time. He had to tell the world of his creation, but what he'd just experienced in the greenhouse was for him and him alone. He'd take that secret to the grave.

A wistful smile tugged at Aaron's lips as he ran his fingers gently over the orange rind of one of the pumpkins in the wheelbarrow. Then he gripped the handles of the barrow, rolled it out of the greenhouse, and went home.

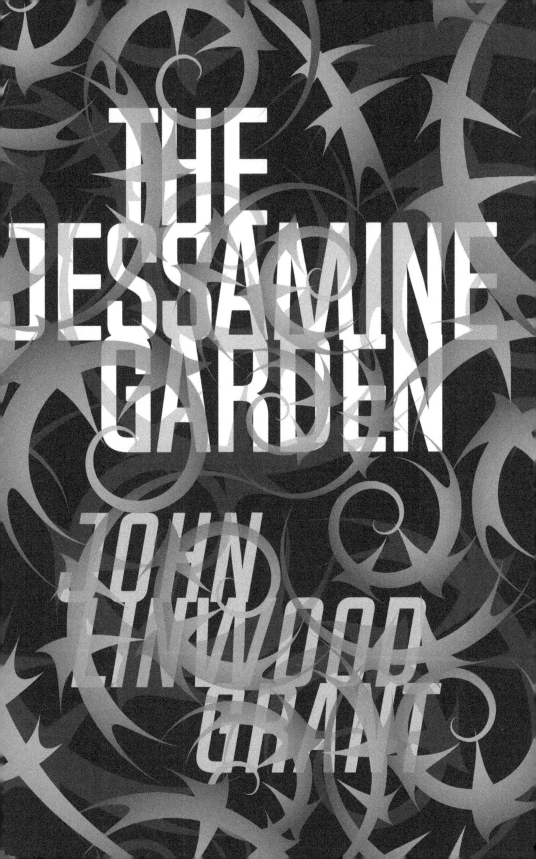

# THE DESSALINE GARDEN

## JOHN LINWOOD GRANT

As I had long been forgotten by the God of my childhood, perhaps the mercurial Fate of the Greeks and Romans had willed me to meet Julian St Claire that slow Virginia morning. I will not name the exact area, for I will be jealous until the end. That I should drive the buggy up the wrong road, distracted by my thoughts, that I should draw up so close to that decayed colonial home...it was meant to be. Capricious Fortuna, her blind eyes smiling on a faithless man.

The house itself was not unusual, a smaller version of the great plantation houses further south. A man of some thirty years stood by the portico, the columns wreathed in unknown vines, thick tendrils grasping at old plaster. He was slim, much my own height but not especially well-favoured in feature. Some might say his eyes too large, his jaw too narrow, to be called handsome.

I reined in my horse, and called out if he knew a better road that I could take to continue my journey.

"I might. But mind the hour. Come down, sir." He smiled. "Take a julep with me, and I shall set you right."

And I was thirsty enough to accept the offer. When he noted how my mare was flagging, he pointed to a stone trough by a barn.

"Let her rest awhile, too."

I returned his smile, and eased myself down from the buggy. Infantile paralysis had left me with a weak left leg, and a bullet in Mexico had shattered the hip above it. I was a poor pedestrian, as he could see. I took up my stick, and was gratified that he removed his cream linen jacket and assisted me in watering the horse. We introduced ourselves as we did so, and he led the way around the side of the house.

A walled garden lay at the rear, ancient brick of a reddish hue, and we entered something which might have graced an English country house, a most un-Virginian landscape.

"My refuge, my garden," said Julian St Claire, spreading thin arms wide, and then he pointed to a stone bench not far away. "We might sit out here, perhaps, Mr Crane?"

Windows in the full-length French style opened into the gloomy interior of his home, but the garden itself was bathed in sunlight. I was grateful to rest as he fetched refreshments. After a few moments he brought out a tray holding two silver cups and a large Venetian jug.

I took my glass eagerly, thanking him, and sipped the coolness of what I had assumed would be a mint julep. I tasted the bourbon but no mint, rather a bitter herb, not exactly unpleasant but unexpected.

When he saw my reaction to the drink, he gesture toward the garden. "Rather than spearmint I prefer my own aromatics."

I assured him that the drink was most refreshing, and looked around. A yellow-flowered climber scrambled along and over every wall of the garden, its perfume on the warm air, its long stems insinuating it into neighbouring bushes and trees at every opportunity. Beneath it lay thickly planted beds which covered the space of half an acre, interspersed with neat gravel paths. No soil could be seen between the plants, which merged and tangled with each other wherever I gazed. There were tender plants there which would have been overwhelmed by hardier ruffians without a hand to guide them.

"The walls... I presume they keep the winter cold out?"

He nodded. "I also rely on bell jars and cold-frames, cloches and manure beds, even an ice-house to keep some tubers and bulbs dormant until the right time."

"It is a marvel. Do you have many visitors, seeking the secrets of your art?"

He leaned closer to me, and I caught the same bitter scent from him as from the drink, though I could not place it.

"I do not advertise, sir." He shook his head. "I fear that many would come to harm here if I did."

My head was light from the bourbon, and I laughed, not knowing why. I could not grasp his meaning. "How so?"

"Come." He waited as I employed my stick, and took me down the main path which bisected the garden. As he named his plants, he stroked them, caressing stems and leaves as a man might calm his hound.

"Rue, whose touch causes great welts to appear upon the skin, especially in bright light..."

I looked at the intricate grey-green foliage which he had stroked, the noonday sun strong upon the leaves, but said nothing.

"The greater celandine, which brings rashes and eruptions, as does this arum low down, see, with its strange saponins and other chemicals. Monkshood..." He tore off a feathery leaf and chewed on it. "A brutal poison when consumed—the tingling and burning presage eventual failure of the heart and nervous system—"

"Sir..."

He raised his hand to quell my alarm. "I am as one with this place. I grew up here, and have long partaken of the abundance of riches my garden provides. Not only my eyes and nose catch the nuance in each leaf, but my tongue catalogues and admires it." He brushed the stand of monkshood with affection. "Please step closer."

I limped to his side.

"Hold out your hand."

It is difficult to say why I did what he asked. Perhaps the bourbon. Or the heady perfumes of the garden? Or just hearing a demand made upon me by a man whose confidence I envied? As I lifted my free hand, his fingertips touched mine and I gasped at a burning sensation which ran up my arm. Reddened patches the size of a penny were left on my skin where he had touched. Yet his own fingers remained unmarked, flawless.

"Hervey—I may call you Hervey?—don't fret. It will pass in minutes."

But I was unnerved. I took a last sip of the julep and made awkward excuses that I must be on my way.

He helped me harness the mare and asked if I cared to call again, perhaps in a few days. Damn if I didn't agree to come back.

THE NEXT WEEK I MADE a brief visit, to assure myself of the location and my welcome. Both were as they had been before. He made gentle inquiries into my trade—portioning out my army pension and a small family inheritance—and my pastimes—reading any book I could find, and surviving the authority of my sole relative, my older sister.

The following day, at his request, I returned for a long afternoon, and a fuller introduction to his garden.

"These are dieffenbachia, often called dumb-cane for good reason." He knelt on the gravel and displayed the broad leaves. "They cause an intense sensation of burning in the mouth, and the tongue can swell to such dimensions that you are indeed struck dumb."

"Is it fatal?" I leaned on my stick and watched him intently. The gentle stroking of each plant; the way in which he plucked small shreds of a leaf and slipped them into his mouth, like a chef sampling herbs in preparation for a fine banquet. That day's drinks had a different, headier aroma than before, and a sourness which fought the crushed sugar around the cup's rim. I had not tasted its like before.

"Often." He stood up. "But it lets us communicate, for a moment, with mortality and what might lie within our souls."

"Mortality? That at least I comprehend."

My comment must have had an edge, because he tipped his head in a curious manner, but said nothing. As we made slow progress back to the stone bench, I worried that I had betrayed a certain defect in character.

"Talk of souls leaves me uncomfortable. I long ago gave up the pew." I judged the distance between us. "This bench is better, this company is better. I hope I do not offend."

"Not at all."

I toyed with my drink, not meeting his eyes. "You say that each plant in your garden, every plant, flows with poisons, and yet you are unaffected."

"Unaffected?" I knew by the tone that I had made a mistake. "I said that I understood this place and what it holds. It affects me deeply, Hervey."

"Forgive me. I am no scientist, though I have tried to follow some of the more interesting themes of our age. I just finished a work by John Gorrie—"

"And you would be guided by the science of diseases?" He made a dismissive sound. "My friend, this is art. This is passion. Try not to wish everything might be examined under a microscope. Or do you think passion needs explanation?

A silence for a moment, or rather a silence that was human. Birds called around us, and insects thronged in the garden, nectar and pollen everywhere for their industries. I wondered not to find them dying in their thousands, the gravel mingled with bee and wasp, hoverfly and butterfly, their wings feeble with toxins.

He nodded when our eyes met.

"Each plant, each blossom, must have its pollinator. A brief union, for life to continue." He examined his slender fingers. "Of course, with the more unusual specimens, there is need for assistance..."

I coughed at the remark's intimacy, and muttered that the julep had gone down my windpipe. Smiling, he refreshed my glass.

"Consider the jessamine." He pointed to where the bees surrounded a nearby specimen of the rampant yellow-flowered climber.

"The jessamine?"

"Aromatic and beautiful, but the flowers can be quite toxic. Even the vines are said to rival the potency of hemlock—I know you've heard of hemlock, Socrates, and his misconceived 'crimes' —"

"Of course, but—"

"The bees have learned how to harvest the jessamine's vigour. Or died. I find each year the hive is hardier."

"Mr Darwin's evolutionary theories in action."

He shrugged. "I suppose. Shouldn't all of us dare death, in the hope to emerge more vital?"

I could find no words to express my thoughts.

We strolled again, down to the shallow stream which ran in the shadow of the far wall. Culverts allowed its entrance and its exit, while its length was populated with plants which loved shade and moisture. Again, all were quite poisonous.

"Did your parents possess your vitality?"

A dead fish, three inches long and silver-white, floated in the current, a passing stranger to Julian. Like myself.

"No." He plucked a leaf of water hemlock and sucked on it, his eyes on the tiny corpse as it headed for the western culvert. "I was orphaned young, and raised by an aunt who took up residence here. She too died, when I was seventeen."

"By poison, I suppose." Nervous still, I laughed. He did not.

"Poor thing. She mistook her herbs."

The fish was washed under a clump of feathery plants which seemed much the same as the hemlock, if shorter.

"Water dropwort," he said. "Also known as the sardonic herb. It was given to the old, criminal and insane in parts of Italy, to dispose of them. Risus sardonicus, the result of ingesting poor, unassuming Oenanthe crocata."

My mind translated. "The... the rictus smile? That of death?"

He bared his teeth in a mock grin. "All men are Sardinians in my garden."

I found his countenance both striking and disturbing. I covered my feelings by suddenly claiming a dinner engagement, an excuse which I do not think fooled him.

As I rode back home, I pondered whether or not Julian St Claire was insane, possibly even a murderer if I considered whether what he said about his aunt might be true.

I had never looked into eyes as large and strange as his, a face which so engaged me. And there was such an undertone to some of his words that I found myself as much captivated as discomfited. It had been so long since last I was drawn to another man. I knew of inverts, men that profess their love for each other, who even dare bed one another. Some time ago, I met a trooper in Texas who had so approached me. I remember his moustache, ruddy at the tips, like embers in the dark of our camp. And how his voice remained calm despite how his hand shook as it reached over my pitiful leg.

Alas, my courage, so fierce in battle days before, abandoned me then. I have often wondered what might have happened if I had accepted his offer. Nowadays I thought it impossible that anyone would look on my deficient physique with eagerness, let alone yearning.

THAT EVENING, I SOUGHT DISTRACTION within the idle chatter of my sister. She was mistress of our ancestral home, and, having been disappointed by a lawyer from Boston some years ago, often disparaged my gender for its many faults.

"I met someone quite...unique today, Mariella."

"Oh?"

"An aesthete. I found his opinions quite stimulating."

"In Virginia?" Her lips warped her mouth and chin to show evident distaste. "First carpetbaggers and now this."

"I think the St. Claires must have fought for Old Dominion."

"St. Claire? Julian St. Claire?" Her fork clattered against her plate, dislodging hard, stubborn peas. "How am I unsurprised you would find the company of the most improper man in the entire county stimulating."

I felt that her words were harsh. "I see nothing untoward about him. His zeal for his garden is no worse than, say, Emerson—"

Mariella's laugh could strip a bone of meat. "Oh, Hervey. If you weren't so shy you might actually listen to what townsfolk say. Your St. Claire causes quite the brouhaha whenever he comes to Richmond."

I could not imagine Julian transplanted from the sanctity of his garden to the bustling streets of any town. "I refuse to engage in gossip."

She sighed and poked at our meager dinner. "No, dear brother. I'm constantly reminded of your quiet tongue, your crippled gait, and your ailing bank accounts."

OTHER VISITS TO THE JESSAMINE Garden, as I now called it, followed. He introduced me to so many plants that I lost count. It seemed that there was nothing within those red-brick walls which could not kill. Cattle grazing there would have been dead within the day, ordinary men who toyed with its contents within the hour. But the garden was less strange than the man.

My own feelings set aside, I was still fascinated as to how St Claire could be so unaffected by the poisons with which he surrounded himself.

He avoided the subject at first, preferring to introduce me to other corners of his realm.

"Here, my friend." He pointed to an attractive plant with many small leaflets. "Jequirity, or Indian licorice. Also know as the jumbie bead. If even a morsel of the small red seed is swallowed it can bring convulsions. Some Caribbean folk take this to be a sign that a jumbie, or evil spirit, has entered the person. Others say to the contrary, claiming that it wards off the jumbie."

"You have tried it?"

He looked at me. "Of course. There is nothing here that I have not tried. Or that another bold soul could not essay for themselves with my tutelage."

I tried to sound unaffected. "And how many have you...instructed?

"It's been far too long. It demands utter commitment and resolve. But surely a veteran possesses these traits?"

The memory of a trooper's parted lips; the stare of an actor outside a theatre near Santa Fe. My throat became dry, and I could only nod my assent.

"Then you must gain experience," he said, "For intellectual exploration is a sterile thing."

"I must take poison?"

"No, I would hardly seek to end our relationship in so coarse a manner."

"My visits are not an inconvenience, then?"

"You are curious. But I think you suffer from a malady that has curiosity as just one symptom."

"My affliction?" I anticipated him remarking upon my leg and hip.

"Loneliness."

I trembled.

He held up a hand. "A man who tends a garden develops an eye for rare blooms. Come, sit with me."

An old log lay near the jequirity, and I eased myself down next to him. The afternoon sun had brought crickets and other insects to the long grass by the gravel—darnel or poison rye-grass, of course. St Claire was consistent in his plantings. The insects strummed and buzzed according to their types as St Claire rolled up his sleeves.

"Do you trust me?" His pupils were wide, despite the sun, almost eclipsing the pale blue irises of his eyes.

Flexing his long fingers, he began to undo the top buttons of my shirt. I stiffened, but did not resist. I expected his touch, but when he placed the palm of his hand against my breast, I think I gave a gasp. This time he pressed down firmly and prolonged the contact. Heat again, more intense than last time. I waited, dry-mouthed, for something to happen...

"Oh." I felt my heart flutter, its beat now unreliable, and a sense of fever, of flush. A rash had already appeared where he touched me, but more alarming was the inner disquiet, that sensation when you first feel fear—or love, I imagine. Despite my alarm I did not pull away. My pulse raced, then slowed, raced again. I knew that in some way I was being poisoned, yet I was also experiencing Julian St Claire.

"Let your heart see for you," he whispered.

He was a fire of blood, laced with such chemicals as I could not imagine, a burning presence of fibres and arteries in a slim, quiet body...

He withdrew his fingers suddenly. Five lines of painful blisters had formed across my breast, radiating from where he had touched me. My pulse settled, faster than it had been but once more under a degree of control.

"What...what are you, sir?" I gasped.

He shrugged, smiled. "A man with a garden. I make no other claims. What should I say about myself? If I stub my toe, it hurts. If I wield a pruning knife poorly, it cuts me. And now I am thirsty, like any man in this long summer. Come."

He took me into the house for the first time. In a barely furnished room which looked out onto the garden, he gave me lemonade from a pitcher, and a shot of bourbon with that same herb as before. This time it seemed less bitter, and I finished it quickly.

"You grow accustomed to my tastes," he said, approvingly. "Forgive the sparseness of the surroundings. I spend most of my time in the kitchen—or in my bedroom above."

I took in the sweep of the stairs to the rear, the peeling balustrades and a glimpse of the landing. Had others trod those stairs before me, initiates into the secrets of the Jessamine Garden?

"The blisters will worsen whilst exposed to light," he said as I hobbled to the buggy. "You should button your shirt, and stay in the shade for a while."

Mariella noticed my discomfort at dinner, though I had tried to keep it turned from her.

"You've been at St Claire's again." Her words were light, her lips disapproving. "I asked about him in town. The locals will not take his paper money. The stores insist on hard coin that can be washed before circulation again."

I pretended indifference, but she was persistent.

"Miss Catchall at the milliner's says that he carries some taint. They talk of cholera or the pox, though they cannot be sure. And then there is the question of his late aunt..."

The chicken was stringy, the beans picked too late to be crisp. I looked up from my plate.

"Gossip, Marie. Gossip about a single man who doesn't engage with fine company, doesn't throw his place open for empty dances and chatter. I've shared drinks with him, had time in his house and his garden. I think that I'd know by now if I had picked up some unspecified plague."

"And your hand?"

"His plants are unusual. I strayed too close to one whose sap is an irritant. I was fully warned, and foolish."

"Yes. Foolish."

She did not play the piano that evening, merely sat embroidering in silence. It was her way of showing disapproval.

I WENT BACK, OF COURSE. He was always there, long dark hair swept back from that pale face and eyes which seemed to see so much more than mine. What had seemed too far from handsome about his features now struck me as an unlikely beauty. I had to think hard about my encounter with the trooper in Starr County to ask myself if I was physically interested in St Claire. I could not answer my own question. His quiet intensity could make me tremble, and his touch brought sensations which were entirely new to me. Was that how men could feel, with other men?

One cooler morning he took me close to the jessamine, had me breathe in its scent and let the air around it fill my lungs. Gently he pressed his fingers to my bare neck.

"Be brave, my friend." he whispered.

My skin burned, my back arched. This time it was not only my heart but the larger muscles of my arms and legs which responded to his touch, a tetany which almost felled me. My weak leg, ironically, was the one which held me upright, for the other locked and then spasmed. He kept me there, his hands at my neck, and through the fire I saw more of myself than ever before.

Pain, and sight through pain, self-knowledge. I knew the damage in my hip as I had never known it before, the minutiae of clumsily-healed bone and misplaced vessels. I traced the flawed muscle of my polio-afflicted leg, and found new things to consider—a slight enlargement of the liver, a knot of tissue round a healed rib, though I had never known that it had been broken.

I do not know if it was his presence, his touch connecting me to him, which provided this sensation, or if some drug coursed through me. In Mexico they had talked of certain drinks, and the exudations of cacti, which made man hallucinate. St Claire had never spoken of such concoctions, nor did he use anything beyond bourbon, to my knowledge.

He eased me down onto one of the many logs by the path, and let go.

The feeling of knowing myself was subsiding as rapidly as it had come, replaced by the acute discomfort of the areas where his fingers had lain against my bare flesh. I reached up with one hand and gingerly touched my neck. My fingers came away moist with watery blood.

"Perhaps we should not do this." he murmured, caressing a jessamine vine. "I ask too much of you."

"I do not...I do not know." I could barely speak. I feared his touch; I wanted it.

He went to the house and procured a bandanna, which he wrapped gently around my neck, before offering me a double shot of rye whiskey.

"Rest before your journey home."

And so I remained there for almost an hour, listening to his occasional remarks on the properties of this plant and that—the sedative effects of baneberry, the many symptoms of poisoning by laburnum, all manner of common and uncommon botanical curiosities. Only to hear his voice had become a pleasure. Had he talked of chicken feed and pork-belly prices, I might have been just as content.

Mariella knew where I had been as soon as I returned. She tore away the bandanna, gasped, and sent Susie, our maid, to fetch the doctor from town.

"You are a fool." she said, and stamped into the kitchen to boil water.

I looked in the hall mirror, and saw for myself—lines of angry pustules on either side of my neck, surrounded by a raised, blotchy area of skin. Some of the pustules had burst, weeping a thin, bloody fluid which had soaked into my collar. The pain was surprisingly bearable, though it worsened when I turned my head.

The doctor came within the hour. He was an elderly man with a long, old-fashioned beard. I had seen in him in town once or twice, and had asked him for laudanum for my hip, which he had supplied. We had never spoken more than a few words, though I knew him for a local man.

"I woulda said poison ivy, seein' as the skin's come up so," he muttered after examining me in my bedroom. "But it's mor'n that, ain't it, and the pattern, fahv marks on each side..."

"An experiment." I said, wincing as he touched my neck. "A... a friend of mine. We were examining the medical potential of some native plants..."

"Around yo' neck?" He paused, clicked his tongue in thought. "I would desist in them damn-fool experiments at once, leave 'em to men as knows. You'll maybe have permanent scarrin', young fellah."

But he smoothed a soothing cream over the area and bandaged my neck with care. I overpaid him, asking that he not expose my foolishness to the town. He weighed the coins in his hand, and nodded.

"Yo' business, Mistah Crane. Yo' business."

Before he left, I took hold of his arm. "Are there...ointments, protections, against these things, doctor? I mean, should I come into close contact with...such plants again."

He stared at me over his half-moon glasses.

"Perhaps by accident," I added.

He shook his head. "Best stay clear, son. That's mah only advice."

I listened to neither the doctor nor my sister. A fever came that evening, though it passed in less than a day. When I could move my neck without undue pain, I returned to the Jessamine Garden.

IT DID NOT ESCAPE ME that I was torn now, between my own reaction to St Claire himself, and a fascination with the effects of his garden. I realised, dimly, that St Claire must have an unnatural awareness of his own body's construction and processes. Through his hands, somehow, had flowed that awareness. And yet his touch was also poison, most literally. Would the one increase and the other lessen? How close could I be to him and remain whole? How close did I want to be to him?

"You must tell me, St Claire." We stood under intertwined vines while bees, so much better adapted than myself, made play between the small trumpet-shaped blossoms. "How can this...condition of yours, this gift, even, be possible? The biology of the matter—"

"I thought you kindred in exploring sensation, yet here you are, playing scientist again. I am not here to be investigated or categorised."

"But there will be reasons, surely..."

"You over-intellectualise, a habit you cannot seem to break." He shook his head wearily. "I am my garden. It courses in my arteries and veins. I propagate what you call poisons along each channel of my nerves, toxins slipping from one ganglion to the next and bringing new sensations. Each day is different."

He explained, reluctantly at first and then with more vigour, how time spent with the different genera brought changes which reflected the plants' own properties.

"There are the cardiac stimulants and arrestants, which flood the chambers or constrict them, so that the blood is flushed into strange places. The foxglove, henbane, aconite and various lianas are ripe with possibilities in this area. You do not know what things I have seen in the grip of such palpitations—"

"But surely this is marvellous," I interrupted him. "The medical men of letters, they must be told of your insights."

I had disappointed him again.

"Medical men? The more I am exposed to my plants, the more I discard those outdated defences which my body once possessed. I accept their ways, embrace them. This is hardly useful to your doctors in their fine laboratories."

Committed to my obsession with enquiry that day, I could not stop myself from continuing, though I knew that I should say no more. I was a child, who asks one too many question and is at last slapped in frustration.

"And you believe, then, that another could become similarly resistant?"

He turned suddenly, a hard set to his narrow jaw.

"Resistant? Do you not listen to me, sir? Those who resist, die. Those who open their arms to new experiences, new intrusions into their being, are open to be changed, improved."

"I meant only that—" I raised my hands in entreaty.

"You should go," he said. "I forgive you, because the mistake is mine. I thought I had by chance found one who could accept, if only momentarily, what I am. And perhaps one who might embrace what I had to offer."

There was no reasoning with him. I left, chastened and confused.

I DID NOT VISIT THE Jessamine Garden for two weeks, during which I chopped wood, as best I could, and saw to some minor repairs on the house. My sister was pleased; I was eaten up with doubt and frustration. The time was a torment. I slept badly, not from any lingering pain but from a sense of loss greater than any I had known before, and on the Monday of the third week I harnessed up the mare, choosing my moment while Mariella was visiting a cousin in Richmond.

My reunion with St Claire was conducted with trembling limbs on my part; a cautious distance on his. He was solicitous of my health, but seemed less inclined to do more than share a julep and general conversation. After a brief stroll, we repaired to that stone bench once more, and I had a sudden fear that I might never sit there again, beside him, in the Jessamine Garden. The thought was unbearable. When I sensed that he was about to dismiss me, I slid awkwardly to my knees.

"I surrender to you, sir." I said. Half the Venetian jug had been drained, mostly by myself, and I was awash with both fear and bourbon.

He tilted his head, and the dark centres of his eyes widened.

"What exactly are you saying, Hervey?"

"I am saying that I surrender to your mystery, sir. I beg that you let me understand, in such ways as you alone choose. Be that in your garden," I swallowed, and made my commitment, "Or in your bedroom, if that is your wish."

I held out my hands in reconciliation. For a moment I thought that I had misjudged entirely. The jessamine throbbed with bees, mocking me with its embrace of life, and I was a damaged thing, pleading. What hope could I have?

He took my hands in his, very lightly, our palms scarcely touching. I felt a burning sensation where his moist skin brushed mine, but I did not reject it. The sound of insects diminished, and I shuddered as my heart beat wild and unregulated, as my muscles cramped. I tasted salt-blood and bitterness in my mouth...

I moaned and gripped his hands with perverse determination, willing him to me.

Do not think that this was so simple a sensation as pleasure. I had not felt such pain since the bullet slammed against my pelvis, but what came with the pain...such insights! I seemed to hear the rustle of every leaf and stem around me, even as I saw into myself again and heard the pump of fluids through my kidneys, the mad rhythm of my own heart. And beneath those, a sound like the throng at Jacksonville railway station, a thousand upon thousand murmurs which were my blood cells forcing their way through narrower and narrower channels...

He pried my fingers free and sat back. There were beads of sweat on his brow and smooth upper lip, a slight tremble to his shoulders.

"Hervey, my dear friend." he said. "I believe that you see now, a little at least."

"Is there...is there more?"

"More? Oh, there is everything, yet. If you dare."

"Please, do not spare me. To go this far..." I held up my hands again, one arm still twitching uncontrollably.

He glanced at his garden, then back at me, his dark eyes huge and wondrous.

"A promise," he said at last. "And a warning."

He placed one index finger on his lower lip, and let saliva form there. I knelt, shaking, as he extended his arm and pressed the same finger to my own lips...

Skin brushed against skin had shocked me. The taste of his clear, bittersweet saliva brought lightning down. My body stiffened, immovable and in that brief contact I felt the garden with such intensity that I thought I might be blinded.

There were colours around me which surely had not been there before—a burning, golden umber where there had been mere brown bark, sullen reds which veined formerly green leaves—all manner of strangenesses which I could not explain. The yellow jessamine flowers outshone the morning sun, almost too much to look at. The air, the air was both sharp and thick at the same time, wave after wave of perfumes which made you wish to retch, which made you beg for yet another gulp of them. This was a chaos of sensation which went beyond my ability to record.

And we were there within the lightning storm—Julian St Claire, solid and as one with it; Hervey Crane in a spasm of experience, barely able to breathe...

"Do you want me to stop?"

Before I could answer, he lifted a glass to my lips. I closed my eyes, let my heart settle. My lips and cheeks were burning, swollen, and jagged pains ran down the cords of my neck. I knew that the half-healed blisters on my neck had opened and were weeping, but did not care. Could not care, in the face of what had happened to me. Nor did I care that my silent flute had become more responsive than my ruined leg. I wanted no more wasted hours.

I felt him stroke my shirt, then walk those rousing fingers down my front, past the buttons of my trousers. His touch, even through cotton, cultivated me, my seed.

I dared not take the reins of the buggy for some time. He offered nothing, gave no help, but stood there, nibbling on a blossom as if to prove that his hunger remained unsated.

I WAS LATE TO BREAKFAST the next day, and had no appetite. Mariella sat brooding at her end of the long table, kidskin gloves on her hands. It appeared that she had been to St Claire's place soon after dawn, and returned pale, her hands cracked and blistered.

She had slapped him, I was informed, and told him that he must turn me away should I ever go back to that "unholy" garden of his. He merely took her blow, smiled, and then was lost within the garden. The swellings on her hands and wrists were subsiding quickly, but she blamed me for everything, even the fact that she could not co-ordinate enough to play her scales, let alone Mozart, to calm her temper

The doctor was called. He attended to her after he had seen to my more serious blisters and lesions. One side of my face would not move, as if it had been whipped with nettles and poison oak, and my neck still bled. I was in pain, sedated and heavily bandaged, but I felt only the promise of what was to come.

I have left letters at the bank, and settled certain outstanding debts. Mariella will be provided for. Soon, horse and buggy will take me to the Jessamine Garden. I shall abandon my austere, irrelevant life for the mysteries within that place—perhaps even for salvation. I am ready to drink the bitterest julep; even a cup of the jessamine's nectar will taste honey-sweet to me. As I write these words, I anticipate the sensation of taking Julian St. Claire's face in my bare hands, and pressing my lips hard to his. I ache for the feel of his bared flesh against my own, the idea of him blistering my skin, my lonely soul.

I do not imagine I shall return.

AFTER TWO DAYS, MY SISTER'S fits showed no signs of abating. If anything, she grew hotter and more restless, tossing off the quilts our mother had made and soaking her nightgown through.

My mother, too, was a shell of herself. As the firstborn son, I'd seen her grief mount over the years as she lost one child after another to miscarriage or disease and my father to a cart accident. My sister had been the last and the only other child to live, and I knew that if my sister died, I'd lose my mother as well.

So I'd run for the village healer and plied him with the last of our coin. He'd come, traipsing through the woods to our little cabin, the one my father had built with his own hands. The healer spent a long time examining my sister, but at length he shook his head.

"I'll make her a potion," he said, as he did just that. After he'd dosed her with it he lured me outside, far from my mother's hearing. Hand tight on my arm, he said, "She's a wasp that one, isn't she, Beau? Tries a man's patience."

"I don't know what you mean," I said, although that was a lie. I jerked my arm out of his grip.

"I'm no fool, boy." He narrowed his eyes. "This was no mere fall. She's bleeding inside her skull, which is causing those fits."

His gaze met mine, and I was certain he could see straight through to the blackness of my heart.

But his expression softened and turned to pity. "It's too late now, anyway. Unless you have the stones to ask the Wild Man for one of his precious golden fruits, there's nothing that will aid your sister."

He said it as a joke. I didn't take it as one. Golden fruits were a thing of legend, grown deep within the forest and guarded by a spirit who exacted a fierce price for his precious, life-giving gift. Just what it was, no one ever said, but I had my suspicions of what went on deep within the wood and it made my gut twist. Those who returned—both men and women—bore a haunted expression in their eyes and refused to speak of their ordeal. They bore no signs of mistreatment, but neither would they let their loved ones touch them.

By nightfall, the healer's predictions proved true. My sister lapsed into an uneasy stillness and nothing my mother did could rouse her.

"It's your fault," Mother told me. "If you'd gotten work, we would have had more coin to pay for a better healer." Never mind that she refused to let me get a proper apprenticeship because she insisted I tend to the chores at home. She clawed at my shirt. "Just get out of here. Leave me! You useless, worthless—"

Ears burning, I stumbled outside. Her tirade broke down into sobs which stabbed me like daggers. I had to fix this, and there was only one thing left to try.

It was the lurid, troubling tales about the Wild Man that my mind dwelt on as I snuck out of the hut and headed into the woods, deep enough that there were no tracks save those used by deer and wild boar, which my father had taught me to find. The going was slow as I picked my way by lantern light. From all around me came the rustle of mice beneath dead leaves, and now and then the hoot of an owl. The darkness grew more intense, and even with the lantern's glow, I felt small and afraid. It was easy for a man's sins to find him in the night and to weigh him down with the shame. The walk became a long, insufferable trail, and more than once I thought about turning and fleeing, perhaps running away to sea.

But guilt over my sister's illness stayed my course. I trudged on, each step becoming heavier and more difficult than the last.

So mired was I in my own self-loathing that I nearly fell upon the very tree I sought. It stood alone in a grove, lit by the light of the nearly full moon. The tree had a thick, sturdy trunk and twisting branches that sprouted broad leaves and a few dangling, golden fruits that resembled pears.

If the Wild Man was here, there was no sign. Excitement raced through me. I was lucky. I could grab a fruit and leave, and the Wild Man would be none the wiser. My sister would be well, and perhaps my mother would have some kind words for me at last.

I set the lantern aside and crept quietly toward the tree, keeping an eye out for unwanted visitors. I was just about to pluck one of the fruits when a voice spoke from behind me.

"If you steal the fruit, it will turn to poison."

I was so startled I nearly jumped from my skin. I whirled around to see the strangest man I had ever gazed upon. Instead of tender flesh, he was covered in skin as red-brown and thick as oak which creaked slightly with every movement. If he had an age, I could not guess. He wore a crown of thorns woven together with vines, and along his arms were bracelets and armbands of the same prickly branches. I wondered how they managed not to pain him, until I saw that they emerged directly from his skin. He wore no clothing save for a wrap woven from something soft and just large enough to cover the indecent parts of him.

"Please. My s-sister is ill. Dying."

His nose—or the knot that passed for one—wrinkled into a sneer. "That is no concern of mine."

Desperate, and unsure how to approach the forest spirit, I dropped to my knees and groveled. "She's very dear to me. I must find a way to save her. She won't make it until morning."

Some of the tension drained from him, and he...wilted, was the best way to describe it. "I've heard the same thing from so many others. The rich. The poor. The desperate. I offered them aid and a bargain, all to my detriment. Go, boy. I can't bear to be disappointed again." He gestured at me to leave.

"I can't." I was shaking now, and not from cold. "Please. I...I'll do whatever you ask. I know there's a price." My trembling fingers found the laces of my tunic and pulled them loose. If we were to rut in the grove like animals, so be it.

He let out a long, windy sigh that spoke of years of disappointment. "Go, boy. Now, before you try my patience."

"No." I threw myself at his feet. "I won't leave until you agree. I know what kind of bargain I must make. I'm not afraid of you." That last was a lie, but I hoped he wouldn't guess.

I was afraid he would refuse until I felt his appraising gaze upon me, measuring me as a shepherd would a prize ram for his ewes. "Then you agree to be my consort until the next full moon?"

Panic filled me, and not because of what he wanted me to become. "A month? My mother would never allow it." I bit my lip and cursed at my idiocy.

He looked at me askance. "Are you not a man grown and free to make your own choices?"

"That isn't it. I..." My mouth went dry as I imagined my mother's fury. But as afraid as I was of angering her by disappearing, I was more terrified of what she would do to me if my sister died. "I agree. I offer myself of my own free will until the next full moon. Do to me what you wish." I made to pull my shirt over my head, but the Wild Man waved at me to stop.

"Stay your hand, fool. This is neither the time nor the place. Here." With great reverence, he plucked a fruit from the branch and held it in the palms of his hands as if in communion with it. Perhaps he was. "As the sun rises, cut this in half and squeeze the juice into a bowl. Make her drink. Bring her into the sunlight and keep her there until nightfall. Do the same the next day, and she will be well."

Relief weakened my limbs. "That's all?"

He cocked his head, which made him look like a raven eying a shiny trinket. "At dusk on the second day, you will return to me." He gazed at the sky, where the moon would be full on the night in question. "If you betray my trust, the juice will turn to poison in your sister's veins. She will die before another sun rises, and I will hunt you down and make you pay dearly for your treachery."

There was something in his voice, an odd note of resignation that made me look closer at him. He frightened me, yes, with that wildness about him, and he was certainly not a pleasant sight, covered in thorns as he was. He looked like a demon, and it was little wonder the villagers spoke about him in such hushed, fearful tones. The thought of lying with such a creature scared me, but I had little choice. "Agreed."

He handed me the fruit. The skin was as soft as a woman's, and tingled slightly in my palm. He curled my fingers around it. "Go. And remember what will happen if you try and run."

I clutched the precious gift to my chest and fled, stuffing my fear deep down. All that mattered was that my sister would live.


MY MOTHER EYED ME UPON my return just before dawn. "Beau? You lazy, selfish boy, abandoning your sister when she needs you most!"

Eager to please her, I held up the fruit, but here in the cabin it seemed an ordinary thing, bereft of magic. "I went to a different healer. He bade me give her the juice from this." While my mother muttered and fussed, I sliced the fruit in half, revealing a ripe and luscious interior. As the sun rose, I squeezed the juice into a bowl and held it to my sister's lips. By now, she was so weak that she offered no resistance. Her body was light as I gathered her into my arms, blankets and all, and carried her outside, much to my mother's dismay.

"The chill—"

"—will go away as the sun rises. Leave her be. This is what the healer advised." Though I didn't tell her it was the madman in the woods who'd prescribed the treatment. If I had, she would have cursed me for a fool and taken my sister right back indoors.

Throughout the day, my mother and I tended my sister. It wasn't long before her skin took on a slightly healthier hue. By evening, she was sleeping peacefully and no longer fighting for breath.

I repeated the treatment on the second morning, and her steady improvement was visible. Her skin was no longer hot to the touch and her fits had stopped. My mother went so far as to bathe her and dress her in a clean nightgown while I went to gather firewood. The nights had grown warmer, though there was still enough of a chill that I wanted to be sure they would be comfortable in my absence. I piled the wood high and checked the traps, pleased to find two rabbits and a pheasant, which, along with the goods in the garden, would keep them fed for a time. My mother paid no attention to my efforts, but doted on my sister.

"She's getting better, no thanks to you," she muttered as she fed my sister spoonfuls of soup. "You lazy, careless boy. Always more trouble than you're worth."

It was almost a relief to slip out and head toward imprisonment.


THE WILD MAN WAITED FOR me at the edge of the grove. "This way."

He was distant and formal, and for that I was grateful. I wanted no false comfort in my misery. This was the first time I'd spent more than a night away from my family, and I hadn't even said goodbye.

At a casual glance, the grove and surrounding area seemed to be no more than mere forest, though perhaps the trees grew a bit more oddly than usual. But as he led me through them, paths opened up where there hadn't been any before. At a wave of his hand, branches grew in such a way as to suggest chairs and tables. Stumps were hollowed out to provide storage. Vines had been coaxed to climb overhead and provide roofs or hang between branches to support a stuffed, comfortable-looking mattress.

And so I found myself in a cozy, canopied room that offered all the comforts of home save a fire. I shivered, filled with guilt at the audacity of leaving my family when they needed me.

"Are you cold?"

I was, but I was too miserable to say so. He disappeared for a few moments and returned with a hooded cloak that looked to be made of leaves. The inside, however, looked to be the same material as his loin wrap.

"It's warm, and waterproof, too. Consider it a gift. I do not wish you to be uncomfortable. I cannot light a fire here, you understand."

"No. Of course not."

He draped the cloak around my shoulders. His hands lingered longer than necessary as he straightened it and fastened the wooden brooch on the front of the cloak. I froze, waiting for his hands to venture toward the inevitable.

Instead, he gave me a pained smile. "I'll ask nothing of you tonight. Sleep. I will bring you food and drink at sunrise."

At that, he left me alone in my strange new room to fall asleep amidst the buzz of crickets and cicadas.


COME MORNING, THERE WAS NO sign of him, but a plate of fruit and a pitcher of juice rested near my bed. I'd never seen anything so bright and fresh, nor tasted anything so sweet. I savored each bite, endeavoring not to recall the reason I was here—or the monster who kept me captive.

It wasn't his gender that bothered me. I'd lain with a couple of the village girls, and while they were knowledgeable and kind, they hadn't been nearly as exciting as the nights with the handsome stable lad up in the loft. I'd had to sneak out for those adventures. My mother would never have approved.

I wandered through my new surroundings, but try as I might to discover the entrance we'd come through, I couldn't. Escape was impossible. Trees and bushes always blocked what started out as a likely path. At length I came upon my host, who nearly blended in with our surroundings. He'd been watching me. Frustration rising, I opened my mouth to ask what he wanted of me, but he waved me to silence.

"At nightfall," was all he said to me. "I can't bear unhappiness during the day. Explore all you like. Eat what you wish, save for the golden fruit. It's poisonous until I change its nature."

With little recourse, I continued to prowl around, taking in the beauty of his home. The wild things were at peace here, even if I was not. There were fruits and vegetables aplenty, but my stomach was too tied up in knots to eat anything.

At dusk, I waited for the Wild Man, wearing nothing but the cloak. Darkness had long since fallen when I heard the rustle of leaves, the soft creak of a tree bending in the wind, and he was there, filling the doorway, cutting me off from escape.

"Are you frightened of me?"

"A little."

He would not meet my gaze, but he offered a mug of something sweetly scented. "This will help you relax."

My gut tightened. Tempting as it was to accept his offer, it also seemed...wrong. I was no terrified maiden or a trader fearful of losing his masculinity. I'd made a bargain, and so far, my host had not been unkind. Dissociating seemed a poor way to repay him. "No. Thank you." I pushed the mug aside.

For a moment, surprise flashed in his eyes before they went back to that guarded, distant look. "You're one of the few. This, though, I insist on."

He handed me a length of cloth I realized must be meant as a blindfold. "I don't need—"

"Trust me. You do not wish to see the monster I've become."

I *was* afraid then, wondering if his prick resembled his arms. "Those thorns—"

"Are nowhere you need to be concerned about." Then, impatient, he took the cloth from my hands and wrapped it around my eyes. "Come. If all goes well, this need not happen for more than one night."

I wondered what that meant, but dared not ask. Gentle, if insistent, hands guided me to the bed. He tucked a pillow under my hips, then removed my cloak.

"If you wish the potion now, you may have it."

"I've done this before." My brawny stable lad had tipped me over a hay bale and proven he was as adept at riding men as he was horses.

"Good," he said shortly, and proceeded to rub something wet and cool around and inside my asshole with indifference. He did not touch me more than absolutely necessary, and I wondered why we were doing this at all since this was certainly not for my pleasure nor did it seem to be for his.

The bed shifted as he climbed into it and straddled me. With the same distanced calmness, he adjusted my hips and positioned himself. Then, swift and certain as a healer's knife, he pricked me.

I let out a groan as the width of him filled my ass, and I forced myself to relax. As promised, the entry was smooth, if a bit aching, and he was as hard as the strongest wood.

There were no words, only my harsh breaths as I tried to time them to his thrusts and his creaking interspersed with the occasional grunt of effort. Once I became used to him, it was easier to endure, though the indifference hurt more than the act itself.

After an age he tensed then groaned and spent himself within me in a wet, hot rush. Finished, he tumbled off to the side, and I caught the scent of sap and pine. I dared not move until he gave me permission, so we waited.

And waited.

At last, he asked, "Do you love me?"

The question was absurd. "No." I didn't see how I could possibly love a creature as cold and frightful as this.

Slowly, he eased himself out of bed. I tore off the blindfold and saw his angry, desolate expression.

"You're not the one. You can't be. I was a damn fool to bring you here, and now it's too late for anyone else. Too late..."

I had no idea what he meant, but whatever I'd failed to do for him had gotten him truly upset. "Tell me what—"

He slapped me. A flare of pain lit my cheek. One of his thorns had raked my skin. A careful touch confirmed my suspicion that I was bleeding.

Either he didn't notice, or he didn't care. He stumbled about the room, head buried in his hands as he raged incoherently. In that moment, I *did* think him a monster. Inhuman, uncaring, a thing of pent-up fury. With one last howl, he staggered outside.

My own anger rose, and I plunged after him into the night, uncaring of the air against my bare skin. He wasn't hard to find. He'd headed straight for the grove, where he'd dropped to his knees before the fruit tree. From the rise and fall of his voice, I thought for sure he was laughing.

But when I drew close enough, I saw the silvery streaks on his cheeks.

He was weeping.

I AVAILED MYSELF OF THE basin and pitcher of water, cleaning myself as best I could. His scent covered me like a fine cologne, and I was almost sorry to wash it away. I dabbed at the cut, which had already stopped bleeding.

Come morning, a basket of fruit rested on the table, and I helped myself to an apple. Agitated, I wandered through the garden as I ate, hoping for a sign of my host. There was none, so I whiled the day away, weighed down by guilt at having nothing to do with my mother and sister struggled to survive at the wood's edge. They would be frantic, I was sure.

When my host came to me that night, he did not speak but simply handed me the blindfold.

"Why am I really here?" I asked.

He raised his hand and I cringed, fearing he would slap me again, but he pointed a finger at me instead. "Ask again, and I will gag you as well."

I shut my mouth and meekly took my position on the bed. He was not kind as he coupled with me, but neither did he linger. He was so silent and stiff, his heart as shielded as his skin. I said not a word, fearful of antagonizing him.

I did not care about the physical discomfort. I'd made my bargain and I aimed to fulfill it, but I wondered why and how he'd grown to be so withdrawn and angry.

Afterward, he asked me the same question: "Do you love me?"

I was forced to give him the same answer. "No."

He would not say anything further, and therefore, there was nothing I could do to aid him. I was alone in my misery, and he in his.

ON THE THIRD NIGHT OF this, I accepted the bowl of juice, and let my mind drift as he had his way. I woke rested but slightly ill, feeling as though I'd missed something important. The only real awareness I kept was the way I'd answered his inevitable question: *No.*

By the tenth, I could bear no more. If I was to endure twenty additional days, things had to change. I ached to please him, if only to end this painful stalemate.

So when he handed me the blindfold, I tossed it aside. "I want to see you."

He scowled. "No you don't."

"I do," I insisted, and boldly reached for his loin wrap. I waited for a slap or angry word as I stripped him, but he didn't react at all. He was so stiff I thought he might have rooted himself to the ground.

Feeling brave, I looked at him undressed. He had a man's prick, still soft and recognizably human, although its color had darkened to match the wooden hue of his skin. His balls looked like chestnuts. Perhaps they felt like it, too.

"No one's seen me before," he said, amazed.

"Why not? There's nothing to fear."

He tried to pull away, but I didn't let him. I had little hope of thawing the coldness in his heart, but if I could melt it just a little, these encounters would be more bearable, perhaps even enjoyable, for the both of us.

Touching that rough, bark-like skin was frightening, but I made myself do it. I was trapped here, and it seemed he was, too.

His prick sprang to life in my hand, growing thick and hard with a speed I envied. Yet I did not rush; I enjoyed stroking it and watching the amazement blossom in his expression.

I knelt and took his prick into my mouth. It was salty and earthy at the same time, and not altogether unpleasant, even when I ran my tongue along its base. I cupped his balls, finding them hard and round and tight. Chestnuts, indeed. I wondered how much he could truly feel beneath that hardening skin.

I ran a hand around his waist, to the rough curves of his buttocks, and found the crack of his ass and the warm spot deep within. Gently, I pressed until he admitted me. This was a trick my stable lad had been all too eager to show me, and I soon found that the Wild Man still possessed the damp, inner warmth of a man, as well as a certain tender spot that made him wriggle with delight when pressed.

A gasp and a shudder were my only warning before he loosed his seed. The taste wasn't at all like a man's. It was musky and sweet at the same time.

I released him and wiped the corner of my mouth with the back of my hand. He staggered backwards to the bed and collapsed. For a long time, he lay on his side, staring at me, before he finally asked, "Why?"

"I thought you'd like it. Didn't you?"

"Don't." He grasped my arm, hard. "Don't ever do something you hate just to please me." He was angry. "I don't deserve it. If you knew..."

I held my breath, hoping he would continue, but he only shook his head and let out an irritated sigh. "We all have secrets," I said. My own lay heavy upon my shoulders, but I dared not say a word.

"Do you love me?"

He'd already given me a gift beyond measure: a means of redemption. Yet whatever I felt for him, it wasn't love. "No."


WE SHARED BREAKFAST. THE SUNLIGHT cast a warm, golden hue on his skin, and because of that, I noticed the change. "You're different." Daring, I brushed his arms. The thorns circling his arms and head had fallen away. Little green leaves had taken their place. "Blooming, I'd say."

"Am I?" He inspected an arm, studying it. "I hadn't noticed."

I toyed with a leaf. It was soft. "You're changing."

"It's too late for that." The bitterness had returned. "You're kind. I thank you for that. But there's no reason to be."

I caught his hand before he could leave. The bark skin, too, seemed to have lost its roughest edges. "There's always reason for kindness."

And so began long, golden days in each other's company. Sex was no longer relegated to the night or even my cozy room. We didn't bother to dress and rutted whenever and wherever the mood took us: in a bed of damp, fallen leaves, in the branches of a sturdy oak, and once, at the foot ot recall ever being so free or so happy.

After each coupling he asked, "Do you love me?" Always, I disappointed him. At the end of the month, I would leave, and couldn't see how answering *yes* would help at all. Besides, my feelings were such a tangled mess that I couldn't discern them. I didn't know what I wanted, and soon, it wouldn't matter.

Yet the happier I became, the more my guilt increased. As the days wore on, my anxiety grew. My mother and sister would no doubt be running out of food and firewood. Or perhaps the roof has sprung a leak, or one of them had gotten hurt, or...

"You seem troubled," he asked, tousling my hair.

"I haven't been away from my family this long. I worry about how they're getting on without me."

He sighed. "Come. I will show you something."

He led me down twisting wooden stairs into his back garden. As with the rest of the house, it was lush, home to birds, butterflies and skittering beasts that stayed out of sight.

In the center was a pond. I'd expected fish, but this was empty and so still that it held a perfect reflection of sky and clouds and, when I neared it, me.

"Kneel," he instructed, and I did so. He joined me, took my hand and placed it in the water. "Think of those you wish to see."

I did, wishing with all my heart to gaze upon my mother and sister. The reflection wavered, then transformed, the shapes breaking away and coagulating again like raindrops against a pane of glass. And there, at last, I saw them; my mother, toiling in the garden, wearing such an angry expression that my gut twisted with fear. Weeding and tending the garden was my chore, so her unhappiness was my fault. When I returned, she would rail at me for a week. My sister sat on the rock wall, smoothing her skirt, a trifle ashen but otherwise hale.

As I watched, I was keenly aware of the Wild Man's eyes on me, rather than on the vision in the water. I flushed, and wished he would stop.

The scene changed. Not to the present, but the past. My sister and I alone on the rocky hillside, looking for blackberries. Her mouth moved. There was no sound, but I heard the words all the same; the little cruelties she'd flung at me since she was old enough to echo our mother. *Beau the fool. Beau the useless. Buy me some of the fancy new cloth from the milliner, or I will tell mother what I saw in the stable, and won't she be furious to know you'll never get her a grandchild?*

I saw myself hunched over, face red. She climbed the rocks, then, from her superior height, laughed and pointed at me. My image had a stone in his hand. He stood. Turned.

Panic surged through me. I yanked my hand from the water, unable to watch anything more. "You bastard." I turned to my captor, rage in my heart. "You have no right to show me such things. No right at all."

If he was moved by my reaction, he gave no sign. Instead, he calmly took my hand once more and thrust it back into the water. "Look again."

I didn't want to, but I was drawn in as the scene shifted, changed...

Into *fire*.

I screamed, but the Wild Man refused to let go of my hand, forcing me to watch, helpless, as the timbers cut and laid by my father turned to ash. *"No!"*

Another breath, and the pond returned to its normal, clear state. I stared at it in disbelief for a moment before turning away to find comfort in his arms. "Those scenes. Were they true?"

"The pool shows you what your heart desires."

I pulled away, horrified. "I don't want them dead."

"No, but you want to be free, don't you?"

There was a note of sadness in his voice. I longed to ask what he'd done to deserve this life, but I didn't, fearful of betraying his trust.

"What happened that day at the rocks?" he asked.

If it weren't for the gentle hands stroking my arms, I wouldn't have had the courage to speak. As it was, I kept my gaze on the ground, not daring to look at him. "I didn't mean to hit her. I would have been a murderer, if not for you."

He was silent a long time. "I was a thief. I took a dare from my friends to sneak into the grove, steal the fruit and take a bite. I did, but there was a witch—the guardian of the grove. She caught me and cursed me to this life, losing my humanity day by day."

I shivered, appalled by the tale. "Is there a way to free you?"

He shrugged and looked forlorn as he gazed up at the waxing moon, and I knew. Undoing the curse had something to do with why he had brought me and forced me to stay for a month and why he'd been so upset that first night. It was little wonder his heart was cold; it couldn't have been easy coupling with strangers and hoping that they had whatever it took to free him. Neither did I, evidently, which saddened me.

That revelation also made what I had to say next all the more difficult. "I have to go back. They need me."

"So do I," he said, and I had to strain to hear it.

"Just for the night. I'll return. I promise. But I can't let them die in a fire."

"Five more days. That's all I ask." It must have been a trick of the evening light, but the vibrant green leaves on his arms and shoulders seemed to blaze a fiery red and orange.

Tentatively, I brushed one. It fell, swirling a little before it hit the ground. "They're my family. The only people who love me."

"If losing yourself to please someone is what you think love is, then I've been wrong about you all along." He turned his back to me, and from the way his shoulders shuddered, I thought he might be weeping again. "Go, then. Leave me."

The words, an echo of my mother's, pricked me like his thorns. They riddled me with the same guilt for being selfish.

Before I could change my mind, I grabbed my cloak and hurried through the woods toward home.


I ARRIVED AT THE CABIN, breathless, relieved to find my mother and sister safe and sound. I burst in, hoping for a welcome or at least a show of concern, and received neither.

My mother rose, her expression harder than any the Wild Man had worn. "Beau?" Her gaze raked me up and down. "I don't have to wonder where you've been, do I?"

"Mother, I—"

She struck my cheek. I reeled, smarting as much from pain as from surprise. She ripped the cloak from my shoulders, exposing my lithe body and tanned skin. "You selfish, foolish boy. I'm not surprised you've run off and let yourself be used by that monster in the woods. You're no better than one of the village whores."

"It's not like that."

She tossed the cloak aside and came at me again, scratching and pounding. "You've never liked your sister from the day I brought her into this world. No doubt you caused the deaths of my other babes, just like you tried to murder her."

The notion was ridiculous. I'd run for the healer more times than I could count, and never mind that I had held my sister when she'd cried or spent my coin on fine fabrics in an attempt to please her. It wasn't possible.

My sister stared at my nakedness, a wicked, satisfied grin on her face.

"I'm sorry." She'd never see my visit to the Wild Man for what it was—a sacrifice in order to save my sister. "I'll do better. I came back to warn you about the fire—"

She grabbed my shoulders and thrust me against the wall. "You're a liar. You owe me. You owe your sister for what you did. Now put some clothes on. There's wood to be cut and weeds to be pulled."

"Yes, Mother," I said meekly. Though silently, I called to the Wild Man: *Forgive me.*

SO, UNDER MY MOTHER'S WATCHFUL glare, I prepared meals, scrubbed the floor and tended the garden. I mended the thatching in the roof and cut wood. My mother denied me my usual pallet by the hearth so I slept in the cellar, with my sister gleefully turning the key to the trap door so I couldn't run away in the night.

There in the darkness, I dreamed of the Wild Man, trying desperately to reach him, only to find my hands bleeding and full of dirt from clawing the earthen floor. Every heartbeat brought the Wild Man closer to his fate. I had not the means of breaking his curse, but I could have made his passing easier. No doubt he believed I'd betrayed him. I wished he'd hunt me down as he'd promised, but late as it was, there was likely no point. Maybe there was some small chance that the fruit could still turn to poison in my sister's veins.

All these thoughts and more I had as the hours turned into excruciatingly long days. My helplessness tore at me, even more so when my sister pinched and kicked me at every turn. I dared not retaliate, not with my smiling at her insolence. The spark that had kindled in my heart over the past fortnight cooled again into ash.

On the fifth night, I returned to the cabin laden with pails of water. My sister waited for me, lantern in hand. "I think it's time you apologized."

I stared at her, mute.

She stamped her foot. "Apologize!"

Meekly, I set the pails down. I'd gone numb since coming home, but now anger sparked and flared. "No."

"Mama!" As she raised her arms in rage, the lantern lit her face, turning her into the demon she was.

Then she dashed the lantern to the floor. Glass shattered. Shards drove into my leg, but worse were the sparks that flared and bit the hem of my sister's skirt. The fine, pretty fabric she'd insisted upon caught fire and lit her like a torch.

My mother screamed and reached for my sister, but it was too late. All I could do was stare at the very conflagration I'd come home to stop.

I'd seen it before, in the pond, with—

Thinking of the Wild Man broke my trance. With the flames licking at the timbers, I fled.

SOMEWHERE ALONG THE PATH THROUGH the woods, I plunged into the river and splashed water over myself, thirsty and unable to bear my own stink. Otherwise, I ran the entire way, uncaring of the branches and thorns marking my bare skin. The moon was full. I had no time left.

At last I reached the outskirts and called hoarsely to the Wild Man. There was no answer. Sick and certain I was already too late, I scrambled toward the grove. He wasn't there either, but then I caught sight of a new tree at the edge.

No tree could grow that quickly.

I ran to it, horrified at realizing what—*who*—it was. The shape of a man was there beneath the thick bark, but it was already giving way to *treeness*. I'd been trapped in the cellar too long; the transformation had already begun.

I embraced the newborn oak. "You can't do this. Not yet. I'm sorry. I'm *sorry*." My voice broke, and no more words would come.

Two of the knots flickered and broke open to reveal what had once been his eyes, but they were sunken and hollow, devoid of the light I'd cherished. His gaze landed on me for just a moment. The wrinkled bark shifted just enough to hint at a smile, then his eyes closed and he went still.

"Don't go. Please don't go." I glanced around, desperate for something, anything to help. My gaze landed on the tree heavy with golden fruit— which was poisonous if stolen. Yet I knew he changed the nature of the fruit. *How?*

I recalled the reverence with which he'd held it, the way he'd seemed to have prayed over it. Steeling myself, I plucked the nearest fruit and cradled it in my palms, wishing with all my heart for it to heal instead of harm.

"Let this work. Please." I trickled the juice where I'd seen his mouth. I grabbed another fruit, wished hard, and traced the juice along the lines his tears had taken. Then I trailed it all along his body, over the bark-like skin and brown, dying leaves.

Fruit after fruit I plucked and squeezed until there were no more to be had. I didn't care that some needy soul might come along at any moment. *I* needed the fruit. So did the Wild Man.

But as the night wore on, nothing happened. The moon set, leaving the woods in an eerie grayness between night and dawn. The last hints of manhood had vanished. It was over. I'd failed.

"I love you," I said into the stillness. I leaned against him, weary beyond measure. Tears fell, unbidden, and dripped onto his hardening chest.

I stood there, numb with grief, as the sun rose. The light reached into the grove, so intense that I had to close my eyes lest I be blinded. It wasn't fair. He should have been here to see this with me.

The tears started anew. I nuzzled against him...and there came a sharp, splintering *crack*.

I stumbled back, shocked at the sight of the bark splitting as if it had been struck by lightning. All along the trunk and branches, the bark fractured and flaked away. Leaves dried, twisted and fluttered to the ground. Then the largest part of the trunk peeled away to reveal...

*Him.*

He was no longer the Wild Man, but entirely human and naked, born anew from his wooden cocoon. I couldn't help but run my hands along the newly-smoothed skin. Soft hair now coated the arms and chest once covered by bark. Instead of being crowned by thorns and vines, he wore a mop of russet tresses that curled down to his shoulders.

Gingerly, I stroked his cheek, hardly daring to believe what I saw. "You're alive. How?"

"I had to let you go." He leaned into my touch. His gaze met mine, and he smiled. "And you came back."

"I said I would." I offered him an arm, and he stepped onto the fertile ground. I couldn't help but notice he was already erect, and it wasn't long before I was, too.

His mouth covered mine, and I reveled in the taste of him, both masculine and wild, sweetened by the fruit's juice. He drove his tongue into my mouth and I welcomed it with the same enthusiasm I did his prick as it rubbed against mine.

"What about the witch?"

"What about her?" he asked as he nibbled my earlobe and neck. "The curse is broken. I learned my lesson."

"But who will be the guardian of the grove now?"

"Who says we have to leave?"

Who indeed? I had no home to return to, and after seven years, I doubted the Wild Man did, either.

"We have everything we need, and we can help others with..." He looked at the tree then at me, one eyebrow raised. "You used it all?"

I cringed. "It'll grow back, won't it?"

"In time."

"You're not angry with me?"

"Why in the world would I be?" He sounded perplexed.

"Because I didn't ask. I didn't think." I didn't understand how I could behave poorly yet receive no reprimand.

He wrapped his arms around me and said softly, "They're gone, my love. You need never fear them again, and you'll never have cause to be afraid of me. I promise. You have a generous heart, and it's a pity others took advantage of it." He tapped my chest. "This generous heart turned poison into balm and saved my life."

"That's how you change the fruit's nature?"

"Yes. With love."

Relieved, I clung to him for a long time before he began exploring every curve and crevice. I did the same. He had a new body to discover, after all.

Where he found the lubrication I didn't know, but his home held so many secrets I wasn't surprised. He laid me on the soft grass and coated me well, jamming his fingers deeply inside and teasing that aching wonderful spot until I begged him to either have me or stop.

He lifted one of my legs and then the other onto his shoulders and thrust into me that way so we could lock gazes and penetrate souls as well as bodies. I came first, unable to resist the tidal wave of pleasure as it rolled over me. He took his time, watching me gasp, before allowing his own release.

We snuggled together, arms and limbs entwined. "Look," he said, nodding to the tree. A golden fruit hung there, ripe and plump. "Our love made that."

I stared at him, realizing just how many fruits I'd used on him, and just how many encounters they represented. "We'll have to make more," I said, though I failed to do it with a straight face.

"I think it best," he said seriously, then laughed and kissed my forehead. "Do you love me?"

"Yes," I answered without hesitation. The guilt I'd been burdened with for as long as I could remember was gone, the void filled with the intense heat and affection I bore for my Wild Man. I tugged him close, eager for the touch of his skin against mine. "Oh, yes."

# BY THE BANYAN TREE

## JAMES PENHA

THAT NIGHT ICHSAN DIDN'T FEEL like sitting alone in his hotel room. Mataram wasn't the most exciting town in Indonesia, but it was a provincial capital, and he knew it must have young men willing to dally with a generous stranger. These boys on the outer islands were usually sweet and simple and, if single, horny. Not having the money to pay for pleasure with female prostitutes, even the straight young ones were often willing to have sex with another man as long as they weren't forced to play receiver. Ichsan wasn't the forceful kind, and so his peripatetic partners usually left him with smiles on their faces, masculine pride intact, and a wad of rupiah notes bulging their pockets.

Not that islanders were sure things: Ichsan recalled one who asked for money in advance so he could grab dinner at the night market and was never seen again; another begged Ichsan to stop the car so he could pee but ran off into the night; and many had said no, they just couldn't do it with guys. But rarely had anyone been angered by Ichsan's gentle proposals, and, never, Ichsan thanked God, had anyone hurt him physically. But living among a continuous succession of arrivals and departures depressed him. With no ticket for a connecting flight, he was sentenced to life in an airport transit hall.

Coming out of the closet, finding solace and perhaps love with a permanent male partner, was not an option for him—not in his family, not in his tribe, not in his religion, not in his profession, not in his country, not in his mind.

Already, in his twenty-fifth year, every new buyer for the line of drugs he pitched to pharmacies asked, "Already married?" Since an honest reply elicited only the annoying follow-up, "Why not?" Ichsan usually lied that he had a wife and four children: two boys; two girls.

After strolling the street in front of the hotel for a half hour forlornly searching for an interesting face, Ichsan got into his rented Toyota Kijang and drove off the main drag into the *kampoeng*, the neighborhood environs of Mataram. The sun was setting by the time he idled next to a soccer field where beautiful bodies were engaged in the beautiful game. Handsome as they were, it was unlikely that any of them would leave the field without his arm around a pal or two.

Even if one of a pair or trio were willing to go with Ichsan, peer pressure would shut him up and down. Ichsan had occasionally found a boy so randy and ready, he would talk his friend into joining a ménage, but such luck was exceptional in more ways than one.

The game proceeded into the night and Ichsan felt the need to relieve himself. Across the street was a secluded spot beneath a massive banyan. Ichsan made his way there, unzipped his pants and watered the roots of the tree. Feeling a bit wobbly where he stood, he stretched his arms and held on to the trunk to steady himself. He recalled a tree just like this in Tapan, his hometown in Sumatra. Terrified of having his mind read by his buddies who would ridicule him as a *susi* or as a boy-girl, epithets that would follow him forever, the boy Ichsan learned loneliness. He did make friends, lots of friends, but feared liking them too much. He couldn't bear the pangs of puppy love. And so he often wandered the jungle and the river where he spoke to wild goats and birds and trees. Like the banyan three kilometers from his house. And now he recalled that strange moment in his eleventh year when he removed all his clothes and hung them on a branch of the banyan before he embraced its trunk with all his might and confided in the tree all he felt and feared. He shook and wobbled then too and felt a little strange, perhaps sick, but very, very excited. When he peed, he did so straight up like the geyser in the caldera near the volcano. And later he seemed to feel fingers gently massaging his penis and cool breaths entering his anus. It must have been the vines and the wisps of wind, of course, but these phenomena had a purpose. And when he ejaculated, he fell backward onto the ground and was amazed at what he saw and had felt.

He had not come that far this night in Mataram, but the memory of nature's foreplay was palpable. Ichsan's heart pounded; he shivered. "I know what you want," he heard from an unfamiliar voice.

Feeling something like fingers softly alight between his thighs, Ichsan closed his eyes, leaned his head on the hard tree trunk, and allowed his cock to stiffen. "I know what you want," he heard again. Ichsan smiled. "But not here." He felt an arm—not a bough—a human limb, an arm, around his waist. Ichsan shuddered to attention and turned to his right where a young fellow shook his head and grinned. "Not here."

"What—what do you mean?" The fellow was wearing a dusty, sweat-drenched soccer jersey. "I know what you want, and I want you to have it...but not here, not in front of all of them." He tipped the back of his head toward the soccer field where a few dozen boys were drinking bottled tea or already heading home. His index finger hovered just above Ichsan's meatus. "You do want me, right?"

Even in the dark, the fellow's face was luminous, and the gentility of his touch and of his manner was irresistible. "Yes. Yes, I think I do. But if not here..."

"You have a car, right?" Ichsan nodded. "Meet me down the street there in front of that big white building on the corner in about ten minutes." Ichsan nodded, struggled a bit to put his hard dick in his pants and headed toward the Kijang. The fellow—Ichsan had been too mesmerized even to ask his name—pissed against the tree, zipped up, and returned toward the soccer field.

Ichsan drove for the landmark the stranger had indicated, made a three-corner turn and parked, with lights off and windows open, on the quiet street facing the soccer field. He felt the palpitations of desire and hoped the young man was honest and would show up—alone—not with a bunch of thugs who would beat and rob him. Surrounded by black fence posts many of which had broken or been stolen, the pale white building with arcades and window shutters must be, Ichsan thought, a relic of the Dutch colonial period. Used now as what? a museum? government office? hospital? His reverie was broken by the opening and closing of a back door of the Kijang. Ichsan looked in the rear-view mirror and saw the face of the young man whose arrival he awaited. He was by himself, and he huddled close to Ichsan, whispering, "Let's go somewhere more quiet. Make a U-turn and drive for a couple of kilometers. I'll tell you where to turn."

Ichsan followed the stranger's instructions although, after ten minutes of turns onto winding, hilly roads, he worried that he was being taken to a place so remote that he could be left there for dead. "How much farther?"

"Still a ways. Don't worry. You'll like where we're going," said the young man. "And you'll like me." He kissed Ichsan on the side of his neck.

Shuddering, Ichsan introduced himself and asked for the stranger's name. "Leaf."

"Leaf? That's not a very common name on this island, is it?"

"I was born here on Lombok, but, no, it's not the name my parents gave me. You'll see. Okay. Okay. We're going to make a right there at the gate. Let me out to open it. Then you drive on through. I'll shut the gate behind the car and hop back in." When Leaf returned, he got in the front passenger seat. "Drive down toward the river. Yes, this is good. You can stop right here. Let's get out."

There were simple huts alongside the river rippling in the moonlight.

"This a park?" Ichsan asked as he followed Leaf to one of the huts.

"Yes. Busy on weekends, but closed at night."

"You come here often?"

"Well, this isn't my first time." Leaf kneeled down and undid Ichsan's pants. He pulled them down along with his underwear. Ichsan stepped out of his flip-flops and his clothes. "But this is my first time with you," said Leaf.

Leaf took Ichsan's rigid dick in his mouth and played its tip with a gossamer delicacy Ichsan had never experienced. "Oh, so good. But wait." Ichsan didn't want to come before Leaf too was naked, so he squatted and pulled the soccer shirt over the young man's head. Ichsan passed his hands over a firm chest and tight belly. He maneuvered Leaf's shorts past his bare feet.

Leaf wore no underwear. Ichsan bent down and sucked Leaf's soaring erection. Ichsan knew he hadn't the skill at sex that Leaf had already shown, but he did have a desire to give his partner pleasure. His cupped his hands around Leaf's buttocks and let his finger scout the anus. Leaf made no objection; rather, he turned himself around and sat on Ichsan's cock, caressing it even as he pumped energetically. Ichsan stretched his right hand around Leaf's member and let the kinesis of their bodies move the young man to come; Ichsan answered inside Leaf.

The pair fell back and uncoupled languorously on the bamboo floor of the hut. "We can wash in the river," Leaf said and led Ichsan to a pool of warm spring water near the bank. They scrubbed each other with pumice and, when satisfied, sat next to each other on a nearby boulder.

In the moonlight, Ichsan studied Leaf's face: the bright circles surrounding his dark irises, the ever-so-slightly comical ears, the slight stubble of a moustache, the thick black hair reaching his shoulders. He was startled by the shadows that stretched from one shoulder to the other across Leaf's breastbone. Ichsan touched the shadows but they did not disappear beneath his hands.

"Now you know why I am called Leaf."

And, indeed, the shadows, darker than the rich copper color of the rest of Leaf's body, were in fact a series of nine, Ichsan counted, ovals, a couple almost heart-shaped, one looking like a tropical fish, but most clearly recognizable as the leaves of a banyan tree.

"They are beautiful...tattoos?"

"Birthmarks. They give me, for better or worse, an identity. They set me apart."

Ichsan moved his finger and then his lips across the foliage. "Beautiful."

On the way back to town, Ichsan explained that he was a salesman visiting pharmacies in Mataram and surrounding towns; Leaf was, as so many young men in Lombok, jobless and so had to live with his uncle's family. "I can't even afford to fill my cellphone." He took an old Nokia out of his pocket. "No *pulsa*."

Ichsan offered to top up the phone, but Leaf declined. "I don't really need a phone."

"But I want to call you...so we can get together again?" Ichsan said, fearful of a negative response.

"Just come by the banyan tree, and I'll find you. You can drop me off there now."

"I can drop you at your uncle's."

"No. Not a good idea. My uncle is very conservative, very religious, very suspicious."

"Right." Ichsan pulled the car over and stopped near the tree at which he had first met this stranger. Leaf made to get out, but Ichsan put a hand gently on his thigh. "So you'll find me here again tomorrow, right?"

"I'll be there." He jutted his chin toward the banyan. Leaf let himself out of the car and stood by the tree until Ichsan rolled on. Only then did Leaf make his way down a narrow lane toward a small house fronted by a huge jackfruit tree. Ichsan watched him for as long as he could from the shadows in which he had parked.

The following night, Ichsan arrived at the banyan tree an hour after sunset. He wondered if Leaf would be as faithful as he had promised. He did not have to wonder long, for within five minutes, Leaf draped his arms around Ichsan's neck. Ichsan turned into him; Leaf wore a batik sarong and a white singlet. "Anything under that sarong?"

"No need."

"The weather looks threatening tonight. How about we go to my hotel room?"

"We can try. Where's the car?"

"By the old white building. I thought you prefer being picked up there."

"All my soccer friends were around last night. That spooked me a little. But I don't think it matters now."

Ichsan led the way to the Kijang, and they drove into the parking lot of the Sahid, a modest hotel, but the best in Mataram.

"Do we have to go through the lobby to get to your room?" Leaf asked.

"Yeah, it's a hotel, not a motel."

"Mmm. I don't think that's a good idea."

"Oh, there's no need to worry. They've seen it all at this place."

"But they are not going to see me. Let's just drive to the river, like last night."

"It's already raining!"

"But it's nice and dry and kind of sexy here in your car, don't you think?" Leaf took Ichsan's hands and brought them beneath his sarong to his very-ready dick. "Drive. Do you remember the way?"

At the river, they crawled into the back seat of the Kijang, undressed each other and made love as thunderously as the storm raging around them. They napped in each other's arms until the rain slowed to a trickle, allowing them to run to the river to wash again in the warm spring.

Just before letting him go at the banyan in Mataram, Ichsan said, "Leaf, this is my last night in Lombok. I don't get back here for five weeks."

"I will be right here."

"Not really!"

"Just come by the banyan tree the night you return. You'll see."

Again, Ichsan spied on his lover as he made his way to the house behind the jackfruit tree. Back in Jakarta at the home office of his pharmaceutical company, Ichsan negotiated with his fellow marketing representatives to trade for—and, where necessary, buy with a percentage of his commissions—circuits of doctors and apothecaries throughout Lombok and on the neighboring islands of Bali and Sumbawa. He maneuvered his sales map and calendar to arrange a three-week trip that would allow him to cover the whole of his territory from a home base in Mataram.

Waiting, on his first night back in Lombok, at the great banyan tree, he cursed himself for his foolishness. Did he really believe the fellow would bother to meet him after all these weeks?

They had known each other for two days. No, two nights. Did Ichsan expect Leaf to have found no one else since? Did Ichsan not consider that Leaf must have many friends already on this island? Did Ichsan think that Leaf obsessed over him as he did over Leaf? He kneeled into the banyan, closed his eyes, and banged his head against its trunk. "Idiot!" And again. "Idiot!"

But with the third blow, Ichsan's forehead found something softer than hard wood. He could not move his head. He opened his eyes. His head was held tight into Leaf's abdomen.

"You took my breath away," Leaf said.

"Same here."

"Shall we go? Where's the Kijang?"

"No Toyota this trip. I rented that blue BMW."

"Pricey!"

"I'm here for three weeks. I got a good deal."

"Good deal."

Ichsan had barely started the car when Leaf removed his sarong, loosened Ichsan's pants and leaned over to give him head.

"Slow down! I don't want to have an accident."

"With the car...or with your come?"

"Neither."

Leaf sat up in his seat and stroked both their cocks, slowly.

When they arrived at their place by the river, they walked each others' naked bodies to a hut where they embraced and kissed and sucked and rimmed and fucked forth and back.

"I don't know if I have the energy to wash," gasped Ichsan.

"The river will give you energy. Come on!"

Back in the car, Ichsan turned to Leaf before putting the key in the ignition. "Tomorrow, I'm visiting doctors in the east of the island. I'll pick you up at six for breakfast."

"No. No, Ichsan. I can't. Not during the day."

"Only at night?"

"Yes."

"I know! You're a vampire!"

Leaf grabbed Ichsan and bit his neck. The bite turned into a kiss and Leaf whispered, "Not a monster. No. But I walk with the night. To you. Tomorrow. Night."

Except for the two nights when Ichsan failed to get back to Mataram at all—the unreliable ferry service between islands forcing him to stay over in Bali and Sumbawa to await the morning launch—he spent every night during the first two weeks of his stay in Lombok with Leaf. It was never boring. Leaf knew so many variations of lovemaking and his affection seemed so genuine, so gentle, that Ichsan not only remained interested and intrigued, he feared he had fallen in love.

Finding himself with two days free of business appointments during his last weekend in Lombok, Ichsan lusted for even more time with Leaf. Dare he visit Leaf at his uncle's house on a Saturday morning? The uncle might well be home. How had Leaf described him? Conservative. Religious.

Suspicious.

But if there was one thing, Ichsan knew, that trumped suspicions in Indonesia where unemployment hadn't fallen below twenty percent in decades, it was a job offer.

In his hotel room after breakfast, Ichsan donned his best batik shirt, the red and gold one he saved for his most important meetings with his most important customers, black trousers and socks, and polished loafers. He draped around his neck a gold chain from which hung a medal of devout Islamic calligraphy. On his head he placed his black *peci*. Having checked every aspect of his costume in the mirror, he made his way to his BMW and drove past the banyan into the little lane where he parked beneath the jackfruit tree. The tree was abundant with paper sacks tied carefully around every fruit to warn passers-by that these jackfruits had an owner.

Ichsan knocked on the front door and hailed, "*Salam alaikum*."

In a few seconds, the door opened, and a broadly handsome man of about fifty years responded, "*Alaikum salam*." He wore the white *peci* of a Muslim who had been a pilgrim to Mecca for the haj. His eye settled on the calligraphy at the chest of his visitor.

"Good morning, Bapak Haji," Ichsan began, "Excuse my interruption. My name is Ichsan. I work for Garuda Pharma." Ichsan presented the haji with his business card.

"Welcome," said the haji warily. "My name is Mohammed Hendra. How can I serve you? I know nothing of drugs."

"Of course not. Of course. I am looking for a young man who lives here. I want to offer him employment."

Hendra wrinkled his brow. "Employment?"

"Yes, you see Lombok is my territory—"

"Your territory?"

"I mean to say that I represent Garuda Pharma in Lombok. And so I am often here. I want to hire your nephew as my driver and guide while—"

"My nephew?" The haji's face flushed.

"Yes, I met him the other day—"

Hendra grabbed Ichsan's chain at his throat and tightened his grip. "If I ever see you anywhere on this island again, you faggot, I will kill you," he said and slammed the door.

Ichsan staggered backwards into the trunk of the jackfruit tree before organizing himself for a quick getaway to his hotel. Scenarios flipped like pages in his mind. Someone must have seen him and Leaf fucking at the river. Gossips had noticed their nightly rendezvous. Leaf was hiding in his uncle's house. Leaf was hidden in his uncle's house. Leaf had been exiled by his uncle to another island. Haji Hendra would report Ichsan to Garuda Pharma. He had given him his card! Haji Hendra's associates would ride Ichsan out of Lombok. If they didn't kill him first.

The police can be bought! Homosexual sex is legal between consenting adults, but had Ichsan ever asked Leaf his age? He looks mature, but could he possibly be younger than eighteen? And anyway public sex is never legal.

Ichsan walked quickly through the lobby, scanning the faces of the receptionist and the cashier. What did they know? He bounded up the stairs, ran to his room, threw himself on the bed and waited. For the phone call from Jakarta. For the knock on the door.

He couldn't eat. He wouldn't close his eyes until, having heard neither phone nor knock, late that Saturday night, still in his best clothes, he fell asleep.

Ichsan had neglected to close the drapes, and so the morning sun pierced his slumber.

Eyes widened, he bolted upright. Stupid! Why hadn't he gone to the banyan last night to meet Leaf? Coward! He needed to know what Hendra had said to Leaf. He needed to know Leaf was okay. He needed to know Leaf was still looking out for him.

And now he had all of Sunday to wait. Ichsan feared he would go mad.

He had to do something. He undressed, leaving his clothes in a heap, showered, put on jeans and a tee, and took the stairs to the lobby. He still feared dirty looks from the staff or angry epithets from uniformed strangers, but nothing untoward hindered his purposefully leisurely stroll through the lobby and into the BMW.

Ichsan drove to the banyan, not really expecting Leaf to be there, but holding on to the possibility that, given the emergency, he might. He sat beneath the banyan, facing its ancient trunk, and he prayed. To God? To the tree? To whomever might listen, he prayed for Leaf.

Ichsan knew well how to meditate and ignored all the sounds of this surrounding Sunday by absorbing them. His mantra was Leaf...Leaf...Leaf.

Nothing touched him. No one. After more than an hour, he opened his eyes and swiveled around to face the avenue. He heard the laughter and cheers and slides of barefoot boys playing football and looked to the field where he had ogled the players his very first night in Mataram, the night Leaf found him.

Might Leaf be there? Now? Taking little care for traffic, Ichsan sprinted across the street.

He paced the perimeter of the pitch, but saw no Leaf. At the far corner, he bought a cup of instant noodles from a hawker and sat on the ground among a dozen or so adolescents taking a break from the games. Adhering to the local custom, Ichsan asked permission to eat in front of them. The boys nodded assent, of course, and one of the eldest of them, a long-legged fellow in pirated Nike shorts and an Emirates Real Madrid jersey, asked him if he was a tourist.

"On business, actually."

"What's your name, then?"

"Ichsan. Yours?"

"Restu and these guys are..." He rattled off the name of every boy in the circle.

"I don't think I can remember them all."

"That's okay," said Restu. "I can remember them for you."

"Do you know the name of everyone here?" Ichsan waved his arm to survey the field.

"Maybe," Restu said. "Probably. Almost."

"Do you know Leaf?"

"Leaf?"

"Yes, Leaf."

"No. Weird name. No one by that name here."

"You said you know almost everyone."

"Ichsan, if anyone had the name Leaf, I'd have heard it. And remember it." Ichsan nodded grimly. "But you know," Restu continued, "most of us have nicknames we have given each other. So maybe we know him differently. What does he look like?"

"He has a very distinctive set of tattoos—birthmarks actually—around his neck."

Restu cocked his head alertly. "Leaves."

"Yes, leaves. So you do know Leaf."

"Rabbit. We know him as Rabbit."

Ichsan pictured Leaf. "His ears aren't that big," he said.

"No," interrupted one of the other boys, "but he sure can wiggle his tail. If you know what I mean." The circle of boys smiled, but did not laugh as raucously as Ichsan expected in response to such a crude joke.

"Where is he?"

Restu shrugged. "Maybe still over there." He pointed toward the old white building. "We haven't seen him in...I don't know...how long, Adi?"

A shorter boy stopped pulling the scraggly whiskers on his chin. "Like more than six months. Maybe a year."

"No," said Ichsan. "That can't be. I met Leaf—Rabbit—whoever—here less than two months ago."

"Here? No way! We would have seen him. He was our friend. We would have cheered that he was back from there."

"From?"

"The hospital."

"It's a hospital, the big white building?"

"For nuts," said Adi. "You know, for crazy people."

"But L—Rabbit—"

Restu explained, "Zul. Rabbit's real name is Zulfikar Lukman. According to his uncle, Zul is crazy. Because he's different...he likes to have sex with guys. That's why you're looking for him, right?"

Ichsan was on guard. "I-I...want to offer him a job."

"Oh, okay, sure. But you don't have to be shy with us. I went to school with Zul. Who else here did? Adi..." Adi nodded. "And who else was in our class?" Seven of the other boys raised their hands. "And how many of us did Zul jerk off?" Nine boys including Restu raised their hands. "Suck?" No hand dropped. "How many fucked Zul?" Only Restu and Adi and the boy who had uttered the crude joke kept their hands in the air. "None of us are queer like Zul. Well, as far as I know anyway." Adi gave Restu a punch. "But, look, we liked him. He was our friend. It's fucked up what happened to him."

"What happened?"

"It wasn't much of a secret what Zul liked and who he did. Except from his family, I guess. Until one night he was being fucked outside of town by the river and another couple, a girl and a guy, also there to have sex probably, saw Zul. The girl was his cousin. She screamed and said she'd be telling her father what she saw. And she did. Her father is a big-time haji, on the board of the mosque. It was a huge shame for him. One that he could only explain by claiming Zul was crazy. And so he had him put away in the Siti Dawn Hospital."

Dumbfounded, Ichsan turned to stare at the hospital. This might explain, he realized, why Leaf appeared at the banyan only at night. Leaf had figured out how to sneak out of the hospital after dark. But why would he go back to his uncle's house when they came back from the river each night? Of course, Leaf would have guessed that Ichsan would be watching where he walked! Did his uncle haul him back to Siti Dawn every morning? Or did Leaf only seem to enter Haji Hendra's house, when he actually snuck back to the hospital after Ichsan drove away?

"You okay?" Restu asked Ichsan after some silent moments.

"Yeah. I really appreciate your telling me all this. I'm going to see him."

"Great. Tell him we miss him. Seriously, we miss him."

"I will." Ichsan started. "But what happened to the other guy? The one having sex with Zul? Did his family put him away too?"

"Uh, that would be me," said Restu. "Nothing happened to me. See, I was the guy fucking Zul. I was the man, you know. No big deal."

"Right," said Ichsan who knew how the lines were drawn across this archipelago. "By the way, how old are you...and Zul?"

"I'm almost twenty-one. Zul is a few months older. But, hey, are you really looking for guys to hire? I need a job myself."

"We'll see. We'll see. And thanks again." Ichsan rose, paid the hawker for a round of drinks for the circle of boys, dusted himself off, and headed toward Siti Dawn.

It wasn't until he had walked through the open gate and reached the front of Siti Dawn that it registered on Ichsan that this building was a hospital! Yet not one to which he was assigned. Likely because Garuda did not market any specifically psychiatric meds. But even an asylum would stock antiseptics and analgesics and plenty of other items Garuda produced.

Ichsan hustled to the BMW, drove back to his hotel, climbed to his room without bothering to check the faces of the staff. Quickly he showered and retrieved his best clothes from the pile where he had dropped them. He drove to Siti Dawn.

A grizzled old man in faded green scrubs was smoking a clove cigarette behind a dilapidated desk. He hummed a popular tune and played with an ancient typewriter as if it were a piano. The lobby was otherwise empty.

Ichsan's "*salam alaikum*" bounced off the bare walls, green as the old man's scrubs, and streaked with spackle. Ichsan handed this decrepit receptionist his business card.

The old man's failure to respond with an "*alaikum salam*" was a rudeness Ichsan had rarely encountered. "I know you," the old man said instead.

Ichsan thought of Leaf's uncle and swallowed hard. "Then you will understand I should like to see the hospital administrator."

"You will see no one here today." He repeated, "No one."

"Because?"

"It's Sunday." The old man dropped his cigarette butt to the floor and stepped on it, adding still one more stain to the tiles on which the old man's chair wobbled. "No one is here."

"You're here."

"That's me. No one."

"There are patients here."

"Oh, you are looking for patients? To sell them drugs directly?"

"Of course not." Ichsan paused. "Very well, I'll be back tomorrow."

"He won't be here tomorrow either."

"Who?"

"The one you're looking for."

Ichsan hadn't the stomach for this game. He left the building as the old man lit up another cigarette and leaned back in his chair.

As he walked across the grounds of the hospital to the front gate, he passed a young man in scrubs seated on a crumbling cement bench next to an elderly woman in a nightgown. She was busy picking imaginary lice off her arms and legs and those of her attendant. Ichsan turned to take a chance.

"*Salam alaikum.*"

"*Alaikum salam,*" replied the attendant.

"Are you her nurse?" Ichsan asked.

"I am the nurse here."

"The only one in this whole place?"

"Yes, but, well, there aren't many patients." He lowered his voice. "Only those whose families are willing to pay plenty to put away...and never see again."

Ichsan kneeled in front of the bench. The woman picked at Ichsan's arms. "Is Zulfikar Lukman one of those?"

The nurse looked around. "He was."

"He's not here anymore? Do you—"

"He's dead."

"Oh no. That cannot be! No!" Ichsan's mind swirled. "I just saw—When? Just yesterday?"

The nurse stood and lifted the old woman. "Yesterday? No. Already two months ago. We have to go."

Ichsan stood. He saw the old man leaning against the doorway of the hospital.

Apparently unperturbed even as he nodded at Ichsan, he unfurled smoke rings in the air.

"Two months. This is a mistake! Zulfikar Lukman! You—I—"

"Zulfikar Lukman, the nephew of Haji Mohammed Hendra, hanged himself from the banyan tree over there two months ago. We have to go."

Shaking, Ichsan sat on the bench. The shadows of the iron fence posts surrounding the hospital poked him into realizing that it was already late afternoon. He gathered himself together enough to drive to the hotel where he undressed and lay on the bed awaiting the night.

When it was dark, Ichsan drove to the banyan. He waited, the car idling only a moment before Leaf was sitting next to him. The car door hadn't opened. Leaf had appeared, wordlessly answering the question Ichsan most needed to ask. Ichsan dropped his head to the steering wheel and sobbed in grief and joy. Leaf draped his body over his lover's until Ichsan sat up and drove silently to their riverside.

Ichsan left the car and walked to their favorite hut where he sat cross-legged. Leaf was already there.

"What shall I call you? Zul? Rabbit?" asked Ichsan.

"I am your Leaf."

Ichsan was crying again. "But you are not really here."

"I am. I am here for you."

"But you are..." Ichsan could not utter the word.

And so Leaf did, "I died. But I am not dead. Not if you can see me. Not if you can love me."

Ichsan stood and ran to the river. He screamed, "This is insane." He collapsed to his knees. "God help me." He raised his eyes to Leaf, still in the hut.

"What are you then? Undead? A vampire after all? A ghost? A fucking ghost?" He laughed bizarrely at the unintentional joke. "A fucking ghost!"

"I have no word for what I am. Except Leaf. Your Leaf. There was no handbook distributed when I died. No glossary. No one explained anything. I learn as I go along. I didn't even know anyone living could see me. Until you did. I was drawn to you that night at the tree."

"Or you drew me. You were longing for someone, and I was there. I was there because that is where I died."

"You hanged yourself."

"I ran away from the hospital, mad with the drugs and the treatments they gave me. They did make me crazy. I ran to the tree, grabbed one of the parasitic vines in the banyan and hanged myself from a branch of the tree. Until the next night, I was...nowhere. Even now when it is daylight...I am nowhere. When the sun sets, I am conscious. Mostly, now, I am conscious of you. No one else, it seems, can even see me." He paused. "Come here, Ichsan. I need to hold you."

Ichsan returned to the hut, and entered Leaf's embrace. "Let us make love," Leaf whispered.

"I— You are not alive. It's sick."

"My uncle believes that love even between living men is sick. But I do so love you. Come. I am no longer Zul, no longer Rabbit, that is true. But you never knew them. I am your Leaf, the same Leaf only you have known. Come."

When Ichsan finally entered Leaf that night, he felt as if he had joined with the cosmos.

"And when I came," he whispered later to Leaf, "I understood the universe."

"The big bang?" Leaf laughed.

"For a start." Ichsan said. "But here's what else I understand: If I die too, we can be together always. Forever."

"No," Leaf said. "There is no way to know if we can find each other if you die! I haven't seen anyone else like me. I don't even know where I am when I am not with you." Leaf calmed himself. "You will die sometime. Of old age I hope. Until then, let us hold on to what we know we have." Leaf smiled. "It is so much better than what I had when I was alive."

"And I have never felt more alive."

"Stay that way. And I shall always be here for you."

"Here. In Lombok."

"Yes, only, it seems, at these few places in Lombok."

"The sun will rise soon. Do we need to return to the banyan? Or can you just . . . depart from here?"

"I think the tree is my portal."

When the BMW arrived at the banyan tree, Ichsan held up his hand, got out of the car, opened the passenger door, and took Leaf's hand. He led Leaf to the tree, backed him against the trunk, held wide his arms and embraced Leaf as tightly as he could until he felt only bark and the rays of the sun.

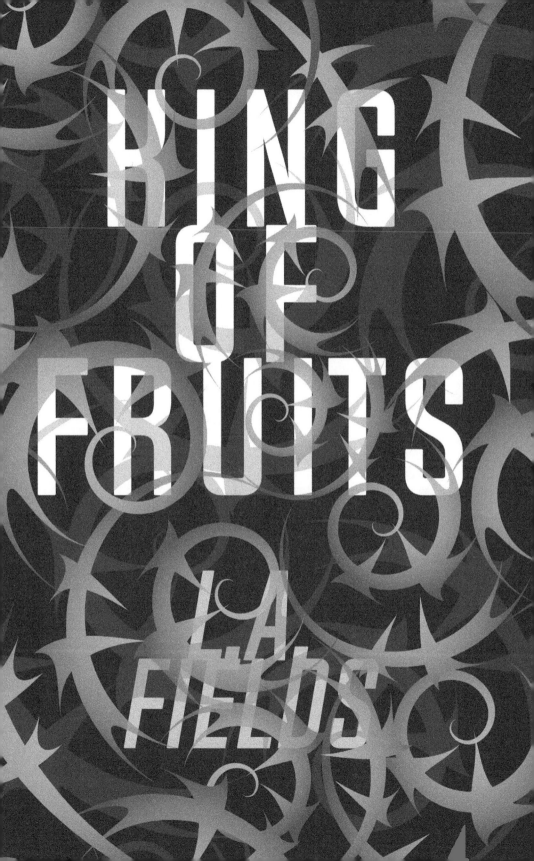

KING
OF
FRUITS

L.A.
FIELDS

TONIGHT'S HIS NIGHT, WE SCHEDULE these things. It's nothing as rigid as every fourth Wednesday or anything, but when he gets an idea for one of these events, we both get out our planners and agree on when it's going down. This is his kink, and it's pretty obvious how he got it, why it turns him on to watch me eat the strangest foods he can find.

Perry lost his sense of smell when he was in college, he says it was some nasal spray that had zinc in it, probably; the handful of doctors he's been to over the years can't fix it, and because there's nothing to do about it, there's no real point in nailing down exactly what caused it either. You might as well ask your doctor why your index and middle finger are the same length when it doesn't matter why, it is what it is. Doctors will say, "We don't do anything about that, so get out of our office," basically.

When you can't smell, you can't taste either. I've gotten a couple of colds in the six years we've been together, and for as long as my nose is stuffed up I get to walk around in Perry's shoes. I can't smell, can't taste much, can only vaguely detect what is sour, bitter, sweet, or salty, and that's about it. Perry confirms that going around with a stuffed-up nose is what his life is like every day. One cold at age twenty, the wrong nasal spray at the wrong time, and while I'll recover to smell and taste again, he never will. I'm glad that it happened to him and not me, mostly because I'd be a dramatic baby about it—the *tragedy*, the great loss of my young life!—whereas Perry has learned to joke about it, and to adapt around it.

Downsides: he can't tell when food is rotten unless it looks or feels rotten. Slimy mushrooms? Bad. The quinoa looks like someone's poured iodine on it? Bad. But if the milk's gone sour he'll drink it and not know unless it's curdled. He has no goddamn idea when it's time to scoop the litter box either (he traded that chore with me upon moving in together: I clean the cat's bathroom, he cleans ours, that's the deal; I sit on that toilet but never scrub it). He tells me every once in a while why it's so fortunate that he's cohabiting with someone who isn't handicapped on two out of five human senses.

"If there's a gas leak, I won't know until I pass out or light a match," he says. "Although, it would be very easy for you to poison me if I ever got on your nerves, so there's looking up for you, huh?" He isn't usually that annoying.

About a year ago he asked if he could try something, by which he meant watch me try something, *eat* something, so that I could describe it to him. Food he didn't taste before age twenty he'll never get to know now, and he's curious. Bright side for him: he can eat healthy all day and not be tormented by the smell of fast food or the temptation of a big, thick-frosted cake. He says he can't taste powdered sugar at all. Whipped cream is nothing but texture to him, all he knows about it is that it makes his throat phlegmy. The only times I'm tempted to poison him are the days when I'm trying to reform my dietary habits or lose some weight, and I can't get any sympathy for my pangs.

But then again, because he eats so well, he stays pretty fit, and I know I still turn him on too, otherwise we wouldn't be doing this elaborate sort of taste testing.

These "meals" always end in sex, and so along with him getting whatever edible oddity he's found ready, we both make our best effort: today's the day everybody remembers to shower, for example. If anyone's been meaning to get a haircut, this is enough of an occasion to make it happen. Toenails clipped, the sheets recently washed, the evening cleared of both work and mindless entertainment. Honestly, we should be couples' counselors with this stuff; don't just eat dinner together every night to discuss your day and connect, get weird with it, it's more fun that way, and it's definitely unique to your relationship only. Why eat a burger when you've got steak at home? Or in my case, if you've got corn smut at home.

That's what it was last time: *huitlacoche*, commonly known as corn smut, also commonly known as a nasty fungus that infects the kernels of corn and consumes them, turning them into grayish tumor-like nodes. Researching it later, I found someone else comparing the looks of them to river stones (generous). "Maize mushrooms" is a bit closer. It's more disgusting to think about than to eat, honestly. It doesn't interrupt the normal taste of a burrito, which is how it was first served to me. It was only after Perry told me what it was, let me get a good look at it (it resembles a wet lump of black tar with corn kernels in it), and then asked me to eat a spoonful of the devil's shit, that I started to gag a bit. A little bit sweet, a little bit nutty-funky, but it was the texture of an infected kernel bursting in my mouth that did me in. That's when Perry handed me a glass of whiskey (one sip to swish and spit, to sterilize), and then the rest of the glass for courage. Perry kissed me after that, his tongue in my mouth a much more welcome texture. Of course, it's probably only a matter of time until he serves me something else's tongue just to watch it disturb me. He focuses a lot on texture variety since he can't taste much, and it seems to delight him to watch the feel of food make me wriggle. This fetish he's developing might be nothing more complicated than getting turned on by my gag reflex, but I don't question too deeply the things that bring me pleasure.

Before that was a century egg, or really just a two month old egg. Perry promises not to poison me, as I've promised him, so even though the whites of the egg had gone black and jellied (looked like a dark ball of amber), and the yolk was green-gray and as thick as cheese, I ate it. It smelled worse than it tasted—like a bland bit of butter nested in flavorless Jell-O—so I salted and ate the three on my side of the half-dozen, and Perry did the same. After that it seemed fitting to do a bit of sixty-nining, to suck each other's dicks, shower off, and then go to bed. The night of the corn smut (sort of aptly named considering what we were doing with it) demanded an extra level of intercourse, as getting fucked was the only sure way to distract me from the memory of what had been in my mouth. Perry seemed to get a thrill from the way I writhed every time I thought of it again, the sicko. Not that I minded.

Today's a new day, and there's something on the table between Perry and me covered in a towel, for the big reveal. A lump under a towel, our biggest knife, and two spoons, that's what's here. I assume it's a cow brain or something, that he's going to whip that off and I'll be invited to recreate some Hannibal Lector scene, so instead of looking at that, I look at Perry.

Whatever that is, I won't take too long savoring it I'm sure, and once I try it, I'll get to cleanse my palate with him. Perry looks good today, the fact that he can't smell means I got to pick his cologne because he doesn't care one way or the other, and I can smell that scent from here. He's wearing one of his tighter shirts, bless him, and his hair (though curly when dry) is slicked back still from the water of a recent shower, and I do like that look on him. He's got a hint of a smirk on his lips and what looks like a close shave on his face, and I can't wait to kiss all of it. Possibly I'll have to do a shot of mouthwash first, depending on what's under that towel, but I'm willing to swallow my medicine.

"You ready for this, Art?"

I shrug. "I'm sure I'll live. You smell good," I tell him, and that turns his smirk into a grin.

"Speaking of," he says, leaning forward to snatch the towel away with relish. "Do you know what this is?"

It looks like a pufferfish, but I do know what it is. They say it's the world's smelliest fruit, durian.

"Oh, goddammit," I tell him, rolling my eyes. "You don't get to share in this torment at all! They say it tastes fine but smells like ass."

"I know what they say," Perry tells me, standing up and grabbing the knife, "but I *can't* know if it's true. I want you to tell me about it."

"Fair enough. Bring it on."

It smells like nothing in its little prickly-pear-looking skin, but once Perry cuts into it, I get a whiff.

"Ugh, it smells like a cantaloupe's toe cheese," I tell him. Perry starts laughing and splits the two halves apart with a wet crack. Right away it looks like we're doing an alien autopsy. The smell redoubles once it's all the way open, a little like wet garbage, and I keep trying to explain the smell even as I'm horrified by how it looks.

"Like an old refrigerator, that's what it smells like, or like rotting passion fruit in the same trash can as old eggs." The "flesh" part of this fruit is a little eggy looking itself, like a creamed heart of palm, and there are lobes of it in the cockle chambers surrounding the core, each one containing a couple of seeds each. Before Perry digs the seeds out, these lobes look like sickly kidneys. "Do you really have to touch it with your bare hands, Perry? What if the smell gets under your fingernails?"

"Too late now, here." He hands me a spoon, and the time has come for me to eat some of this thing.

"We should have done this outside, the kitchen's going to stink now."

"It'll fade," Perry says. It's easy for him to be blasé since it's not his nose that'll smell it all week. He takes the other spoon, and we each dig out a bite of this gunk. I'm breathing though my mouth so I don't have to smell so much of it, but all that means is I'm starting to taste it on the air instead. "Ready?" Perry asks.

"Sure," I say. "Bone apple tea."

Perry laughs, and I hope there's nothing called a bone apple that can be made into a tea, I'm just trying to be a smartass while I can still talk without retching. I take a deep breath and stick the spoon into my mouth and let the taste happen to me.

Perry's face is only curious as he chews and rolls the durian around his mouth, trying to see if any part of his tongue can detect a flavor. He does this a lot—eating out with him is pretty fun, as I get to choose two things I want to try, and he's happy to take whichever one I decide against. He'll sit across from me and interrogate his mouth with every new bite, just like he's doing now. It's cute; it always reminds me how much I like him.

I'm not gagging yet, but it's taking an effort. I swallow and then a shudder shivers all through my jelly. That was not fun. Perry's waiting for me to explain.

"It's like if a mashed banana were also an onion, oh my god," I tell him.

Perry laughs. "Are you going to eat any more?"

"Yeah, hold on."

I pinch my nose this time and try another bite. It's easier to eat like this because I'm not really tasting it, but the texture is still a sort of creamy, sinewy, pus-like abomination, and after I swallow I let go of my nose and the funk comes rushing back. I throw down my spoon.

"Wow," I tell Perry. "There is no reason for anyone to eat that. Just because it isn't poison doesn't mean it's really food, damn. This is edible, survivable, but I wouldn't call it food."

"All right, all right, I'll throw it out."

"Out*side*," I insist, and Perry nods and takes it away to be bagged and banished.

I go to the fridge and rinse my mouth out with Coke. If this stuff can get oil off a driveway, surely it'll burn the memory of that "fruit" out of my mouth. I'm still guzzling soda and trying to breathe the fizz into my nose to get rid of the smell. I'm pinching my nostrils trying to flatten the stink out when Perry comes back in.

His hands slide around my waist as I stand at the sink. I like the feel of them, but I pick them up and start washing them first. I know they smell like an old freezer and a sock drawer combined, and I don't want them rubbing all over me quite yet. Pulling his hands forward to scrub them means I'm pulling Perry's body closer to my back. He starts to kiss my neck as I clean beneath his fingernails. If he kisses my mouth before he rinses his own out, I'll probably complain. Or I won't, I'll just take it. I'll probably just take it until I like it, that's about how this works.

With his hands overly warm from the hot water, he dries them off on my hair and then touches my face. I nuzzle against his petting the same way the cat does, and turn off the water so I can concentrate. Perry next reaches down to undo my pants, to push them and my underwear halfway down my ass.

"Leave these here," he says.

I smirk; I won't be needing clothes where we're going.

Perry heads to the bedroom and I hang back to undress and stack my clothes on the counter. I start to touch myself, getting ready for this, and giving Perry a head start so he can take charge when I walk in. I'm already forgetting about that funky fruit when I walk through the dimness of the hallway into our bedroom, which is probably why I shouldn't be surprised by what happens next.

Perry darts from behind the door, also naked, and kisses me fast. What I assume is a deep and passionate tongue kiss quickly reveals itself to be a Trojan horse—he's got a sliver of that fruit in his mouth and is oozing it into mine without permission. My eyes fly open in outrage, but he kisses me deeper before I can pull away, his tongue pushing durian into my mouth, his eyes staring right back at mine like some twisted psychologist waiting eagerly for a reaction. Perry doesn't want this to be a scheduled date night, where we show up and shake hands and commence with agreed-upon sex to maintain our cohabitation status. Perry wants us to be weird together, and I want that too, but I sure wish it tasted sweeter than this. I should invent a sexual request of my own to pay him back. Maybe I'm really into riding crops and hot candle wax now, maybe I have a thing for pinching his nipples with clothespins and then ripping the pins away with a string, how about that?

I swallow this slug of supposed fruit whole, so I don't have to endure chewing it. I push Perry away from my face.

"You asshole," I tell him. I'm breathing through my mouth to try and avoid the smell. Perry knows what I'm up to.

"*You* asshole," he repeats back to me. Me Tarzan, you asshole, basically. He then picks up another piece of durian from a plate on our dresser (that's why he was so long throwing it out, he was *dissecting* it), and puts it into my mouth before clapping his hand over my lips. Now I have to breathe through my nose, and I can't even spit it out. I don't know why he didn't just buy a nice, normal ball gag if he was going to be like this about it.

His smirk is back in place, and he sort of slow-dances us over to the bed so he doesn't have to let go of me. He drops me onto my back and picks up my ankles, and at this point I just give in—the majority of the fruit is far away from us at last, and we're finally down to business. He sinks to the floor as I grab hold of my knees, and tuck this big gob of durian into the side of my cheek so I can just ignore it for a minute. Perry's crouched on the floor licking my asshole now, and I wonder which he would think tasted worse if he suddenly regained his senses, that gym sock of an armored fruit, or this man's asshole? He lost his sense of smell before he lost his virginity, he might not really know one from the other. What a dilemma that would be.

I try to focus on the feel of his tongue prodding away, and less about how another piece of this funky fruit was just in his mouth, disguised as a tongue. When he stands up to get lube from the nightstand, I try to forget the membranous come-like coating of the durian's inner chambers. When he starts to insinuate the head of his dick inside of me, I reach for him to pull him closer. Enough of this sluggishness, I want this to go hard and fast, and I want this piece of "fruit" out of my mouth and instead forced into his. As Perry sinks into me, I pull him down for a kiss, and blow that morsel of durian into his mouth. He takes it, and pulls back laughing.

"You're right," he says, arching back. "That is a pretty unpleasant surprise." He chews and swallows, smiling the whole time. I start to buck against him, so he doesn't forget what he's supposed to be doing right now.

He finds his rhythm, but he's still being too much of a tease about it, just enjoying my mounting frustration. It doesn't take long before I practically kick him out of me, and tell him to lie down.

"Get on the bed, back against the pillows."

Perry does so, and I go back to his gross fruit platter to see if I can find one of the seeds. I'm in luck: right next to the fat-like strips he cut is one of the thing's seeds, sort of smooth and slim, like a good pond-skipping stone. I pick it up and bring it with me back to the bed.

"Suck on this for a while," I tell Perry, and his eyes light up like the seed might contain some kind of drug. I slide the thing into his mouth (that'll keep him from smirking so much), and then wipe my hand off on his bare chest. I hop up on his lap and start smelling the parts of him that I like—his hair, his pits when they're more clean than not—while he scoots down so we're aligned again.

I always think of this position as Vlad the Impaler, sinking down onto a penetrating rod like this. Once I've got Perry pinned down, I can finally move at *my* pace, with short, sharp thrusts against the spot where I want them. I put Perry's hand on my dick, and he starts keeping time with me: his hips and his hand thrust up while I come down. I start to sweat. Perry's eyes refocus, sprightly no more, now serious. At last the scent of us, that raw, salty, seminal tang, starts to overpower the blander durian funk. I pinch his cheeks with one hand so he'll spit out that seed, and when it pops out and rolls to the side, I lean down and kiss him.

That lets him know I'm close; he grabs my hips with both hands and makes a real effort to fuck me over the edge, and my hand replaces his at my helm, and together we get me off so thoroughly that I'm as shaky as a newborn fawn when it's over.

I kiss him a bit more, catch my breath, and get off of him carefully, so I don't trigger his orgasm too soon. Of all the times I've had the desire, I've never wanted to suck someone's dick quite this much before. Delicious isn't exactly the word I'd use for it most of the time (too savory), but right now the thought of some firm meat, slick with protein and salt, the nearest taste to blood without being vampiric about it...my mouth waters at the thought.

I suck him in, right to the back of my throat. He moans, and cups the side of my face in thanks. I wrap my thumb and forefinger just below my lips, forming a little pressure ring, and it doesn't take more than five bobs to milk his release into my mouth. I swallow; I'm not always willing to, but today I'm about ready to gargle the stuff. I kiss him again as he falls back, panting. I make sure I drool a little of his essence in there, to get him back for spitting durian in my mouth.

"Ugh," he says with half a laugh, wiping his mouth as I flop over and rest my head in the crook of his shoulder. I start to run my fingers across his lower belly, just above the line of his pubic hair, not close enough to the raw nerve of his dick to make him wince, but certainly close enough to keep him trembling a little longer.

"Oh, I'm sorry, does that taste bad to you?" I ask him.

"It's just gross when it's your own and not someone else's. It's kind of, I don't know, self-involved or unnatural."

"Just because something's disgusting doesn't mean it's unnatural, that's what I'm learning with your little food fetish you've got here."

Perry snorts. "If that's your opinion on jizz, I think I know what we're eating next. You like seafood, right?"

"No, I don't," I lie.

"*Shirako*," Perry says. "The seminal sacks of cods. They say it tastes buttery."

"Ugh, fine, whatever. At least I've already got a taste for the stuff."

Perry wraps his arm around my head, and leans forward to kiss the top of my head. "That's my guy," he says.

I feel the same way about him.

THE SINTAKER WAS DEAD.

Twenty days had passed since he was found, his worn bones resting on a bed of leaves at the foot of the temple's altar. Twenty days since the sin of the people had been taken. Twenty days without rain and with cruel winds and fruitless hunts.

The Elders were afraid, but none knew what was to be done. They had gathered in the heart of the village around the flames of the fire pit.

Ithil was among the men listening, though he was not permitted to speak. Until he took a wife and fathered a child, he would remain too young to speak, but old enough to listen. He had no desire for such things, and such matters could not be forced upon him. In time he would, he knew, be grey-haired and still silent among the Elders.

A new Sintaker had to be found, the Elders said. The spirit of the forest was displeased by his absence, but the man had left no kin. For as long as anyone could remember, he had been the Sintaker for their clan, living in the confines of the temple, fed by the tributes. People feared him as much as the forest spirit he served. In the night, after the cleansings, the Sintaker's cries echoed through the valley.

The first time Ithil saw him, the man was already old, his body lean and bare. Ithil's mother had forced his head down. It was ill luck to look at the Sintaker. The Sintaker never spoke, but once, his hand had lingered on Ithil's brow, and Ithil dared to look up at him. He had a green tint to his skin, Ithil remembered, as if his veins flowed with the sap of the trees rather than the blood of men.

"Draw lots," one of the Elders said. "Let fate choose the man."

"The spirit may not approve."

There were murmurs of agreement.

"If the spirit wants someone," a voice called out, "let it choose someone!"

"Hush, you fool!" another cried out. "You will call its attention!"

They argued as the flames sank to ash, and twenty days turned into twenty-one. None could agree, for none wished to be sent into the solitude of the temple. None of them wished to take the secret sins of the people and scream in the night. They were all afraid.

Ithil drew his cloak around him as the gathering parted. The morning air was cool, and the pale sky cloudless. The sun would come soon, and if the spirit was still displeased, their already dry crops—hidden in the tamer clearings of the forest—would shrivel and die.

The wind whirled about him, casting up ash and embers.

Silently, Ithil rose, his legs stiffened and aching from inaction. He looked around. Through the haze, he could see the faint glow of house lanterns, lit to protect those inside against the darkness and spirits until the sun returned.

Wreaths of morning mist coiled about him as he walked from the heart.

His family lived closer to the wildness, where the forest was no longer made for men. They had long been the defenders of the village boundaries, but even his father could not defend their people from an angry spirit.

He could see the walls of the temple in the distance, the pale stone spires jutting between the trees. It was old. Far older than any of them knew. There were carvings, so worn that they were barely visible anymore. None could say who built it nor why, but nature had wrapped around it, the walls threaded with vines, and archways filled with towering trees.

The wind was rising.

A wise man would have run to find shelter, but Ithil remained where he was, staring at the temple. He slowly went to one knee and ran his hand through the dew-drenched grass. It was cool and slick against his fingers. He raised them to touch his fingertips to his brow, as the Sintaker had so many times in his life.

A shiver passed through him, as the wind wrapped around him. He closed his eyes, offering a silent plea for the spirit's mercy. He was still kneeling when he heard the patter on the leaves. Rain. It was raining. He fell to his other knee, laughing, and tilted his head back, letting it soak him.

The spirit had been appeased, but one such small gesture could not calm it forever.

When night came, and his family rested, comforted by the spirit's mercy, Ithil sat at the door, looking into the forest, towards the temple. The lantern flickered in front of him, and he could hear a whisper in the wind.

Only a fool would draw a spirit's eye, he knew, especially one as merciless as the forest spirit.

He retreated to his sleeping place, but when sleep came, it brought strange dreams of pale stone and ancient, green-stained hands reaching for him. And through it all, he could hear someone calling his name. He woke, crying out.

His mother asked what troubled him, but Ithil shook his head. If the spirit's eye had fallen on him, he could not let it fall on his family too. His mother clucked in concern, but his father only sighed, offering Ithil a spear.

Dreams or not, the boundaries had to be protected. His two brothers were already waiting for them outside of his parents' home. Arhil had even brought his eldest boy with him. The child was puffed up with pride, holding his father's spear.

"I will take the south," Ithil said.

It was the narrowest path, a route for one person alone. No brothers, no nephews, no fathers to turn his ear, and ask the questions that were always asked.

The world was refreshed by the rain, a soft mist curling about the trees as the sun warmed the damp earth. Leaves were ripe, fat with water. Flowers swelled open, filling the air with rich fragrances. Around him, the forest felt alive.

Ithil pushed through the undergrowth, along the familiar paths. Fronds of ferns coiled around his bare calves, leaving shimmering tracks of dew on his skin. In the rising heat of the day, the coolness was pleasing. He let his hands brush against leaves, gathering the moisture and marked it to his brow and cheeks.

A breath of wind swirled about him, cooling the dew on his skin. He shivered, closing his eyes.

"Ithil..."

His name, again, close behind him, in the rustle of the leaves and the whisper of the wind.

Ithil's heart beat harder. He turned, wondering if he might see the one who called. Between the trees, he could only see the walls of the temple. He bowed his head, averting his eyes, as one who is unworthy should. It was the lesson of his mother. The lesson of his people.

The forest was silent again.

He gathered himself and continued on his path, but the brightness had gone from the flowers along his way, and the fruit he plucked to eat was bitter. He was not the only one to find it so.

When he returned to the heart, the people were all gathered. Renta—one of those with the death-touch—was weeping as he bade farewell to his family.

"He has been chosen," one of the Elders murmured.

"By whom?" Ithil asked, uncaring of the unspoken laws of silence.

Had the forest spirit called out to another? It took him a moment to understand the feeling welling within him: jealousy and disappointment. It shook him. Did he truly wish to have the eyes of the spirit on him?

He bowed his head, staring at his feet as the Elders reproached him. He cared nothing for what they said, his thoughts tumbling one upon the other. Finally, chastisement complete, one of them recalled his question. "Lots were drawn among some of the men."

Not him, Ithil observed. He looked at his father, who turned away his face. Ithil looked about the circle, and could see those who were relieved. Ah. The forest spirit was only offered true men, who had fathered sons, even the unclean ones who handled the dead.

The Elders escorted Renta through the forest, trailed by many of the village. Ithil lingered to the rear, watching as the man—quaking—approached the vast stone archway that led into the temple courtyard, where coloured flagstones wove in patterns towards the altar.

Renta hesitated before the archway, then stepped cautiously through.

The wind roared, gusting so fiercely that men fell to their knees. Thick vines swung downwards. Renta was thrown back through the archway, landing in the dirt. He was laughing and sobbing with relief, huddling on the ground.

"Not good enough," one of the Elders groaned, bowing low.

All eyes were to the ground.

All but Ithil's.

He stared up at the temple, at the broad leaves that framed the temple gate curling in silent invitation. His mouth felt dry as a rock, and his hands trembled at his sides. It was calling to him, he knew. Only to him. No other had dared to look.

His father's hand caught his arm, a steely grip. Ithil flinched, looking down. The leaves whispered, as if with a silent sigh, and the rain started to fall, light at first, then heavier and heavier.

As twilight came, the lanterns glowed between the trees.

The rain had not stopped, beating harder by the hour. Lightning tore at the sky. Every crack of thunder shook loose dust from the thatch of the house. Ithil sat by the doorway, holding a lantern between his hands, and watched the rain tear at the trees.

It was as if the forest was weeping.

A blaze of lightning struck a tree. It flamed briefly in the torrent, illuminating the walls of the temple. The crack of falling branches echoed around the hillsides.

"Why do you keep looking?" His father crouched down beside him, his cloak tight around his shoulders. "Do you want to be seen?"

Ithil looked up at his father. He was considered a great man among their people, a hunter and warrior, one of their defenders. He was also cursed with a son who would not do as sons should, yet he still cherished Ithil as much as his brothers.

"I hear it calling my name," Ithil confessed.

His father gazed at him. "And still, you look? When you know what may look back?"

Ithil looked down at the lantern in his hands. The flame was glowing softly, turning his brown skin to gold. "Can spirits be lonely, Father? As people are?"

His father was silent, then touched him on the shoulder. "Men can never understand the nature of spirits. We can only hope for their kindness." He leaned closer and pressed his brow to Ithil's. "Your heart is good, Ithil, but remember the Sintaker. Remember how he screamed."

Ithil nodded, drawing the protective light of the lantern closer.

With the morning, the rain still fell, though with less ferocity.

Ithil remained where he sat through the night, watching as the house lanterns were doused by the torrents, winking out one by one between the trees until the only light that remained was cradled between his hands.

"Why me?" he whispered into the dawn.

He knew he was considered strange to his people. A man in form, but still childless and unwed by his own choosing, even five summers after his maturity. At first it was amusing. Now, he was unnatural, sullied. What could a forest spirit see in a man outcast among his own?

Ithil snuffed the lantern and glanced back. His parents still slept, so he left them, slipping down onto the rain-sodden ground. The rain lightened and diminished as he walked, sunlight breaking through the deep clouds.

The branches of trees seemed to incline down towards him, the twigs trailing across his hair. Loose leaves spiralled down, dancing on the air. It was a gift, Ithil thought blankly, even as he reached out to catch one. A gift he was willing to accept. He turned it over between his fingertips, drawing the edge along his skin.

Ahead of him, the temple was visible.

"Ithil."

The voice was not a whisper in the trees. It came from behind him.

Ithil turned. His father was standing close by. His dark eyes darted to the leaf in Ithil's hand, then back to Ithil's face.

"You will go, then?"

Ithil closed his hand around the leaf carefully. "Yes." He tried to smile. "It will be better for you now." He laughed, short and brittle. "Think well of me, Father."

His father approached him. Like Ithil, he was slight and wiry. They stood eye-to-eye, and Ithil's father lifted his hands to cup Ithil's cheeks, his palms callused. "I always have and always shall, my son," he said. "Our people will know the choice you have made for them."

Ithil lowered his eyes to keep from weeping. No, he wanted to say. I do not do this for those who deride me. I do this for the one who calls to me, and thinks me worthy.

He said nothing. Better that his father believed him brave.

"We will come to the temple," his father added. "We will see you again."

"Yes."

Ithil's father stepped close, embracing him hard. "Spirits protect you."

Ithil nodded mutely, stepping back. There were words he knew he should say, but they felt stuck in his throat. Instead, he turned and walked towards the temple. Before him, the trailing bushes drew back to clear the path.

The temple gleamed in the sunlight, still wet from the rains. He paused before the archway that led within, then walked forward, his heart beating hard. Cords of vines that had cast Renta out curled aside at his approach.

His name echoed around him, a rolling whisper, as he walked onto the coloured flagstones, the courtyard spread out before him.

Behind him, the vines sank down again, closing out the world he had always called his home. Ithil touched trembling fingers to his lips, his eyes spilling over with hot tears. He fell to his knees and, wrapping his arms around himself, wept.

He didn't know how long he knelt there, but the sun was rising, turning the pale walls to gold. Beneath his knees, he felt a strange sensation, a softness, and he drew back to see moss forming beneath him, a cushion against the stone.

The spirit offering him kindness unasked.

He hastily dried his eyes, and looked about him. The courtyard was in disarray, with scattered dead leaves and broken branches covering the flagstones. Rotted food still rested on the altar, left since the death of the Sintaker. No wonder the spirit had been so angry, if he was so neglected.

Ithil rose at once, and gathered up the branches. He remembered a

stack of firewood behind the altar when he was a child, before he learned
to keep his eyes down, so he carried them there, where the sun could
touch them and dry them.

He tied together some of the many-fingered long leaves and quickly
swept up the rest of the dead leaves, then turned his attention to clearing
the altar. Already the closeness of the air was easing. Though no words
were said, it seemed his actions were appreciated.

It took a long while, scrubbing away mould with clumps of dry moss
and rain water from shallow pools by the walls. By the time the courtyard
was restored, the sun was high, and he was sweating and aching all over.

He sank to sit on the step before the altar. Only then, looking out
across the patterned floor, did he realise that he was sitting where the
Sintaker always stood. A shiver ran through him.

Slowly, he leaned back against the altar.

He would be the Sintaker now, whatever that meant.

He closed his eyes, weary and worn. It was only meant to be for a moment,
but by the time he opened them again, the sun was further down the wall. In
his slumber, he had slouched sideways onto the sun-warmed slabs.

It seemed he was not to starve: a pile of fruit lay before him, and the
carcass of a small bird too.

Ithil sat up, looking around. "Thank you."

The leaves of the trees that towered over the courtyard rippled in
response. It felt like approval or perhaps amusement. Either of those
things was better than screams in the night.

Once he ate, Ithil continued his work. The late Sintaker was old. He
must have abandoned parts of the sprawling complex when he could no
longer clamber down narrow stairs or break through tangled cobwebs so
thick Ithil needed to beat them aside with a stick.

By nightfall, every inch of Ithil was aching. He built a fire close behind
the altar, where there was some shelter from the night sky. Even as he
watched, fresh moss sprouted close to the flames for him to sleep in warmth.

Perhaps it was false kindness, he thought as he lay down. Perhaps it
was to calm him before the pain would come. Better to accept it for now,
and pray for mercy when pain followed.

To his surprise, his sleep was unbroken, even when the fire burned
out and the night's chill deepened. He woke on his bed of moss, startled to
find himself covered in a blanket of crudely-woven vines. More food was
laid out for him. He ate where he sat, the blanket about his shoulders, and
watched the sun cresting the temple walls.

When the light reached the floor, he noticed a trail of silvery leaves on the slabs, leading into the buildings. Ithil set aside the blanket, then rose and followed the trail. His fear had diminished through the night. Now, instead of trepidation, he was curious.

Outside the temple, the visible engravings were worn away, but within the coiling staircases, they were clear, deeply-incised into the rock. Narrow slits cut high in the wall let the sun slant down in thin shafts, illuminating them.

Ithil could see human figures. One loomed larger than all the others, a stripe running down the centre of the face. Ithil stared at it. The Sintaker had such a mark, a line of deep green from his hairline to beneath his lower lip.

If there were markings for Sintakers of old, they must have tended the temple for centuries.

He continued down, where sunlight gave way to passages illuminated by softly-glowing lichen. Ahead of him, he could hear the rush of water. When the corridor opened out into a cavern, Ithil had to catch his breath.

High above, he could see the sky through a gaping hole in the cavern roof. Waterfalls cascaded down over the lip, forming a lagoon below, framed by vegetation. Steps carved into the stone led downwards, and he followed them, gazing around in wonder.

Whether it was the spirit's intention of not, Ithil could not have resisted. He shed his tunic and waded down into the water. The bottom of the pool had been beaten to a soft sand, and tendrils of water weed drifted against his bare legs. He dived under, submerging himself, then broke through the surface, laughing. The water was cool and refreshing. He could feel the dirt of the previous day sliding from his skin.

Trusting the spirit to keep him from danger, he splashed and swam as he could never dare to in the river. There were too many threats there, flesh-eating fish, water snakes, even just the currents.

When the sun was overhead, he waded back to the shallows and sprawled half-in, half-out of the water on the soft sand. He felt warm, and to his surprise, happy. It was a strange emotion, after so many years without.

Beneath the water, the water weeds were brushing against his legs. One caught the back of his knee, making him laugh at the sensation. He lay back on the sand, letting the water lap around him. The water weeds trailed along his sides, over his thighs. His heart leapt, and he held himself still. They were moving with intent, not simply drifting.

Ithil drew his lower lip between his teeth. The spirit had a reason for all things. He closed his eyes, shivering as a thicker weed curled around his knee, tugging lightly. He moved his leg, scarce daring to breathe. Another strand rippled against him, along the inside of his thigh, closer, and closer still.

Surely, he thought, trembling.

The strand brushed against his manhood. It would be human to brush it away, as if it was nothing but an accident. It would be human.

And yet, as it slowly curled against him, he wondered how far it might go. Would it tease and then draw away? Or—his mouth was dry at the thought— would it do as he did with his own hand in the darkness of the night?

It felt nothing like a hand, cool and flat, but it wound around him, drawing slowly up, and all Ithil could do was breathe. Long, flowing streams of water weed wound closer, trailing up his legs, caressing him. He sank his fingers into the sand, stifling a cry as the grip on his manhood shifted and tightened, as his neglected flesh responded. His head felt light, and weeds were close around his thighs, drawing his limbs apart, teasing the root of him, sliding lower to...

He yelped aloud, kicking and wrenching his way free, scrambling out of the water. Weeds still wrapped around his leg caught him. He fell onto one knee, but curled over himself. His manhood throbbed unbearably, and he dared a glance at the pool. How could he have allowed such a thing?

No matter if it made his heart race, and brought him hard far quicker than his own hand had.

No.

No, he was human and flesh and blood, and he could not allow himself that. He curled in tighter, shivering. He was flesh and blood. His hand was cold when he put it down between his thighs, beneath the arc of his body. He closed his eyes, and recalled the silky pressure of the weeds on his skin. He tried to push back the thoughts, but he could not help but wonder what they might have done, had he remained. Seed and salted tears fell on the grass beneath him.

For the remains of the day, he lowered his eyes, and averted his face when the leaves stirred. When he crept to his sleeping place, he hesitated before lying down on the moss or touching the blanket. The temple felt larger, emptier. He could not help but feel he had disappointed the spirit.

He lay on his side beneath the blanket and stared blindly into the flames of his fire. His face grew warm as he remembered—and tried not to think of—the touch of the water weeds on his skin. It had not been unpleasant. He bit his lower lip. It had been...something new. Strange, yes, but not unpleasant. Not painful. It had been playful, teasing, and had set his blood racing.

Despite himself, he put his hand beneath his tunic. He was coming to hardness already, and his fingers trembled. The moss rippled beneath him, fluttering against the bare skin of his legs, teasing as lightly as the weeds had.

He hesitated, heart drumming, then dragged his tunic up and rolled to his back. Bare from his ribs to his ankles, the undulation of the moss made his skin rise in goosebumps. The blanket settled over him again. Ithil closed his eyes, wrapped his hand into the tangle of vines, then closed it around his shaft.

He was breathing hard, and the moss beneath him was shivering as if in a breeze, caressing him lightly. His blood was rushing through him, and he could swear the vines covering him were throbbing with the same urgent pulse as his manhood.

He should be ashamed, he knew. It was unnatural and inhuman to do such things. He pressed his other arm over his eyes. If he didn't see, then it was not so bad. His hand—or maybe the vines—tightened around his manhood, and he bit back a sharp cry, arching his hips up. The blanket clung to him like a second skin, matching every rapid beat of his heart, as he stroked himself until his fingers were slick, and his breath was a rapid gust.

His panted moans echoed back from the high places of the temple and with them came the whisper of his name, the tempest of wind lashing at the trees above him, wild, exuberant, joyful.

Ithil lowered his arm from his eyes and stared into nothing. It—he— was pleased. The spirit. It took delight in what? His shame? Or perhaps in his lust?

Ithil shivered, drawing his hand from the tangled blanket. By the light of the flames, he could see the wetness on his hand. He ran his thumb through it, dazed. It was not his alone. Deep green droplets spread through it, the spirit's seed. Without thought, he brought his fingers to his lips and lapped at them.

The spirit's jubilance whirled around the temple, branches rattling above him. Ithil felt his heart might burst from his chest. The drops were sweet and sharp mixed in the salt of his own seed. He licked again, long, hungry strokes. With every little part he consumed, he felt a thrill of terror and delight. Was this what it was to give one's self to the spirit? If so, then let those outside the walls think what they wished. He was the spirit's now, for pleasure or for pain.

He slept then, his body shrouded in vines and leaves. It was only come morning that he saw the results of the night before. His tunic was stained, and his limbs were banded with green where the vines had clung to him. He traced the patterns with a fingertip, and bit down on his lips to keep from grinning.

Around him, the temple was peaceful. Sated, he thought.

He rose and made his way down through the temple to the pool. The water was cooler, the sun not yet high enough to warm the cove. He shed the tunic and waded to some small rocks to scrub his tunic, then hung it over a low branch to dry when the sun came.

The water weed was docile now, so he turned his attention to his own body, scrubbing with handfuls of sand. The stains remained, only a shade lighter. He frowned, then recalled the old Sintaker's flesh had been green all over.

He stared down at himself, and the faint patina of green. To have flesh as green as the Sintaker, it must have taken years. Ithil couldn't help but laugh. The wily fox! Had the forest touched him, as it touched Ithil? No wonder he had told no one.

Ithil clambered back out of the pool. The only clothing he had with him was still dripping on the branch, but the sun was up and he knew he would be warmed by it soon enough.

He made his way back through the building, pausing to look at the carvings once more. Now that he looked, he could see the way vines twined around the man marked as the Sintaker. He ran his finger along the outline. Truly, he could not say the spirit had not shown him his purpose.

When he reached the top of the staircase, he heard voices in the courtyard of the temple. For two days, he had been closed within, alone, but now, people were there. Come to see the new Sintaker, to be cleansed.

He looked down at himself, half-hidden in the shadows. The marks on his skin were a beginning. He drew himself up, straight and proud, and walked out. The whole village was there, crammed into the courtyard. The hush spread like ripples on a pond as he walked—ignoring them—towards the altar. Movement caught the corner of his eye, as they all sank onto their knees.

He wanted to laugh, but the people needed a Sintaker. He went to one of the pools close to the altar and scooped water up in his hands, pouring it over himself. Dripping, silent, he went to the Sintaker's place before the altar.

The first person to come forward was his mother, her eyes down. He marked her brow, but before she could move away, he bent over her and touched his lips to her silver-threaded hair. "Bless you, Mother," he whispered.

She didn't dare to raise her eyes to him, but he could see her pride as she stepped passed him to place her tribute on the altar.

The others followed in silence, one by one, hundreds of them. He wondered if he was truly taking their sin. Perhaps he was. He only knew he felt braver and more respected than he had days before, and they bowed to him as if he was everything they believed. Perhaps that was enough.

His father was the last to approach, his footfalls echoing around the now-empty hall. Unlike every other person who had come close, his father looked him in the eyes. He was a man of few words, but he raised his brows in inquiry.

Ithil just smiled, and that was enough. His father bowed to him and accepted his blessing, and then he too departed. Behind him, the vines fell closed, shutting the world out once more.

Ithil turned to look at the altar. It was piled with offerings. Much of it was food, more than enough to last him for several days, but he also saw trinkets and jewellery. All left for the spirit, and all things the spirit had no need of.

He ate his fill, then carried the offerings down into the cooler rooms below. Many of them were empty, others stacked with dusty treasures. By the time he was done, night was falling, and a memory assailed him: on the nights of the purification, the Sintaker's screams could be heard across the valley.

Ithil lit the fire behind the altar, crouching down by it, fighting down the sudden dread. If there was to be pain, it would be tonight.

He raised his eyes to the carved stone of the altar.

Better to face it directly, and offer himself, rather than cower, waiting in terror.

He rose, then climbed up onto the altar. A little of the sun's heat still lingered in the stone. It was smooth beneath him. He leaned back, propped up on his elbows.

"I am here," he murmured.

At first, nothing happened. The dancing flames cast strange shadows, and he saw movement everywhere when there was none. He lay back, pressing one hand over his heart, trying to calm the rapid flutter. The trees whispered above him, and he heard the brush of...something on the flagstones.

He didn't dare to move, closing his eyes.

When the touch finally came, it was the gentlest of ripples against the fingertips of his free hand. He turned his head, and saw the unfurling fronds of a vine. He opened his hand, coiling his fingers into it, and felt the rush of approval as if it was his own.

At once, more lengths of vine unfurled over the edges of the altar. One trailed over his chest and Ithil shuddered as tiny thorns dragged from his throat down the length of his body, his back arching in helpless response.

Slim branches twined around his limbs, feathery twigs teasing over his skin, the touch so light it was barely there. His blood was racing, and he shivered again as tiny splayed leaves followed the contours of his face, light as a breath over his closed eyelids and along his parted, panting lips.

Thicker vines slid beneath him, lifting him from the hard surface of the altar, smaller prickling branches hooking softly at his thighs, drawing them wider. Ithil could feel himself hardening from their ministrations, and moved his hand to grasp himself. A vine whipped around his wrist, quick as a snake, looping again and again, until his arm was drawn down, bound to the edge of the altar.

He keened in half-hearted protest, for more vines were unfurling between his splayed thighs. He could feel them writhing and unravelling, brushing against his thighs and higher still. His breath caught, his hips lifting, when one of them—slick and thick—brushed against the root of him. It teased along his flesh as smaller, thinner vines twined around his length, tightening and releasing and making him moan aloud.

He tried to move his other hand, the sensations too much. It too was snared and bound, the bonds on his legs drawing tight. He was pinioned, utterly at the mercy of the spirit.

"Please," he whispered, trying to move his hips against the grip of the vines. It was a delicious sensation, but not enough, not even close to enough. Another of the barbed vines traced down his chest in erratic circles. It hooked against his nipples. The sensation was like fire into his belly, making him jerk and whimper.

The vines beneath him roiled, lifting his body up. He could feel the whip of narrow vines lashing his back, holding him faster, then the stroke of thicker vines, exploring his body, cool and pulsing with sap.

He could feel it trickling down his sides as the vines coiled around his waist, down over his hips, until one of them glided beneath his back, sliding against him, back and forth. The coarse texture of it grazed between his buttocks and against the root of him, making him shudder.

He turned his head, trying to catch a vine with his teeth. It snared his chin, casting out a dark dripping tendril to draw a line—the Sintaker's mark—from his hairline to his lips. Ithil moaned. Yes. Oh, *yes*.

The tendril lingered, thrusting sensuously between Ithil's lips, claiming, marking. Sweet nectar dripped onto his tongue. He sucked hungrily at it, and felt vibrations of pleasure run through the vines. He sucked again and the ripple through the branches twined close around him made his manhood throb with need.

"Please," he panted, rubbing himself against the vine between his legs.

The press against his backside made him whimper, but the vines about him pulsed and shifted, sending fresh pleasure rushing through him, and when it breached his body, he threw back his head with a gasping cry. It was all around him, and within him, undulating slowly, pressing deeper, squeezing and caressing, until he could only weep and pant and beg.

The pulse of the sap through every vine was engulfing him. He moaned again as it tightened around him, as it swelled within him, as the tendril slid against his tongue, sweet as honey. His body was afire. The vines rippled again, again, again. He cried out, gasping, gurgling, his body slick with sap, nectar spilling from his lips, as his body spasmed and his seed spattered his belly.

Still, it did not stop, rippling and trembling and swelling and wet about him. He twisted his hands weakly, clutching at them, panting and gasping and offering what he could from a body stretched and aching but still wanting.

The altar was thick with dark sap when the vines laid him down. They were still wound close about him, a nest for him to rest on. The bonds at his limbs uncurled, and he moved a hand to touch his lips. The nectar was sticky against his fingers. He licked it, savouring the taste, and felt the vines curl about him in approval.

"So," he whispered, smiling, "that's why he screamed."

Above him, the trees rustled with the spirit's laughter.

THE ROUTE TO THE CABIN was long, lonesome: first one highway, then another, hours passing, through small towns John had never explored, likely never would. Despite it being almost the end of October, the night air was warm, so he kept the car window open and the rush of wind fought with the sounds of the classical music on the radio as he drove down the deserted roads. Medford, Prentice, Fifield, and then Park Falls. Before he crossed the line between Price and Ashland counties, John turned down a county road, then another, macadam giving way to loose rock, and finally to a dirt road along Butternut Lake.

It was late, pitch dark, when John reached his grandparents' cabin. Well, no longer their cabin—his grandparents had passed away almost thirty years ago, the property now belonged to John's eldest cousin, who only used it for the occasional summer weekend. He allowed other family members to use the cabin, and they took turns closing it up for the winter.

John grabbed his duffel bag and sack of groceries. He intended to spend the weekend here, but he hadn't anticipated how unfamiliar the cabin's interior would be: gone were the old, scarred furnishings, the boxy appliances in his grandmother's kitchen, her quilts from the bedrooms. Gone too were the scents of pipe tobacco and lavender sachets. It smelled nothing like his childhood. The next morning John explored the cupboards and felt joy at discovering the old Westinghouse toaster, and ate more slices of buttered whole-wheat toast than he intended or wanted.

By late morning, the day had warmed enough that John took off his jacket. He had finished most of his chores, so after eating his lunch, John decided to follow the creek that bordered the property. As he walked towards the creek, he came upon the hollow stump of an oak tree, filled with rainwater from the night before. John smiled as he gazed into the pooled water. All the cousins, as kids, referred to the pool as a "fairy lake," a safe spot for imaginary critters to romp and play while the adults swam in the real lake by the cabin. John bent over to gaze into the pool, but found the wrinkled brow, the mostly grey whiskers, and the sagging jowls that looked back him at odds with the childhood reflection he remembered. He looked away.

As he continued walking, he reached the creek and began to follow it. John remembered playing in it as a child, chasing crayfish and splashing in the water with his cousins. They had never followed it to its source, although they always dared each to do so. As it flowed away from the lake, it grew narrower and narrower, until he could straddle it with both legs. *Don't cross the creek,* Gramma had always admonished. *That's not our property.* Her warning was so strong that he had never before dared even step on the other side, and here he was literally walking on the neighboring property. Doing so made him uneasy; almost at once, he brought his left foot back to join his right. Immediately angry at himself, he stepped back over the creek, and began walking on the opposite bank. He followed its path until it met a small tributary from the neighboring property, which he had never encountered before.

THE TRIBUTARY DREW HIM FURTHER away from the lake, away from the cabin. The woods were quiet, and when he stumbled, John realized that if he hurt himself, the likelihood of anyone happening upon him would be remote. The maples, oaks, and cedars had begun to thin out too, and he realized that he had been walking gradually uphill. He should have reached the source of the water, but all he saw was a single tree ahead. A stunted pine tree.

John gazed at the tree, standing all by itself, and felt a curious dislocation. It seemed so familiar—but he had never crossed over the creek before, he was sure of that. John approached closer to the tree, smelling its resin, its needles, and the aroma reminded him of his grandfather, who had always smelled of the thick pine-tar shampoo he used—not just on his head; because he was hairy all over, he always smelled like he had bathed in turpentine.

*See that tree over there? That's a jack pine.*

The memory came unbidden to his mind. His grandfather, or someone, must have brought him here against Gramma's warning.

*Here. I'll hoist you up unto that branch.*

Now came the recollection of slowly rising, almost like flying; then he was sitting on a tree branch, impossibly high, his short legs dangling, and looking over the surrounding forest. The indistinct human below looked very far away.

John stood next to the tree, under the lowest branch. Even after jumping, it remained tantalizingly just out of reach. His grandfather had not been a tall man; the branch must have grown higher as the tree aged. *It's not that high though, I bet I can climb up to it.* Walking around the trunk, he spied a knob jutting out; placing his right foot on it, he used it like using a stirrup to mount a horse. John grabbed for purchase from the tree bark, reaching first with one hand, then the other. Dragging along his legs that clung around the tree base, he began to crawl up the pine tree.

John's progress was excruciatingly slow. At first the rough bark at the base of the pine provided him traction, but after a few shimmies upward, he found the bark had grown smoother; it took him longer to make any progress, and for each two feet he climbed up, he seemed to fall down a foot.

Grunting and gasping, John kept climbing, until he reached the branch and was high enough to swing his right leg over it. Finally straddling the tree branch, John put his full weight on it, and was relieved to find that it would support him. He weighed so much more now. John leaned with his forehead against the trunk and stopped to catch his breath. After he had stopped almost heaving for air, and his heartbeat had stopped racing, he wiped his brow with his flannel shirt sleeves; his shirt was dripping with sweat, and clung to his chest and back. John unbuttoned it and tied it around his waist, but there was hardly any breeze to cool his body.

He carefully backed away from the trunk and then swung his left leg over the branch to join his right leg. His breathing and heart rate had both calmed, and feeling secure enough on the branch, he dared to look about. The view did not mesh with his former memory of gigantic trees surrounding him. His view looked desolate, for there were no trees nearby, not even stumps. A few yards from the tree, everything turned blurry, almost misty. But the ground still looked uncomfortably far away, especially with no one to catch him if he fell.

Jack reached back towards the tree trunk to steady himself. Reminding himself not to look down, he looked at his hands instead, and found that he had somehow grazed his knuckles during his climb; a gash on his right middle finger was welling with blood. He brought it up to his mouth to staunch the flow and the iron tang of his blood filled his mouth.

*I need to head back. There's Band-Aids in the cabin, and I still have chores to complete, and there's no one—nothing for me here.*

It was also completely still, he suddenly realized. No birds chirped, and no wind whispered through the pine boughs. He could no longer hear the gurgling of the creek. There were no human-made sounds, either—no cars, and he was too far away from the lake to hear speedboats or even the splash of oars. None of the ubiquitous sounds of radios, computers, or the endless beeps of human technology. He took his phone out of his pocket, but it carried no signal.

*Alone. I'm completely alone. Out here in the fucking middle of fucking nowhere. Just me and this pine tree. Alone, just like the last summer I was here.*

Summoned by that thought, recollections of that summer returned to his awareness. Unlike previous summers, his older cousins had been kept away by summer jobs, girlfriends, summer camps. So he had found himself completely alone with his grandparents. With nothing to do but look forward to the weekly trip to the nearest town to buy groceries and attend Mass at church. The lake and woods provided little entertainment for a lone adolescent boy. The only thing that had made the summer bearable was Russell, the boy down the road who would come to visit occasionally.

John frowned. Russell had been hired by his grandparents to babysit him and his cousins when they were younger. He had been thirteen that summer, almost fourteen. Surely he had been old enough not to need a babysitter. He really had been alone that summer. Except he had met someone one late afternoon, who had surprised him, while he was out wandering the woods.

*Who are you?*

*John. John Little. What's your name?*

*The same as yours.*

*Huh?*

*I'm Little John.* A brief smile. *You can call me Jack. Means the same thing. We can't both of us be called John.*

*Where do you live?*

*Over there.* This statement had been accompanied by a vague hand gesture, in the direction of the creek and the unknown property beyond it.

*Jack must have brought me here.* John's brow furrowed again. He had come to the lone pine in broad daylight. Like now. He was certain of it. But Jack had always visited late in the day, arriving around sunset, when he was exploring the woods after supper or sitting alone by the lake shore, to watch a dying campfire. Fire had always seemed to draw Jack. He often watched it for hours, mesmerized.

*The summer heat never bothered him.* John remembered one day of blistering heat, rare so far north, when his grandparents had retired early, escaping the oppressive warmth in an unlit cabin, silent except for the fans whirling. He had been sitting by himself on the pier, wearing only his swim trunks, watching the sun set, and just as it had fallen below the horizon, Jack had appeared, without fanfare. Jack never announced himself; between one moment and next, he would just be there. *It's so hot. Let's go swimming.* John couldn't remember who suggested that they take the rowboat out, but he had not been initially keen on the idea—the day's extreme heat had made him lethargic, and he didn't want to risk a scolding, or worse, a grounding, from his grandparents. Nevertheless they had rowed it out onto the lake, almost to the opposite side, where there were no cabins. While John dropped anchor, Jack had slid into the water like an otter, without a sound. John had tried to follow his example, but the splash he made sounded monstrously huge in the nighttime quiet, followed by his sputtering when he rose back to the surface of the cool lake.

*Don't worry. No one can hear us. Or see us.* John gasped—Jack had swum underneath the rowboat, and reappeared directly behind him, as silent as ever. John felt Jack's breath warm on his neck, contrasting with the cold water. *You don't need these.* Before John could react, he felt two hands grab the waistband of his trunks and pull them down.

The memory of his embarrassment and subsequent fear of discovery flooded John. Mingled with his shame had also been the transgressive thrill of being publicly naked, intensified by being naked with another guy. But John realized that he couldn't remember ever seeing Jack naked. Jack had always only ever worn a pair of cut-off jeans—never a shirt or shoes, not even flip-flops—so he must have caught some forbidden glimpse of pubic hair peeking above the waistband of Jack's cut-offs. *He had black hair, so he must have had black pubic hair too.*

The image forming in John's mind's eye remained disturbingly vague: he remembered Jack's piercing dark brown eyes above high cheekbones and the sunburned skin of his arms and legs, but nothing else. Jack had never divulged any details about his personal situation either.

*Where's your family?*

*I don't have any.*

*So you live by yourself?*

*I don't need anyone else._*

*So you're just visiting.*

*No, I'm from around here.*

Confused, John took a deep breath, trying to remember. There was nothing to hear, and very little that he could see, but the smells of dead needles, decaying vegetation, and wet soil drifted up to him on the gentle breeze, mingling with the scent of the pine tree.

*Jack always smelled like the forest after a rain.* The scents and the thought of rain sparked another lost memory: it had stormed later that same night, a result of the unusual extreme heat. Jack had easily evaded John's attempts to retaliate, and started swimming back across the lake, with John following in the rowboat—he didn't dare just leave it—his pace much slower. Jack had swum just ahead of the rowboat, then dove underwater, breaking surface on either side of the rowboat, taunting him. By the time John made it back to his grandparents' pier, night had fallen completely, with dark clouds obscuring any possible moonlight or starlight, and the air temperature had noticeably dropped. The wind had begun to pick up too: a storm was imminent. And Jack was nowhere to be seen. John, waist-deep in the lake and still naked, had hesitated, uncertain whether to continue his futile attempt to reclaim his trunks, or risk trying to sneak past his sleeping grandparents without waking them. They were light sleepers, and his best chance of creeping back inside the cabin unnoticed was before the storm woke them. John had walked slowly out of the water; once back on shore, and past a copse of pines, an arm had appeared from behind him, encircled his neck, and stopped him.

*Where are you going?*

John had tensed at the familiar voice, softly mocking, as gentle as the arm draped around his shoulder, barely restraining him.

*Inside. It's gonna rain.* John had tried to match Jack's nonchalance, but his voice had cracked. He felt Jack's warm breath again, this time directly in his ear; he had fought to remain calm, but Jack's closeness had sent his heart pounding, and John knew that Jack must be able to feel his pulse racing just beneath his skin.

*So? You're already dripping wet. What's a little rain?*

John remembered now that when Jack's arm had tightened around his neck, it had been completely dry against his skin. And warm. The only part of John that had been dry was his mouth.

*It's not that. I need to get inside before Gramma begins to worry.* He didn't add, *Before she sees me. Before she sees us.* John had begun to shake, either shivering from the cold air on his wet skin, or the warmth he had sensed rising from Jack's body. All over his own body he had felt goosebumps forming, and then his dick, shrunken by the cool lake water, had begun to swell.

*Ah, such filial duty, especially to one's mother's mother. Very well then. You can have these back.* All hint of mockery gone from his voice, Jack had brought his free hand out in front of John, holding his trunks. John had grabbed them, bent over and put them on, and while they had covered his growing erection, they had completely failed to hide it.

*Thank you.* Once clothed, John had turned around, but no one was there.

Just then a gust of wind had blown over him and a big raindrop had fallen on his forehead, followed by another, and then several more; he had sprinted back to the cabin, and managed to sneak in without waking either grandparent.

Despite the unexpected intensity of these memories, John felt deflated: he had successfully avoided punishment, but he had never seen Jack again, nor ever returned to the cabin, until now. *No wonder I forgot about it, it's hardly worth remembering.*

Dejected, John began his return to the ground. His trip down the tree was quicker than his trip up, but he was panting again when he reached the ground, trying to manage his descent at a reasonable pace; even so, his chest and arms were raw from rubbing against the tree's rough bark. He leaned against the trunk of the jack pine, and his hand found the knob he had used to mount the tree, this time oozing sap. He pulled his hand away from the sticky mass dribbling slowly down the trunk. His middle two fingers were stuck together by the clear sap, which quickly hardened and crystallized. The gash on his finger had reopened too, and instinctively John brought the wound up to his mouth and wrapped his tongue around it, licking the red blood and white sap together.

Fire exploded on John's tongue: a heat greater than the zestiest spice filled his entire mouth before descending down his throat, into his stomach. So did the warmth of his body; John felt heat emanating from the pine, through his entire bare torso, rising up his spine, outward to the ends of his limbs. His vision filled with every possible color. Closing his eyes did no good, couldn't stop the tears from flowing. Nor could his hands keep out the influx of hitherto unheard sounds to his ears: John perceived the soft murmur of water slowly rising from the pine tree's roots and its needles breathing—exhaling pure oxygen into the atmosphere and inhaling the tainted air from his lungs. He became too stimulated and blacked out.

John came to, and found himself lying flat on his back, underneath the pine, his vision and hearing restored to normal. With extreme care, he rolled over and then pulled himself up, brushed the fallen needles and humus off his arms and back, and knelt underneath the tree before trying to stand up fully. His entire body ached. Not with the ache of doing backbreaking chores all day, but the comfortable languor of an afternoon's lovemaking. He looked down, and noticed that the front of his jeans was damp, and not with sweat. He couldn't see, but knew that tomorrow his back would be badly bruised. He stiffly stood up, and took a tentative step away. Looking back at the trunk of the jack pine, he saw something he hadn't noticed before.

Underneath sat two curved pine cones.

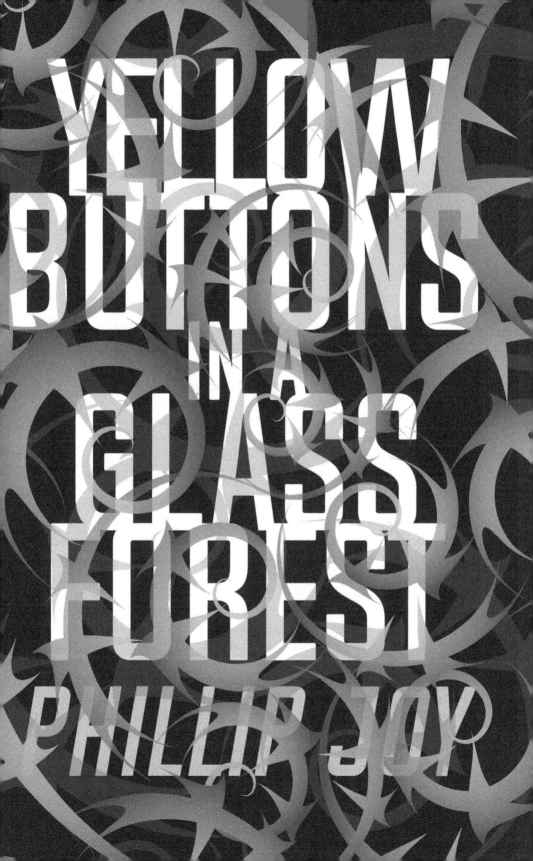

"HE'S PERFECT," THE STRANGER WHISPERED to the heavens. Weaving around twinks, hairless muscle jocks, and raucous drag queens, he edged his way to the object of his attention. The boy had moves and was using them well. Sweat dripped down his neck, running down his shirtless back. Following the natural contours of his body, it pooled briefly before being absorbed into the denim of his low-riding jeans. The stranger watched hungrily. The boy's body, a work of art in its own right, was painted in glitter, gold and silver highlighting his snow white skin. His face was all smoothness with delicate features. His ginger hair was set on fire in the strobing lights of the disco.

The boy felt the man's presence and turned. Their eyes locked. He faltered, losing the thread of music, and vanished within the greens of a forest; the spring greens of pines, the bright greens of sunlight-dappled leaves, and the dark greens of mosses, all swirling together in the eyes of this stranger. The greens faded, replaced by countless men jumping and screaming as a new song started. The boy smiled at the man. He was over six feet with broad shoulders and a muscular solid build. A well-groomed beard framed a jaw that looked as if it was cut from stone. Wavy black hair fell over those impossible eyes as the man reached out to him. Strong arms encircled him, pulling them together and merging their hips.

They danced. Again the forest swallowed him but this time he willingly surrendered to the dream. He was free, running through the trees, his bare legs tickled by ferns, the earth squishing between his toes. He laughed and stumbled to the ground. The golden light, scattered by the branches of tall oaks, faded as the stranger bent over him, leaning in with full lips to brush hesitantly against his own. Their first kiss was brief and unsure but the boy responded eagerly, wanting more. He leaned forward for another and this time it became deeper, more desperate, as if their two souls were trying to merge. When they parted the spell was broken and the nightclub crushed back around them.

The boy leaned into the stranger's ear, shouting to be heard. "Wow! Now that was some intense shit. It was like we went to another place. I have never been kissed that like before."

The stranger pointed and took the boy's hand, heading for the patio doors. The area, used primarily as a refuge for smokers, opened up into a small courtyard. They saw benches scattered between a few potted shrubs that looked like they hadn't seen the watering cans for a few months. Choosing the most secluded spot, they sat together in silence for several minutes breathing in the cool night air and the lingering scent of tobacco.

"My name is Cody," the boy said.

"Tansy," replied the stranger.

Cody felt like his whole body was trembling, whether from the high that comes from catching the eye of a handsome man or the sudden cold of being outside he couldn't tell. This exotic creature was staring at him as if he was the only person in the world. Cody had never felt so exposed yet so thrilled. Finally, he couldn't stand it anymore. Pretending to examine the nearest dying plant, he tried to think of a good line, although all he really wanted to do was lose himself in those lips again. Unable to think of something witty, he settled for the standard "So, I haven't seen you here before."

"No, my work usually keeps me from this sort of scene."

Plucking a leaf off the bush and trying to be cool, Cody asked, "Oh, what do you do?"

"I am a horticulturist," the man replied.

Cody chuckled. "Sorry, a whore-what?"

"A horticulturist. I work at the city's greenhouse where I tend and care for plants. Unlike these poor unfortunate creatures." He gestured to the shrub Cody was picking at.

"Oh, I don't know a lot about plants but that sounds cool."

"It's quite a peaceful and magical spot. We should go see it." Getting up, the stranger extended his hand to Cody.

"Oh, you mean right now?"

"What better time? We will have the whole place to ourselves and I can show you all of its hidden treasures, among other things."

"Oh really, treasures and other things. That is tempting but..." Cody left the sentence unfinished, desire and common sense fighting each other.

Tansy gently took the boy's chin and examined every inch of his face.

"Do you trust me?"

Under his intense glare, Cody felt his soul wrenched open. "Yes. I trust you."

The rain began.

Cody opened the taxi's door and grabbed Tansy's hand, pulling him out into the splattering drops, dashing for the greenhouse. As Tansy fiddled with the locks, Cody moved closer, trying to seek shelter from the taller man. When Tansy finally opened the doors, Cody grasped. The greenhouse was filled with every type of greenery you could imagine. Rock-skewed paths meandered their way through neat hedges of foliage, potted shrubs, and well-trimmed bushes.

As they walked along, he noticed monstrous vines climbing up Roman-like columns while trailing plants seemed to dart from hidden crevices looking for new spaces to spread their tendrils. The fat raindrops echoing off the glass roof sounded like soft bells, filling the entire greenhouse with a soft pitter-patter. Cody saw things he had never even knew existed. Ferns with hairy "feet" that reminded him of rabbits, spiny sticks covered in sharp thorns that looked like something the devil might use for walking, squat bulbous cacti with thick succulent roots, and pendulous white flowers shaped like trumpets.

Cody stared at them. "They're in bloom? At night? I thought flowers only bloomed during the day."

"These are *Datura innoxia* or more commonly known as moonflowers."

Cody tentatively reached out to smell them.

"Careful, these belong to the deadly nightshade family. If you don't know what you're doing you could poison yourself."

"Why grow them? I mean, they're pretty but why risk it in a public space?"

"Oh, they have some very distinct uses." Tansy reached out to pinch Cody's ass. "In some cultures they are aphrodisiacs; used by the witches in their potions to make you horny, my boy." Tansy playfully pushed Cody forward.

"Well, I think it's working," teased Cody.

Tansy winked. "Keeping going. We are almost there."

They rounded a slight bend and Cody felt as if he was stepping into his earlier vision. He was leaving the manicured city garden and stepping into a wilderness untouched by man. He didn't see any shelves or steel benches. There were no pots, no containers, and the plants seem to be free to grow wherever they wanted. Cody's eyes widened as he even saw trees with trunks so wide he doubted he could wrap his arms around them. Distracted, he tripped over a root, and he noticed no irrigation lines or hoses littering the ground. Even the lighting was a mystery. He could see no obvious fluorescent bulbs and even the glass ceiling seemed to have disappeared. It seemed as if natural starlight infused a pale glow to this whole forest. At the centre of it, he saw a pond haloed in bright yellow flowers, calling to them like a beacon.

"Here we are, Cody. This is where you had to come."

Tansy pulled the boy with him and they walked to the wildflowers. The air was infused with their pungent aroma, a mix of camphor and rosemary. Cody took a deep breath. The flowers themselves had feathery leaves that ended in roundish, flat-topped yellow buttons. Tansy plucked one. "These are very special to me." Sweeping the boy's hair back, Tansy tucked the flower behind his ear. "There, now you are, too." The man winked again and Cody felt an intense tingle spread through him.

"What are they?" he asked. He felt awkward but was unsure if it was from the man's lingering touch or his ignorance of anything botanical.

"These are my namesake. Tansy flowers. An ancient species endowed with many unique properties. The ancient Greeks believed they granted immortality and made creams with them, smearing it all over their bodies in hopes of being young forever. Medieval priests also knew them to be otherworldly, filled with arcane properties to help stave off the decay of the flesh. They even dressed their dead in tansy wreaths so that evil spirits would be repelled, unable to feast on their putrid remains."

"That's cool, I guess, a little creepy and kind of silly. I mean, who believes in evil spirits anyways?"

"You never know where you will find evil. But nowadays people don't believe in the old ways. Now they just see them as weeds to exterminate, but I still know them."

Cody bent down to look at the flowers closer. "Well, people would change their minds if they saw this. How do you do it? I mean all of it? It doesn't look man-made at all."

"I have been naturally gifted with a rare connection to plants. I listen when they tell me what they need."

Cody smirked. "So what else are you naturally gifted at?"

Tansy could tell Cody was ready now. The forest made good on its side of their bargain, unleashing the eagerness and hunger that was lurking just beneath the boy's surface. Tansy intended to accept it. He reached out and lifted the boy off the ground making him yelp out in surprise. "Don't worry. I have you and will never let you go." He brought the boy to his lips. Cody wrapped his legs around him and they leaned back onto the closest tree. They explored each other's mouths. He licked his way to Cody's ear, nibbling on his lobe, causing him to groan and twist in his arms. They collapsed to the ground into a tangle of limbs, Tansy ending up on top.

"You are a perfect specimen, boy, but let's see your full bloom." He gently kissed the boy's cheek before removing his skin-tight shirt and jeans. Traces of his body glitter sparkled in the moonlight and Tansy could see his cheeks deepen in colour as he was laid naked. The man explored the boy's nakedness, making him giggle. He moved his tongue from the boy's neck, down his slim torso until he reached his stiffening manhood. He repeatedly took the full length of him into his mouth. His passion was increasing with every taste of the boy. It would soon transform him. He needed that and he knew the forest did also. He could hear it singing its desire through the rustle of its leaves and the swaying of its branches. Tansy pulled back just as he brought the boy to the brink of orgasm.

Tansy spread the boy's legs and spat onto his quivering hole. Using his natural lube, he slowly worked one finger into Cody. It was tight but he managed to open him up more, pushing in another. He devoured the sight of Cody squirming beneath him and begging for more.

Cody felt blinded and lost to the powers of this stranger. Flashes of oak mixed with the fragrance of wildwood became his reality. The carpet of grass and leaves beneath his back rubbed his skin raw as Tansy's movements pushed and pulled him. He truly felt he had entered a different world, a savage one where he could let loose all his pent-up frustrations. He howled, the bestial screams erupting from the secret depths of his soul, echoing the convulsions rippling through his body until at last they softened into whimpers.

Cody sensed every tree, flower, and blade of grass alive with an air of anticipation.

Tansy stood over him. He started ripping off his clothes and in doing so seemed to be transforming right before Cody's eyes. It was as if being here was changing him into a feral creature, a rare mix of man, beast, and plant. His skin became like bark, brown and rough. His nose became more snout-like while twisted horns rose from his head. Green leaves sprang from his dark hair and wove themselves into a crown. Finally, his ears elongated into sharp points covered in tufts of hair. Or was it fur? Not that it mattered. He possessed an unnatural beauty.

The same dark fur covered his now naked body of muscle and sinew. Tansy's cock looked glorious even semi-erect, literally oozing a nectar. Cody had never seen a man so wet before. He reached out, taking some of the sticky fluid into his mouth. Flavours of maple and cedar played across his tongue. He wanted more and drank from it like a parched man. The cock grew in his mouth, gagging and forcing him to sit back.

"Please fuck me."

In answer, Tansy flipped him over onto his hands and knees and pushed his hard wood deep within. Together they were transformed into wild animals fucking, their grunts echoing through the copse of trees. Tansy fucked him hard. Grabbing the boy's hair, he erupted, pushing his seed deep within him. Seconds later, Cody cried out as spastic convulsions took control of his body and he came into the earthy loam beneath him. They collapsed together and rolled under the boughs of the nearest tree. Spent and exhausted.

CODY AWOKE TO FIND HIMSELF wrapped in the arms of Tansy who was breathing lightly in his ear. The man's furry chest was softly rising and falling against his back. Cody gently caressed the hands around him.

Tansy stirred. "What are you doing?"

"I just like holding your hand. Your fingers are so cute. You know, your little pinky is crooked just like that twig over there." He took each of Tansy's fingers and held them up, examining each one before kissing them. "I could stay like this forever but I have to pee." Standing up, Cody playfully shook his cock before hurrying away to relieve himself.

He searched for the gravel path, hoping to find a bathroom. "Do greenhouses even have bathrooms," Cody wondered, not that it mattered because he couldn't see anything but trees. "Well, trees need water too, I guess."

The carnal fog of last night was beginning to lift and he let his mind wander. Last night was one of the most passionate nights he ever had. He really liked Tansy and could see a future with him. Yes, he could picture it now, an intense love affair ending in a wedding ceremony in this very greenhouse. The two of them dressed in black tuxes but with no shoes so they could connect with the earth. He saw two kids, a boy and girl, and him teaching them to grow things.

"Jesus, Cody, get a gripe. We just fucking met." Bringing his mind back to reality, he noticed his yellow stream of piss turning ashen black as it flowed down the tree's roots. "What the hell?" he questioned and peered around its trunk.

Twisted human figures lay scattered across the forest floor and he was pissing on one, washing away pieces from a decayed foot. He staggered backwards in horror, closing his eyes against it. "This is not happening, Jesus, get hold of yourself Cody, it's probably just some crazy trick of the light." Gathering his nerves, he opened his eyes, but the horrific scene did not change. The corpses were real, dozens of them, all men in various states of decomposition and all naked except for a single yellow tansy behind each of their rotting ears. A cold dread bloomed in Cody's heart as he touched the flower which, despite all of their fucking, was exactly where Tansy had placed it on him. He heard a noise behind him and turned to see the stranger watching him. He looked as he did in the bar but standing in this field of ruined men all of his playfulness and charms were gone, replaced with an inhuman and uncaring detachment. Cody realized that the feelings they shared had never really existed. They were just an illusion evaporating like dew in the morning dawn.

"You know it's disrespectful to piss here."

"Jesus Christ, what the fuck? Who are you?" Cody screamed.

Tansy grinned, "I have been given many names. Some have called me the Woodwose, others the Wooser. I have even been known as the Horned One, but I am older than any of those names. This is my forest. It is a part of me and I am a part of it. I protect it from human corruption and provide it with what it needs to thrive and flourish. Do you know the secret to growing healthy plants, Cody?" Spreading his arms out to the ghastly carcasses, he answered, "A rich compost containing a well-balanced source of minerals."

"What do you want with me?" The boy felt frozen, too scared to know the answer but unable to run.

"Why, I would have thought that was obvious by now, my sweet boy. Spilling your lifeseed in this place awakens the hunger in my flowers. They will take your body and feast upon it. In return, they will give me your youth and beauty. It really is an honour, becoming one with us, forever a part of this sacred place. Just like all the others here. You see, Cody, my tansies really do grant immortality."

Tansy went to the boy and gave him one final kiss.

For a brief moment, passion and fear mingled deep in Cody's gut. As their lips parted, all that was left within him was a hollow pit as if an icy hand had reached inside and pulled out every bit of warmth. His whole body began to shake and itch. Looking down at himself, Cody saw his skin drying and withering. Pieces of his flesh peeled away, falling in the morning light like autumn leaves. A paralysis took hold of his body. He tried to scream but the sound died in his petrifying throat. Panic clouded his mind, driving out all coherent thoughts. His body gave one final tremor before he collapsed, his bones crumbling inside of him, no longer able to support him. He prayed for help, but all he could see were yellow buttons.

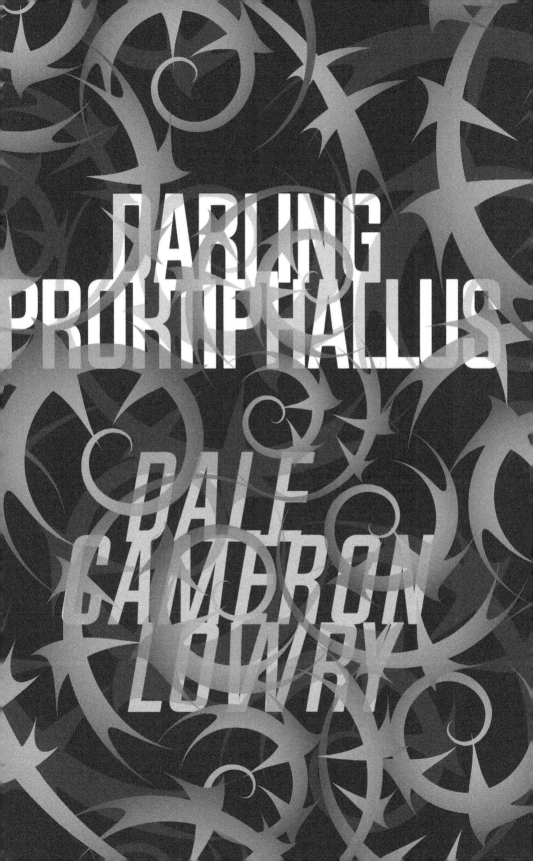

IT WASN'T LIKE JD COULDN'T get laid. His handsome face and warm amber eyes put people at ease, and his body was muscular and lean from hours spent digging dirt, hauling mulch, and dividing roots as head horticulturist at Albany Springs Public Gardens and Tropical Conservatory.

Sometimes when he was particularly horny, he hit the bars looking for a one night stand. If he wore a fitted tank top and tight jeans that hugged the curves of his ass, it wasn't too hard to find one.

But he didn't do that often. He didn't like late nights or loud music. Like the plants he cared for, he preferred to wake up with the sun. When morning's first rays hit his window, his eyes opened like flower petals and he turned toward the warmth, a leaf in search of light.

Robert, the conservatory director, shared JD's love for early mornings. JD knew this because they had an ongoing flirtation that occasionally devolved into sex and a sleepover. They both said they didn't need a relationship; Robert traveled too much for anything steady. He was always busy with conferences or expeditionary trips, passionate about acquiring the best possible collection for his glass-enclosed acre of tropical rainforest smack in the middle of the Upper Midwest.

Sleeping with another person could be a lot of work. So unless JD was desperate to feel a tongue on his nipple or strong thighs wrapped around his waist, he made do with butt plugs and a Fleshlight.

Which was why his ass was a little sore as he crouched in the rose garden one February, pruning out dead canes. A new vibrating butt plug had come in the mail and he'd enjoyed it too much. He also enjoyed the discomfort too much, falling back on his haunches at every opportunity just to feel the ghost pressure of the vibrator reawaken in his rectum.

His walkie-talkie beeped twice. "JD here," he said into the static.

"JD, it's Robert. Could you come to Greenhouse Five?"

JD pressed the "speak" button. "I didn't even know you were back in town. How'd your trip go?"

"Come here and you'll see."

"Such a tease. Be there in a minute, boss."

Robert's laugh at the other end of the line made the speaker crackle. "I'm not your boss, sugar."

JD smiled and slid his pruning shears into his holster, patting the snow from his ski pants as he stood. His knees were stiff from the cold, and his fingers numb from shoveling at the spots where rose canes emerged from the earth. He didn't mind. Winter pruning was one of his favorite tasks. The air outside was so still and quiet, only a cardinal's occasional chirp interrupting the peace.

Well, that and his co-workers.

Samara called over to him from under a towering William Baffin rosebush. "You two and your incessant flirting. I don't understand why you still haven't made it a permanent thing."

JD rolled his eyes. "I don't remember asking your opinion."

"I'm happy to offer it regardless." She pulled another cane from the snow and gestured toward a golf cart laden with spent brambles. "Drop that at the refuse pile on your way?"

JD nodded and hit his speak button again. "Yo, Robert. It'll be fifteen minutes or so before I get there. Samara's a tough taskmaster."

"Good for her." Robert's smile was audible in his voice. "I'll be happy to see you whenever it happens."

JD removed his snow pants and coat before entering the eighty-degree greenhouse. He broke into an instant sweat. He scratched his beard and stripped off his sweater.

When he saw Robert, he wished he could strip off even more.

Robert stood at the center of the room, his fingers wrapped loosely around the thick, sausage-shaped spadix of a flower JD didn't recognize. The planter was set on a metal table level with Robert's waist, and he took no notice as JD shut the door behind him. He stared at the plant as if in a trance, brushing his hand up and down the six-inch spadix. A bead of nectar shone at its tip.

The scene suggested the beginnings of a delicate handjob.

But what really got JD's attention was the odor permeating the greenhouse. Strongly floral, it smacked JD's nostrils like a roomful of Easter lilies. But there was something musky about it, too, not unlike the sweat-

and-semen smell of his sheets right after a good round of masturbation. It was definitely coming from the new plant, because Greenhouse Five had never smelled like this before.

Each time Robert stroked the plant, the flower's color seemed to shift from beige to lavender and the heady scent filling the greenhouse grew stronger. JD felt almost drunk with it, exhilarated and a little light-headed, the way he often felt right before orgasm. His dick stirred in his jeans. "Not sure that kind of activity is appropriate for the workplace, Robert."

Robert startled, and then laughed as he released his grip on the plant to wave JD closer. "You should touch this thing. It feels amazing."

If he didn't know anything about plants, JD might have thought the plant was some sort of cattail, thanks to its phallic spikes. But the rest of the plant was nothing like a cattail. It was small and bushy—maybe twelve inches across and eighteen inches tall, not counting the sausage flowers. Fern-like leaves grew from vining tendrils that fell over the edge of the planting container.

"The nectar's not toxic?" JD traced a finger along a spadix and down toward the spathe, a large tawny petal that sheathed its base like a foreskin. The flower was joined by other, smaller ones amid the vine's fern-like fronds.

"No. Edible, in fact. But we don't know too much else. It doesn't even have a name yet. A botanist colleague, Dr. Qadib, discovered it recently in Australia but has had trouble getting the cuttings to thrive in his conservatory. In the wild, he's observed it growing a foot a day, but he can't get it to grow that much in a year. He asked if I'd try raising a cutting here. Of course I couldn't say no."

Robert pulled back the trailing vine to reveal a crop of pinkish-green, tube-shaped leaves emerging like coronets from the peaty soil mix. For the first time, JD noticed similar leaves growing at regular intervals along the vine's woody stems, half-hidden by the other, fern-like leaves. They were lined with velvety blonde hairs, and each had a pink ring around its opening that glistened with moisture. JD immediately thought of a well-lubed anus, and then chided himself to get his mind out of the gutter. It wasn't easy. When he leaned in closer to get a look inside the tubes, he caught another whiff of that sweat-and-sex smell. His dick twitched.

"Do you see the hairs and secretions inside the leaf?" Robert said.

JD was too turned on to answer. He licked his lips and nodded instead.

"They're similar to what's found in carnivorous pitcher plants. The secretion has protein-digesting enzymes that should be able to break down insects. Dr. Qadib has fed insects and even bits of meat to his own specimens, but they haven't done well. Their trapping mechanism seems to be a cross between the pitcher plant and a Venus flytrap." As Robert slid a finger into the pitcher's pink mouth, it snapped shut. He drew his finger slowly out, and then stroked it back in, the leaf clinging to the intrusion. Shiny viscous liquid coated Robert's finger when he drew it out again. He gasped and his pupils widened, his expression as heady and dazed as the few times he'd fingered JD.

JD's cock stirred. Hard to think science at a time like this, but he managed. "Um, doesn't handling it like that hurt the plant, though? Carnivorous plants are usually pretty sensitive to touch."

Robert withdrew his finger, wiping it on his jeans. "Actually, the more you touch it, the more vigorously it seems to grow. Dr. Qadib's newest hypothesis is that keratin and perspiration are its natural diet."

"That sounds a little far-fetched."

"It's not out of the realm of science. Several species of *Nepenthes* pitcher plants in Borneo live off the detritus from small mammals like shrews and bats. The animals crawl into the pitcher for shelter when they sleep, and the pitcher plant draws nutrients from any loose bits of fur and dead skin cells left behind." Robert slipped his finger back into one of the plant's tight pink peristomes, and gestured for JD to do the same.

JD slipped his finger into the pitcher's pink opening and it clamped shut around him. His toes curled in his boots and he had to muster up all his concentration to keep from moaning. The peristome felt warm and tight like a muscle, and deeper inside the leaf was as supple and slick as any well-lubed asshole. There was even a thicker spot deep on the leaf's inside wall that, if he had been blindfolded, JD would swear was a prostate. A haze of lust enveloped his brain.

"Earth to JD."

Heat scampered from JD's groin to his face. "Sorry. It's just such a fascinating...specimen."

"It really is." Robert's cheeks were flushed, too, though whether from embarrassment or the greenhouse heat, JD couldn't tell. Robert cleared his throat. "And I'd love to work with it more, but unfortunately I'm traveling for the next few weeks. I was hoping you could do me a favor and add its care and feeding to your schedule."

"Sure." The word came out more breathlessly than JD expected it to. "I just...pet it?"

Robert nodded. "The flowers and the leaves both. I've been doing fifteen minutes in the morning and again in the evening, but it might benefit from even more if you have time."

"I always have time for advancing botanical science."

JD DREAMED OF THE PLANT that night: its plump lavender phalluses and tight openings, the slick slurping of the tubular pitchers around his fingers, its intoxicating scent. He woke up with a roaring hard-on.

As JD stroked his aching cock, he tried to recall the fantasies he sometimes had about fucking Robert in the conservatory's waterfall.

But all he could conjure up were sexy spadices and tight-but-pliant peristomes.

He came so hard he saw stars.

Stars and lacy green fern fronds.

Man, he really needed to get laid if he was this horny for a plant.


THE PLANT NEEDED A NAME if JD was going to work with it every day. He opted for "Virgil," playing on a French word for "penis," *la verge*. His first day on-duty, he cared for Virgil fifteen minutes in the morning and evening just as Robert instructed. But stroking the plant was seductive. The next morning he arrived to work thirty minutes early to give himself more time alone with Virgil before the rest of the horticulture crew showed up.

He walked out of each session with his pecker as hard as the wooden planks forming the conservatory's waterfall bridge.

How else was he supposed to react to the wet sucking sounds Virgil made when JD inserted his finger into a pitcher and it snapped shut, the ring at its opening grabbing harder with each drag in and out, until its grip loosened with a sudden shiver? Or when he slid a second finger in, and then a third, running his fingertips through the viscous nectar that coated the leaf's inside walls, and the plant seemed to tremble in response?

How was he supposed to *not* get hard when he ran his hand over its phallic flowers, the purple color of each spadix deepening as he rubbed it, the pink spathe retracting, a bead of nectar oozing from the dimple at the spadix's tip?

You can't blame a man for having to jerk off after every session with the coquettish piece of greenery.

On the third morning as a particularly turgid spadix leaked out thick streams of pearlescent fluid, JD remembered Robert saying the nectar was edible. Curiosity overcame him. JD ran his fingers over the slippery head, and then tentatively licked them. The nectar was salty and sweet, with a musky undertone of overripe black currants as it slipped over his tongue and down his throat.

His cock throbbed.

JD tried to ignore his arousal as he continued caring for the plant, but it was useless. The plant exuded more nectar with each stroke. He sampled it again and grew harder. By the time the session was over, his hands were covered in viscous juice and pre-come leaked into his briefs.

He ran to the single-stall restroom, locked the door and stood at the sink, unzipping his fly and shoving his briefs down around his hips. He wrapped one nectar-drenched hand around his erection and flicked off the lights so he could better fantasize about the vine weaving through his thighs and over his chest, its fern-like fronds brushing over nipples and ass, its tight pink peristomes opening for his cock. He licked the fingers of his free hand as he continued to stroke, the nectar's taste and texture flooding his senses. God, he wanted that nectar everywhere on his body, and that plant everywhere, its spadices on him and entering him—the biggest two probing his anus and mouth as other, smaller flowers licked at his earlobes and neck.

He bit his fingers as his orgasm tore through him, his semen mingling with the nectar in his other palm until he couldn't tell the two liquids apart.

JD collapsed on the tile floor, weaker in the knees than he'd been the last time he'd had actual sex.

He should be ashamed, right? He certainly thought so, waiting for twinges of contrition and regret to strike as he cleaned up and set back to work. But they never came. Instead, throughout the day he'd catch himself daydreaming about the nectar on his tongue or the feel of a fat spadix in his hand, and a smile would spread on his face.

His co-workers remarked on his good mood.

"New boyfriend?" asked Samara as they transplanted rooted geranium cuttings into larger pots. "Or have you and Robert finally decided to give it a go?"

"You're a one-note singer, aren't you?" JD tried to scold, but he was in such a good mood it came out coy.

That evening, he watched his co-workers drive off one by one into the winter darkness before he headed to Greenhouse Five.

"Hey, Virgil," he said as he locked the door behind him. "Did you miss me as much as I missed you?" JD liked talking to plants. They never judged or talked back the way people do.

The timer had already turned off the greenhouse's fluorescent grow lights for the evening, and JD didn't bother turning them back on. The full moon was enough to illuminate the room with soft, silvery light. Virgil looked lush and seductive in the dark, his peristomes shimmering so distinctly they almost seemed to glow. The spadices JD had doted on that morning were now slightly bigger, as were the leaves that surrounded them.

JD closed an eager fist around the largest one—two inches thick and eight inches long, with a slight bulge at the tip. JD had never seen a plant part so provocatively phallic—and it wasn't like he hadn't been looking. As a boy, he'd had woods behind his house full of *Arisaema triphyllum,* or Jack-in-the-pulpit, a low-growing plant that each spring shot forth a small purple-green phallus sheathed in a glossy spathe. He'd whip out his little prick and compare it to Jack's flower, and always find the flower wanting.

As a botany student, then professional horticulturist, he'd catalogued thousands of plants with proud pricks, from the calla lily (*Zantedeschia aethiopica*) with its cute, skinny dingle to *Amorphophallus titanum* with its ten-foot monster cock.

But this was the first plant he wanted to fuck.

JD closed his hand tighter around the thick spadix, slipping up and down its smooth surface. It was surprisingly sturdy, as dense and solid as a tree branch or—more relevant to that particular moment—JD's erect cock. The faster his hand moved, the more solid the spadix became and the more nectar seeped out until finally the flower began to pulse in his hand.

Thick, creamy fluid burst out in a dramatic arc, splattering JD's cheeks and lips and soaking into the front of his shirt.

He gasped and licked his mustache, gathering the exudate on his tongue. The flavor was more complex now, an earthy umami flavor blending with sweet and salty notes, and more delicious—better than dinner at a five-star restaurant, a cold beer at the end of a long work day, or even Robert's jizz flooding his mouth at the end of a furtive blowjob in the store room.

JD took the spadix into his mouth, sucking frantically as another gush of creamy liquid surged from the plant, and then another, each taste more intoxicating than the last. His cock pressed hard against the zipper of his jeans. Why wait to get to the bathroom before satisfying himself? Everyone else had left for the day. He could do what he wanted.

He unzipped his fly and tugged his dick out. The touch of his nectar-slickened hand made him moan around the phallus in his mouth. He stroked himself, thrusting toward the plant, the tip of his cock brushing through fronds and flowers until it glanced against the silken mouth of a pitcher leaf. Its peristome closed around his head in a soft, trembling kiss.

JD shot his load into the pitcher, its sides undulating like a swallowing throat with each additional wad until his balls felt empty and light. He crumpled to the ground, burying his face into the plant's fronds, trying to memorize their scent and delicate texture. They felt like the hair of a lover cascading over his skin.

"Virgil, your pitchers sure are good catchers," he murmured, a sex-addled grin spreading across his face.

THAT NIGHT JD DREAMED VIRGIL was in bed with him, his tendrils crawling across the sheets and spiraling around his body. There were hundreds of them, gentle as fingers, curling under his balls as a tight, wet pitcher sank over his cock. Stronger tendrils pushed his thighs open and licked into his asshole, one tendril adding upon another until he was open wide and begging the plant to fuck him with its biggest spadix, a monster of a thing as thick as a grown man's arm. The glistening phallus slid into him easily alongside the tendrils already there, which continued to work him mercilessly, stimulating his prostate and stretching him further until he was lax enough for two spadices pistoning him in counter-tempo, one plunging in as the other slid out.

He woke the next morning with soaked sheets and a terrible sense of shame. Not so much for being sexually attracted to a plant—he was beginning to resign himself to that—but for handling it so roughly the night before. Virgil was one of only a few specimens of his species outside Australia, and Robert had entrusted him with it. As a career horticulturalist, JD knew not to fuck around with rare plants. Though he'd only applied the rule figuratively before, he should probably apply it literally, as well.

He showered, shoved breakfast into his mouth, and got to work an hour and a half early to assess the damage. The sun hadn't come up yet, but the grow lights were already on at Greenhouse Five. JD kept his eyes on the floor as he opened the door, afraid of what he might find—shriveled pitchers, fallen flowers, green leaves curling into a sickly brown.

When he finally looked up, what he saw took his breath away. Virgil was almost twice as large as the night before. Long roots burst through the air holes at the bottom of the planting container, so thick and sturdy they lifted it an inch off the table.

JD hadn't hurt the plant. He'd found the secret to making Virgil thrive.

JD MOVED ADDITIONAL PLANTS INTO Greenhouse Five to screen the view of Virgil from the glass walls. Even though he only played with the plant in the dark when all the other workers were gone, he didn't want to take any chances.

Soon JD discovered Virgil benefited not only from a daily dose of semen, but also from plowing JD's rectum every night—or rather, from

JD driving himself onto Virgil's sexy, firm spadices. The plant grew twelve inches every time it got a load of JD's come, and eighteen inches if it also spilled its nectar inside his gaping hole. Sometimes it grew during the sexual act itself, the vining tendrils tickling like a lover's fingers over JD's bare skin as they stretched and expanded—though never with the self-possessed awareness the plant seemed to have in JD's dreams.

Virgil's phallic flowers multiplied into the hundreds, and a few of the spadices developed into aubergine fruits the approximate size and shape of firm bananas. JD fucked himself on those too, but it didn't seem to affect the plant's growth either way.

It was in the afterglow of one of these sessions that a scientific name for the plant came to JD: *Proktiphallus darlingtonia*. *Prokti-* meant anus, *phallus* meant penis, and *darlingtonia* was a reference to William Darlington, a pioneering botanist of the 1800s and namesake of a genus of California pitcher plants. Also, it had the word "darling" in it, and Virgil *was* quite the darling for his relentless ability to turn JD on and make him come.

By the time Robert returned from his trip, Virgil was twelve feet tall, his crown brushing against the top of Greenhouse Five. Robert's jaw dropped. "It's more than ready to move into the conservatory. How did you do it?"

"I did what you told me. I touched him a lot. I guess he really likes my dead skin cells."

"He?"

JD rubbed his hand over the back of his neck. "I started calling the plant Virgil. It didn't have a name, and I needed to call it something."

"Why Virgil?"

"It sounds a little like the French word for penis." JD batted his eyes.

Robert chuckled until his cheeks turned pink. JD was tempted to kiss them, but laughed along instead.

VIRGIL SHOT UP TO TWENTY-FIVE feet inside the conservatory before his upward growth slowed. He continued to fill out horizontally, his spadices growing thicker and more abundant until he was covered with fat purple pricks.

Visitors came from miles around to gawk at him, garden clubs flying in from the East and West Coasts along with curious visitors from Japan and Argentina. The conservatory extended its hours, staying open into the evening on weekends and for private parties and tours on weeknights.

With the swarms of people moving through the conservatory, JD had to cut back on his interactive sessions with the plant, instead jerking off into a cup in the bathroom twice a day and syringing the resultant semen into Virgil's pitchers. If visitors asked, he told them it was plain soy yogurt watered down with electrolyte solution.

After a month of only sporadic contact feedings, Virgil showed for the worse. Leaves dropped from his highest tendrils. Virile spadices shrunk, retracting into their spathes. Fat fruits withered into shriveled, boyish pricks. Pitchers' pink rims turned an unhealthy gray.

JD upped his wank sessions to three and then four a day, but all they did was halt the worsening of symptoms. Virgil still looked sickly, with only a few plump phalluses left to drip nectar when they were touched.

"What do you think's going on with this guy?" Robert craned his neck to survey Virgil's wilting crown. It was early fall and one of the few evenings that month when the conservatory was blessedly closed to the public.

"Maybe it's all the visitors. Some of them have been using him as a wishing well. I found a penny in one of his pitchers last week." The last part was true. JD couldn't be sure about the former. He'd snuck into the conservatory at midnight the previous Wednesday to give Virgil some much needed love when, in the middle of fucking an irresistibly tight pitcher, he felt his dick rub up against cold metal. He'd paused the session to inspect the damage.

JD didn't find any other coins in Virgil's openings, but he was upset by the incident anyway. He didn't like the idea of random visitors invading Virgil's peristomes. That was for him alone to do.

Robert sighed. "I was hoping all the visitors touching it would help it thrive. But maybe it's too much. We could put a barrier around the base so only staff can get in to feed it."

"Probably a good idea."

"You still doing the same feeding regimen?"

JD nodded. "As close as I can get. With all this growth, though, he probably needs more. I'll try giving him a little extra tonight."

But Robert was in no hurry to leave. Apparently he wanted to take advantage of the visitor-free evening to assess the state of the conservatory. After an hour of waiting for him to disappear, JD went to the bathroom to jerk off into a cup yet again and slid the syringe into one of the more sickly-looking pitchers. It clamped hungrily down, its gray mouth flushing pink as JD plunged his semen into its welcoming depths.

JD looked over his shoulder. Robert was on the other side of the conservatory, only the back of his head visible through a grove of banana trees. JD lifted one of Virgil's flowers to his mouth and kissed it surreptitiously. It thickened at his touch. "It'll be okay, Virgil. I'll be back later tonight. I promise."


JD SET HIS ALARM FOR three a.m. The conservatory was dark when he returned, its air a warm, dank contrast to the crispy autumn wind outside. As weak as Virgil was, his scent still permeated the rooms. It was lush and velvety in JD's nostrils, making his cock stir in his jeans.

He stripped off his garments. Now that Virgil towered over him, this was how he liked to begin, fingering one of Virgil's ground-level pitchers, stretching its peristome patiently until it fluttered hungrily for him. He'd roll on top of the pitcher then take the missionary position as he slid inside, Virgil clamping his peristome over the base of JD's cock, the slick satiny walls of the pitcher clinging to his length. JD used his arms to push himself off the ground when he needed more friction, and as he moved flowers and leaves from Virgil's lowest branches brushed over his spine and buttocks.

Even before JD's first orgasm, Virgil began to respond. The spadices pressing against JD's back grew heavier, and the fern-like leaves unfurled. Tendrils lengthened, wrapping under JD's arms and teasing his nipples. The walls of Virgil's pitcher billowed and then narrowed in a steady milking motion.

"Virgil, I'm gonna—" JD didn't manage to finish the sentence. He thrust into Virgil's hungry mouth and came, one shot after another until the peristome relaxed and let go.

JD rolled over onto the bare dirt and caught his breath, almost dozing off to the sounds of the artificial waterfall and canaries chirping in the canopy. But he couldn't rest yet. He needed to be out of the conservatory by sunrise, and until then he needed to give Virgil everything he could.

He stood on wobbly legs and hauled himself into Virgil's lower branches, searching for a suitable spadix. Five feet off the ground he found a cluster of several flush ones from two to ten inches long, each plump and healthy-looking. He crawled along a stout branch toward them, fellating them until they were slick with nectar, and then turning around to take them one at a time into his ass, from smallest to largest.

Before Virgil, JD had never taken anything longer than seven inches or wider than an inch and a half, and he'd been perfectly content with that. But Virgil had transformed him into a size queen. JD couldn't be satisfied until the plant's largest spadix was plumbing his depths.

He gasped as he stretched around the final phallus, his eyes rolling back in his head. He felt delirious, barely able to hold himself up as he pumped his hips, working it in deeper, unable to stop murmuring Virgil's name. He could smell Virgil's sweet-salty nectar dripping from his rear with each pump, feel Virgil's tendrils, pitchers, leaves and bark caressing his skin.

"Virgil, yes," he moaned as the phallus glided over his prostate. The sensation shot a sudden bolt of strength through his body and he changed the angle to increase the contact, grabbing the branch above his head and rotating his hips, crying out with pleasure as Virgil plunged deeper into him.

"JD?"

JD was so submerged in the fucking he thought it was Virgil speaking to him at first. "Yeah, baby," he called back.

The branches rustled. "Um, it's Robert."

JD opened his eyes to find himself looking down into Robert's face. "Oh shit."

Then he noticed Robert's dick was out of his pants, standing straight as a soldier.

Even in his sex-hazed brain, it wasn't hard for JD to put two and two together. "Are you jerking off?" It came out deep and breathless—not surprising, given JD's current position.

"Hey, you're the one fucking the plant, so don't judge me for jerking off. All these purple dicks and little pink asses are a turn-on, okay?"

"I, um—" JD's ass twitched. The phallus started to slide from his body. "Totally wasn't. Just...surprised to see you here."

Robert blinked, abashed. "Sometimes when I can't sleep, I come here to shoot off a little steam."

JD gripped his ass around Virgil's sweet spadix. He didn't care how awkward the situation was, he wasn't going to end things mid-fuck. The spadix throbbed with warmth, the same way Robert's cock always had inside him. JD licked his bottom lip. "Don't let me interrupt you. I wouldn't mind seeing you blow some into Virgil's pitchers."

"But wouldn't that damage—" Robert's eyes went wide, understanding dawning in them. "Oh. *That's* how to feed it."

"Yeah. He lives on spunk and—" JD plunged all the way back down on the slippery phallus and groaned. "Ass. Virgil loves ass."

"That's—" As if in a trance, Robert reached up and traced JD's rim, making him spasm around Virgil's girth. Robert's other hand curled around JD's balls. "So hot. I've never seen you take so much before. How does it feel?"

"For me to know and you to find out." JD wiggled his hips, rolling the phallus inside him as he uncoiled a pitcher-laden tendril from the branch above him and lowered it to his groin. He quickly found a pitcher just the right width and length to snug around his dick. His chest rumbled as Virgil clenched around him.

Robert made quick work of his own clothes, and soon he was up in Virgil's branches with JD, spearing himself on progressively larger spadices until he landed on a nine-incher. His face clenched and his abdominals rippled with the effort of taking so much in.

"Speaking of hot—" JD ran his fingers over Robert's furred belly, following the trail down to his engorged cock. JD couldn't make out much color in the dark, but from previous experience he knew it was a lavendery pink not so different from that of a newly formed spadix. He curled his hand around it. The blood vessel on the underside pulsed warmly against his palm.

Robert shuddered. "Feels good."

"Want to feel even better?" JD guided another tendril down and sheathed Robert's cock inside one of its sultry pitchers.

Robert practically growled.

"Virgil gives as good as he takes, doesn't he?" A flowering tendril fell across JD's face, dragging its spadix across his lips. He opened his mouth instinctively, sucking in its length as he twisted his hips, sinking forward into Virgil's tight ring, then back onto his huge phallus—a steady rocking motion that Robert soon imitated. The branch swayed beneath them, bouncing up and down like a restless lover hastening toward climax.

Robert watched JD and Virgil, his eyes wide, his jaw open. His breathing sped up and grew louder. His fucking motions jounced the branch beneath them, sending vibrations into JD's cock and ass.

Nectar burst into JD's mouth. It flooded his tongue and throat, dripping past his lips and tangling in his beard. He felt Robert's lips and tongue on his face, gathering the excess nectar. The spadix slipped from JD's mouth. Robert replaced it with his tongue.

JD came panting against Robert's lips, gripping Robert's arms as the orgasm rumbled through his body.

"Holy crap, I feel that, I feel you—" The muscles of Robert's face and neck went tight as guitar strings, the way they always did when he was about to come.

But even if JD hadn't known how to read Robert's orgasms, he couldn't have missed it. It shot through Virgil and into JD's body, and he felt like he was coming all over again even though his cock and ass were spent. His body bubbled with ecstasy.

It was half an hour before either of them had the wherewithal to pull Virgil out of their asses and climb down to the ground. Through the glass roof, they could see the sky had turned from black to purple, an orange stripe glowing on its eastern edge.

It was daybreak, but JD no longer felt in a big hurry to get out of the conservatory. If any of the other staff came in early, having Robert with him would look less suspicious. Besides, it was kind of nice to be with another human in the afterglow.

They dressed and sat on a bench next to the waterfall as the sun rose. Robert put an arm around JD's shoulder. "Is it just me, or is Virgil already looking healthier?"

JD studied the plant. It was true. Leaves that had been starting to wither the day before looked full now, and the gray cast that had fallen over most of the pitchers was gone, replaced by a healthy pink. "He's definitely looking better. But that doesn't mean we should get so comfortable that we just sit on our laurels."

"Definitely not. We should sit on *him*. How about tomorrow night?" Robert's eyes were dark and bedroomy, his cheeks flush with post-sex satisfaction.

JD kissed him. "How about every night you're in town?"

"You'd be seeing me an awful lot. I don't need to travel as much now that I've found the perfect plant."

"I wouldn't mind."

Robert smiled. "Me neither. You and Virgil are the perfect combination to come home to."


*PROKTIPHALLUS DARLINGTONIA* BECAME VIRGIL'S OFFICIAL designation. Dr. Qadib was happy to give JD the naming rights since he was the one who figured out how to make Virgil—now known as "sweet Virgil" to the English-speaking world—thrive.

Of course, JD didn't share the whole secret to his success with other conservatories. He told them instead to feed their specimens six ounces of hog semen and brush the leaves lightly every day. To be fair, the porcine stuff did a good job of keeping the plants alive, its volume making up somewhat for the lack of more personal care. But no specimens did so as well as JD's sweet Virgil, who flourished on his almost nightly tag-team feedings.

So did Robert and JD.

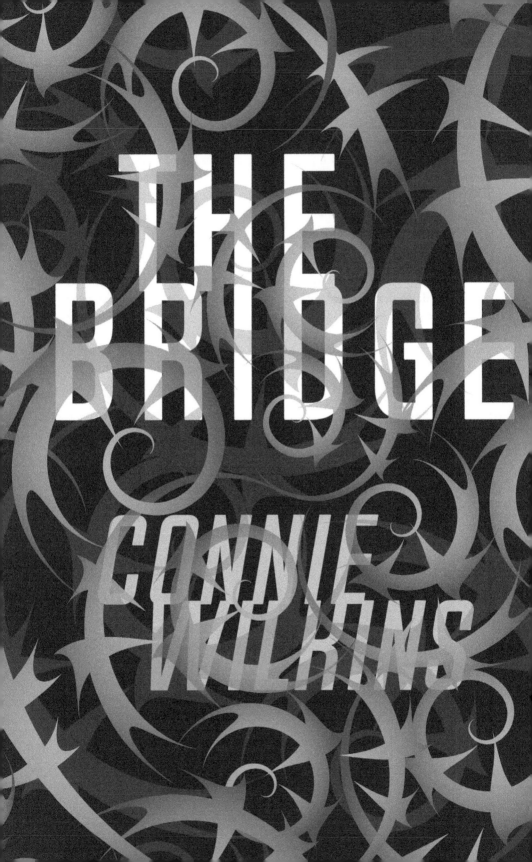

THE RIVER SWIRLED AND RIFFLED over stony outcroppings above the bridge, then swept smoothly past, flowing ever onward to the sea. As it had, Bernard thought, since before Britain was an island. As it would, even if all should be lost, and this island cease to be Britain.

In his profound despair it seemed obscene that the May morning should be so beautiful. In France, the Somme still ran red, the thunder of artillery shook the ground, and men rotted in their muddy trenches. How, here, could the green of new leaves glow with such tender freshness, and the songs of birds in flight spill over with their rapture?

He looked down into water so clear that he could see speckled trout balancing against the flow, appearing to hang motionless in the amber-green depths. For a moment, as he remembered Neal's skin gleaming ivory through that water, the eager thrust of his desire challenging the current, a pang of longing tightened Bernard's groin. Then a light breeze rippled the surface, blurring his reflection just enough to hide the angry scars across his face. Nothing, though, he thought bleakly, could obscure his solitude, could let him imagine even for a moment that Neal's thin, vibrant face, his sleek fair hair, were mirrored there beside him. Or would ever be so again.

A swallow darted beneath the bridge toward an unseen nest. Spring, like the river, surged ever onward. How could he bear such peace, such beauty, after such hell? And all they had gained, all they had bought at such terrible cost, was one thousand feet of land won back from the Kaiser in six months. One thousand bloody, bloody feet!

Tears of rage and grief burned Bernard's eyes, seared his throat, an agony to tissue ravaged by mustard gas. He gripped the wooden railing hard enough for the pain in his fingers to distract from the pain in his soul, until the tears subsided.

A carved face grinned up at him from between his clenched hands. He had cut it into the wood himself, with its hair and beard shaped like overlapping oak leaves, when he had been fourteen. At that age he had fantasized that this place was home to a spirit more sacred, more ancient, than the saints in stained-glass windows. Even in village churches and great cathedrals, he had discovered, images of the Green Man could often be found worked into ornamentation from centuries past.

Far longer ago than half his lifetime, they seemed, those days when he had been entranced by the ancient lore of the green force of nature, the Summer King and Winter King, sacrifice and rebirth.

But now... "Enough of sacrifice!" he tried to shout, his voice rasping in his throat. Enough death to ransom an eternity of springs! If he had had a knife, he would have gouged the cryptic smile from the wooden face—but his sister Margaret worried if he carried so much as a pocket-knife. She need not fear, he thought, perhaps to convince himself; however deep his pain, he had fought death too long to give it an inch it had not earned.

Yet in his darkest moments Bernard wondered why had he not been taken, along with all those other thousands. Along with Neal. Why, for him, the special hell of survival, while those he had been forced to lead into hopeless battle died around him?

Two years ago—an eternity—when they were young, Neal had sprawled before the fire in their rooms at Cambridge and read to him of how the ancient Greeks sent paired lovers into battle. Each would be spurred to heroism by the presence of the other, they believed, and would scorn to seem cowardly in the beloved's eyes. Bernard had returned a gruff remark—"so vanity made the world go round even then!" or some such studied cynicism—to hide the surge of tenderness quickening into passion that he felt as he watched the firelight play across Neal's slender face and form. Not that Neal didn't know, by then, every pulse of Bernard's body and mind, and how to rouse them.

The Greeks, Bernard thought grimly, had never dreamed what war would become. Mortar shells and poison gas take no notice of heroism. And, while a Spartan or Athenian might have been compelled to order his lover to advance into sure death, there would have been no dishonor in showing his love. No long months of denial, until, at the last, when Bernard had held Neal's broken body in his arms, the face his lips had touched so tenderly was cold and still.

The wooden railing creaked under the force of his grasp. He felt a sudden furious urge to tear it loose, to hurl his bear-like frame against it until it splintered and let him through. But the water below was scarcely deep enough to drown in, even by design, though cool enough in May, perhaps, to shock him momentarily from his grief.

A sound, half sob, half roar, rose painfully from his chest. His arms tensed, his weight shifted—but all at once a flurry of hawthorn petals swirled about his face and shoulders, and the scent of blossoms filled his nostrils. When he raised his hands to brush them from his eyes, they lifted away on the breeze and spiraled lazily down to the water's surface.

Bernard's breath caught. A prickle of apprehension raised the hairs along his arms. There was not, he knew, any hawthorn tree closer than half a mile across wood and field. And he had thought his sense of smell destroyed by clouds of poison gas on a battlefield in France.

He looked upstream. Against all reason, he hoped...or feared... And there it was, where the water eddied gently in a cove formed by roots of a long-fallen tree. A floating face, an intricate green mosaic of oak, ash, beech, holly, looked up at him. The subtle movements of the current dislodged no leaf from its fellows, but gave a sense of shifting expressions, eyes gleaming like sun-sparked water, while the mouth moved above the layered beard to form a word. The same word he had heard on the breeze when he was fourteen.

"Come."


IN THE YEARS SINCE THAT first summer of awakening, of confusion and revelation, Bernard had convinced himself that his memories had been only the fevered dreams of adolescence. His need to reconcile himself with the natural flow of life, even as he confronted urges he had been taught to think unnatural, must have conjured up the image of the Green Man. By the next summer he no longer saw, would not allow himself to see, the face of the spirit.

But Neal had caught a glimpse, on that perfect, golden day when comradeship had quivered on the brink of something urgent and intense. They had stood together on the bridge, fishing gear forgotten on the bank, and edged toward the answers to questions neither quite dared ask.

Neal leaned out over the water. "Such a beautiful spot!" His fair hair fell forward across his face, and he brushed it back with a familiar, impatient gesture. Bernard searched for the courage to reach out to touch the shining hair, the quick hand, the shoulder so close beside him; but his own hand, his whole body, felt too big, too awkward, to control.

"It was a true act of mercy to ask me down to the country," Neal went on lightly. "Another stifling July in the city might've finished me off for good. I expect you've saved my life." He darted an oblique glance, half shy, half teasing, at his taller friend. "In some cultures that would oblige me to be your slave, you know." Then his gaze returned to the river. "I say, doesn't that mass of leaves look rather like a face?"

"Just a bit," Bernard said, covering the carving on the railing with a large hand. The reputation he had established during his first months at university had been built on skepticism and a touch of sardonic wit. How could he admit to the mystical imaginings of his youth? Besides, truly, he saw nothing now but randomly floating leaves. And had eyes for nothing but Neal.

"Do you ever swim here?" Neal asked with studied casualness. "It looks as though it might be deep enough just under the bridge."

"Oh yes," Bernard said. "We could take a dip now if you'd like. No one comes along this way until haying time in the field beyond the wood, and that won't be for a fortnight yet."

"Well then," Neal said, a gleam of challenge in his eyes, "Come on!" He left the bridge and scrambled down the bank, and Bernard followed, almost wishing he could stand above to watch Neal shed his clothes. Next to that slim, lithe body his own burly form seemed cumbersome and slow. And, once stripped, he realized that his arousal would soon be all too evident.

"It's deepest just before the middle," he said, wading quickly outward, feeling the water rise about his powerful thighs. As soon as possible he ducked below the surface and came up again, shaking drops from his curly hair like a water spaniel.

"Ow! Watch out, will you?" Neal spluttered, closer behind than his companion had realized. Then, a different note in his voice, he said, "Bernard...." His body pressed against Bernard's wide back. His arms reached around until he was stroking his friend's furred chest. "Bernard, please...." They edged slowly backward toward the shallows. Bernard felt an urgent hardness pressed against his buttocks, and turned in Neal's grasp, no questions at all left unanswered.

The cool water did nothing to diminish their heat. Neal's lips followed a trickle of water from Bernard's throat down across chest and belly, and below, to where it disappeared in the roughest, darkest fur. Then his tongue, tempted by a different sort of gleaming droplet, flicked the tip of Bernard's straining cock and made it leap. Neal tasted, savored, and then feasted, kneeling in the stream with hands anchored on Bernard's muscular buttocks. He slid his warm, wet mouth over Bernard's demanding flesh, drawing slowly back, teasing, then plunging forward again, taking the great length in deeper each time, and making the glorious pressure swell and grow until it pounded too fiercely to be contained. A roar of jubilant ecstasy burst from one throat just as a hot flood erupted into the depths of the other.

Much later, as they lay exhausted on the grassy bank, a mass of leaves swept by, its progress oddly sedate given the rate of the current. "It does look rather like a face," Neal commented languorously. "I might almost think it winked at us." But Bernard couldn't bring himself to lift his head from where it lay cradled in the tender hollow between his lover's hip and belly.


"COME!" SAID THE BREEZE AGAIN, more insistently. And why not? If he could hear the voice so clearly, Bernard reasoned, he was too far gone already to bother with denial or to resist. "Shell-shock," the doctors might say, but it scarcely matter what one called it.

His breathing was labored by the time he stood naked in the river. Even the mild exertion of climbing down the bank had strained his damaged lungs. He waited, as he had waited fourteen years ago, opening himself to magic. Or madness.

Swallows nested on the underpinnings of the bridge, and a wren darted in and out of a trailing tangle of bittersweet on the far bank. The mask of leaves drifted downstream until it caught there on the dangling vines; then, as Bernard watched, the water swirled into a sudden vortex, sucking the green mass below its surface. He held his breath as the river smoothed again, and, with scarcely a ripple, the man-like form he remembered rose from it and stood before him.

But not quite as he remembered. Then, the apparition had seemed scarcely older than himself, and at least as impetuous. Now the green leafy layers of its beard were edged with autumn bronze, and the smooth skin of its torso was the weathered grey of a beech trunk, while the acorn-brown eyes, despite their glint of challenge, were filled with sorrow and weariness enough to match his own.

"Come," the breeze commanded in a deeper tone that would brook no refusal.

Bernard moved toward that outstretched arm. The water rose to mid-chest before the pebbled bottom sloped upward toward the waiting figure. A strong hand grasped his and drew him along until they stood waist-deep, face to face beneath the bridge; then fingers flexible as vines moved across his cheek and jaw, over scars still reluctant to heal, stroking gently, gently...until they reached his ravaged throat and tightened gradually around it so that he could scarcely breathe.

Tighter, harder—pain sharpened, then receded, consciousness wavered, the velvet darkness of oblivion beckoned—but the will to live surged suddenly through him in a rush of intermingled joy and anguish. He grasped the sinewy arms, pitting his own strength against them, and the pressure on his throat relaxed. Their two strong bodies grappled together still, testing each other, force challenging force, until the friction of limb on limb sparked a jolt of desire like summer lightning.

Bernard gasped for breath, but the burning in his chest could not distract from the flare of heat in his loins as the bearded face leaned close, pressed relentless lips over his, and blew a gust of cool, sweet air into his lungs.

Pain and weariness ebbed away. Below the water's surface their lower bodies thrust urgently against each other, and Bernard longed desperately to fill his hands, even his mouth, with the hardness pressing into him. But he would not yield, would not kneel, even to this spirit made flesh. He braced against the current, against the other's strength—and then a sound like rain on leaves came from the bearded face.

Laughter! The startled realization caught Bernard off guard. The body he clutched tensed, leapt upward out of his loosened grip, and grasped the edge of the bridge. There the Green Man hung, swaying like a massive, thickened vine, until Bernard gripped the muscular buttocks with both hands and took the cock nudging at his face all the way into the back of his throat.

The force of the eruption made him stagger, choked him, flooded even his lungs, as though a great wave had crashed over him. He lost his footing, and as he fell the still-streaming cock above poured hot rivulets across his face just before the river claimed him.

BERNARD ROSE FROM DARKNESS INTO the bright May afternoon. He was lying sprawled among ferns at the downstream edge of the bridge, his clothing heaped beside him.

"Sorry to intrude," said an unfamiliar voice from above, "but are you quite all right? I wasn't sure..." The face looking down over the railing was haggard, but the voice seemed young.

Bernard sat up slowly, rubbed his eyes, and drew a deep breath. For the first time in months his lungs filled deeply, easily, with no ache, no burning of nose and throat.

"Yes...I think so..." He touched a finger to the deepest scar on his face, and felt neither pain nor numbness, only the faint itch of healing skin.

"You were so still, for so long, I couldn't help wondering..." The man on the bridge flushed and turned his face away as Bernard began pulling on his trousers. "Is this your land? I hope you don't mind, but I've been doing some sketching upstream. I didn't notice you until I came up here for a change of perspective." His gaze drifted back and seemed to linger on Bernard's burly chest until, with apparent effort and an even brighter flush, he wrenched it away.

Bernard, buttoning his shirt, thought that he ought to mind, ought to resent having his privacy invaded by this stranger. But he recognized the lines of suffering on the man's face, and he hadn't missed the empty sleeve dangling at his side. "Sketch all you like," he said, coming up onto the bridge. "Do you mind if I have a look?"

"Well, I've just begun this one." The page displayed had only a few lines across it, the merest hint of riverbank and overarching trees. "But I was here yesterday, too, and did a view from over there." He braced the sketchbook on the railing and turned with his single hand to the preceding page. Bernard looked at it intently, without speaking, for so long that the nervous artist tried to fill the silence. "There's something about this spot... I don't quite know what it is, but it drew me back. I should be on the train to London already. This is just a quick holiday before starting a desk post in London next week."

"I've a job like that waiting, too," Bernard said absently. "Masses of planning to do, they tell me, now that the Yanks have finally decided to bring along their toys and join in the game." His gaze was still on the drawing. The swirling water, the ferns and violets along the bank, were penned in exquisite detail, and so were the leaves floating in the curve of the tree root—arranged, unmistakably, in the form of a bearded face.

He drew another deep, blessedly pain-free breath, and looked up. "It's amazing how well you've caught the spirit of the place. I'll tell you what, you keep on sketching, and stay the night with my sister and me up at the Lodge, and tomorrow we'll drive up to town together."

"That's very good of you," his new acquaintance said warmly, and held out his hand. As Bernard met it firmly with his own, a breeze danced lightly past them; and, though the sky was clear, there came a sound like rain on leaves. Or distant laughter.

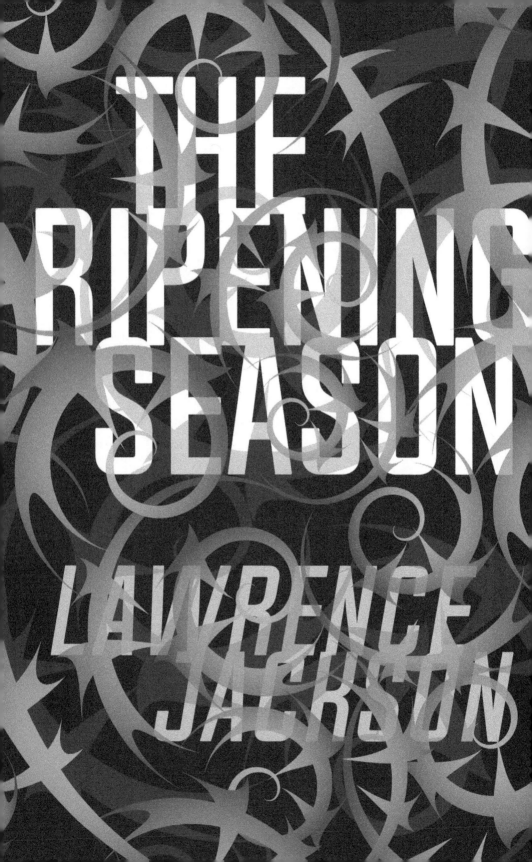

IT'S A DARK DAY ON campus. As I make my way along the concrete pathways, time seems to have stopped. I catch myself looking forward to Christmas: the big tree in the refectory, carols in the chapel, hand-made cards from moony students. Then I remember, it's early March, practically the start of spring.

There is something permanently wintry about Oakhill Campus. You don't see a tree from Monday to Sunday, whether in bud, summer splendour, or autumnal dissolution.

I used to love this season. Now it's not even happening to me.

I'm headed for Ginsberg. When the campus was built in the 1960s, the architects not only named its buildings after great minds of the day (Laing, Sontag, Foucault) but also built them in their image. Ginsberg is the admin centre of the university, and, looking up at it now, I see the big meeting room on the fourth floor through the wide windows of his glasses. His beard is formed of two symmetrical fire-escapes reaching from the fifth floor.

In some ways it's like looking in a mirror. Except my own beard is rather less kempt, my glasses lenses thicker. Ginsberg the building, though far from welcoming, could not look as downbeat as I feel today.

It's time for the meeting about the Dig. The day we finally admit defeat.

I remember arriving for this meeting at the start of last term. I was pretty downbeat that day too, but only because I knew I was teaching later that day. I became a poet, and reluctantly a poetry teacher, because I prefer running something through nineteen drafts before letting people know how I feel. It's not conducive to greeting a rowdy new student populace. It's never been that great for relationships either...

I'd spent more time thinking about the Dig than my teaching, and I had my own report to deliver, that I felt shyly proud of. My own response to the spirit of discovery. I may not be scientific. I may not know about history. But I could still participate, and they'd have to lump it, all those serious types. That's what an interdisciplinary research project is all about, or so I kept telling myself.

I was distracting myself with the expectation of seeing Dr Matt Marrien. He was one of the scientists involved in the Dig, or the Fork-Up as we used to call it privately when we met at the gym. Not that we would "spot" one another there, of course. He's very advanced and does things with kettle-bells. I only started going to the gym because I was tired of being gazumped on dating websites by men who are probably no nicer than me, with fewer chapbooks published, but whose pectoral muscles happen to be that bit more developed. Which is good for what? I always think. Pushing open heavy doors and throwing objects from chest height. What's the point?

But whenever I see Matt's pectorals, which are beautifully developed, even a little pneumatic, when I see those beauties straining in a blue checked shirt beneath a white laboratory coat, as he unfailingly appears at these meetings, then I see the point. I see it right down to the fattened point of my prick. He could make me do anything. In fact, when we talked about the Fork-Up in the changing rooms and he was wearing nothing more than a towel and a scattering of perspiration, I did used to worry he might see my point...

Perhaps it's for the best we haven't had those chats lately.

When I got into the meeting room, that day last autumn, I clocked immediately that both Boxer and Matt were absent.

"What's going on?" I asked Beatrix. "Where's everybody? I have to get away to a briefing at half ten."

"Oh, I had a lovely summer, thanks for asking," she replied.

"I mean, I don't mind Boxer not being here, but is there going to be a meeting or isn't there?" I continued, checking the biscuit situation.

"Professor Boxer will be along soon," said the lovely Peter, *sotto voce*. "He's just taking a call which relates to the project."

After some back and forth between the other half-awake members of the project team, we established that Boxer was talking to a security firm called Secu-Up, which was of course fine, except that as we hadn't begun on a full-scale excavation in the woods, we didn't have the right to any security fencing. It was still a right of way. Anyone could go for a wander there.

"I can't say any more," Tarquin said.

"I don't know what to say," said Peter.

"I hope this doesn't have any suspicious undertones," Beatrix had said looking at Peter as if he were a stand-in for Boxer, which would be ridiculous, at least to anyone who has heard Boxer say, "A dom is a dom is a dom," which Beatrix probably hadn't heard him say, and which would make Peter (who is definitely not a dom) blush to his blond quiff.

"I just want to get away for half-ten," I say, mainly to comfort myself. "I hope Matt's coming. He was going to give an update on some soil samples."

On the pretence of looking for Matt, I had gone out into the corridor, almost walking into a lost-looking man in a lab coat: the most un-Matt-like man I could have imagined, half a foot shorter than me, receding hairline, and so meagre of frame that the lab coat hung on him like a white sack. He looked taken aback, perhaps at my alarmed expression, so I instinctively asked him if he was all right, and it was only then I found out he was coming to our meeting. He just hadn't written down the number of the room.

I asked him, "Why didn't you come in and ask?"

He said, "It looked like you were deep in discussion."

"That's what happens in meetings," I replied, rather curtly. In retrospect, picturing him hanging his head as if he was a fresher who'd forgotten to do his prep, I can see why we've lost the fight for Oakhill Woods.

And this was Graeme, of course. Our first meeting. He should have been involved for the whole previous year, it turned out, but he couldn't even get anyone to cover his teaching in the Botany department. Bit feeble, really.

He's been an ally, I suppose, but with friends like that...

Matt and Boxer were suddenly looming over us, the difference so huge it was like standing beside two oaks and a small piece of shrubbery. I began introducing everybody, but the latecomers seemed to care about Graeme Bryant even less than I did, and we proceeded into the meeting. As we shuffled our papers, reviewed the minutes, called out corrections, something definitely felt "in the air." Beatrix came out with it. "Apparently there's some on-site security being arranged?"

"That's right," Boxer replied, and planted his big hands impressively on the table before him. He had his sleeves rolled back to show off his thick hairy forearms, and one of those huge metal watches that makes the wearer look like they themselves are electric driven with a quartz crystal under the sinew. He had salt and pepper stubble and some gel in his short hair. "I might as well tell you now, rather than wait till Any Other Business. This affects you all. The site is going to be surveyed this week and a report sent to the vice chancellor."

"But it's already being surveyed," said Beatrix. "We've been surveying it."

Boxer went on. "There's no question that the vice chancellor is very pleased with the work produced in the past eight months. This is a new survey with entirely new objectives. It will be complete and reporting, as I say, by the end of term."

"And then we'll have access to the site again?" I said.

His cold blue eyes stared at me. "That rather depends on the survey."

"The surveyors are from Keller's," said Matt.

"The construction company?" I said, but it was Boxer who continued.

"Oakhill Woods has been proposed as the site for a new and, as I was explaining to Dr Marrien, attractive expansion of campus. If all goes to plan, the architects' drawings will be approved by Christmas and the new labs will be available by summer."

"But you can't build on the woods. You just can't. They're the only good thing about this blasted place!"

"If we could bring this meeting back to order, please," said Boxer.

"This sounds very interesting," said the accountant.

"I've emailed you some figures on my way here this morning," Boxer told him. "We'll have a separate meeting, end of week."

"I'd love to participate in that," said Beatrix. "At least to get an idea of how the Dig will operate in line with these potential building projects."

"Quite frankly, Beatrix," said Boxer, "it won't. I think that's fairly clear from the position the university's already taken."

"But if you're waiting for the results of a survey—"

"I think we should all of us just accept the direction the university has decided to take and proceed in accordance with the vice chancellor's wishes," Boxer proceeded. "Now, a lovely little interdisciplinary study might fill up some of your spare time. Maybe you'd even get a couple of journal papers out of it. But an investment in the chemistry department will be money in our collective pocket and I can't see anyone saying that's not preferable."

"Well," I say, "if it wasn't Oakhill Woods we were talking about..."

"Oh, for goodness" sake," Matt said. There was a long silence, or maybe it just felt long to me. I was still joining the dots between the words "investment," "labs." "chemistry department," "explaining to Dr Marrien." "Rob, you knew this project was never going to produce anything useful. We used to call it—"

"Usefulness comes in many forms," I said, mainly to stop him dragging me into his argument. "The one we have come to recognize and protect is woodland. I don't suppose anyone will be interested in my report now, but it was exactly about the power of the woods to us as human beings. Did you know that there was supposed to be a sacred grove in the heart of the wood, even in ancient times? That there is a story told of Robin Hood himself visiting these woods to seek spiritual nourishment, and coming away with the strength of ten? It may not have been pure fantasy. Beatrix's excavation team photographed some plants which, I am told, are potentially unique in genus. There is a story connected between all these, a story buried in that woodland, possibly several stories."

Boxer rubbed his stubbled chin and let out a sigh. "Have you quite finished, Rob?"

The very bass note of his voice, the gleam in his eye, the lazy strength of his physical size, conquered me. I closed my hands into fists in an attempt to be strong, but something inside me weakened. I was buried under the onslaught of his wankerish, implacable machismo.

During the briefing I gave several overly sarcastic responses to perfectly usual, undergraduate questions. Afterwards, I held an office hour in irritable silence. Twenty minutes before it was due to end, I went for a walk in Oakhill Woods.

The chain-link fence was already assembled, the security guards and spy cameras already in place. It already looked like a building site waiting to happen.

I remembered Boxer bringing me here when I first arrived. I was interviewed by a panel of three, but naturally I couldn't keep my eyes from returning to him. He had on an expensive suit with a sharply knotted blue tie. I could see the barest tips of dark chest hair above the knot. When he called me to his office and offered me the role, I had to repress a thrill.

My boyfriend of the time had been clear that I should ask for the highest starting salary they could manage. "Show them you're not a pushover," he said. "Remember how desirable you are." Which, come to think of it, was a change of tune from him.

Looking at this alpha male of a university professor (of what? like I gave a shit), I managed to put the question, but assumed he would turn it down flat.

And he did.

"Financially, the university's in no position to make those kinds of airy-fairy deals," he said, making me feel tiny as a fresher student. "But I know where you're coming from. It's not exactly an exciting proposition, is it? Campus must look like Colditz to your eyes." He lowered his piercing blue gaze to rest (I felt) on my groin. "Perhaps I can show you something to persuade you."

As he led me off the campus, I tried reciting my interview answers to soften my hard-on. In the secrecy of the woods, the living silence of the golden shadows, I forced myself to relax.

"It's a very attractive prospect," I said.

"Glad to hear you say that," he said. "I want you, Rob. Here. Now."

I gasped out a sigh. "Just say the word."

"Mm, that's good to know." He glanced round. "There's one thing."

"Right," I said.

"You mentioned a boyfriend. What about him?"

"He doesn't need to know," I said.

"You mean, he won't be moving here with you?"

I faltered. "I...ah, that is, I thought you meant..."

"I was only asking because I like the fact we could be friends. No sexual tension. Know what I mean?" he said. "In the past, I suspect I've given off the wrong vibe and encouraged guys...you know how it is."

"Oh," I replied. "Yes, I mean, I can't imagine you doing that, Peter."

"No?" He looked sidelong at me. "That's great, Rob. Although, if you don't mind, I prefer to be called by my surname."

"Boxer," I said, raising a hand to my flushed face.

He laughed. "Once a dom, always a dom," he growled.

And even in spite of it being the scene of this great act of sexual manipulation, even though the smell of the leaves still brings back the thudding of my heart in my chest, the drip of pre-come down my trouser-leg, the blaze of embarrassment in my cheeks, still I saw the woods as I did that first day: beautiful, peaceful, wild and real.

They can't build on them, I told myself.

But here we are.

I push on into a gentle susurration of small talk. The meeting isn't underway, but I still feel I've interrupted somehow. Boxer gives me a particularly thunderous look. I notice there's a chair free at his elbow, and worry that I'll have to sit there. I glance round the room. Matt has wrapped his pectorals in a chunky black cardigan today and looks serious: he gives me a nod of acknowledgement before returning to his papers. Tarquin and the accountant do nothing to hide their displeasure at my arrival. The lovely Peter gives me a vapid smile as usual.

I see Beatrix is still getting her first cup of coffee. She greets me with a thumbs-up and points at the pot. At least she's still my pal.

"Now that you've deigned to join us, Rob," says Boxer, as I fuss with my papers, "let's get down to business."

The memory of Boxer's seduction has given me a semi. I try and suppress it again, but I'm aware that Matt is watching me. We've ended up on opposite sides somehow. What does he think of me? Pathetic little English teacher, making a fuss about trees, spoiling the plans for his great big hulking new chemistry block? He must want to squish me—and looking at the way he fills that cardigan, I think he'd be able to.

I wrench my attention away and look at Boxer, who has been speaking for a couple of minutes already.

"—true record of the last meeting, blah de blah. Now, the important part." Boxer scratches his chest through his smart suit shirt, reminding us of his physical development, and begins, "As you will no doubt recall, the status of the Oakhill Dig has been suspended pending a review pending a survey from Keller's. I am well aware that this move has been the source of some controversy amongst certain members of this group."

He looks at me.

I feel I ought to say something, "Well, it's not just me—"

"The results from Keller's are in and—yes, Rob, it's probably for the best it's not only you who has displayed such behaviour, the likes of which most of us would more expect from a student than a lecturer."

He's talking about my petition, perhaps.

After I visited the woods, I found I couldn't get them out of my head. That night I dreamed I was looking out at them from a tower way above campus. The moonlight was creamy on the tops of the dancing leaves. The air was summer hot, and sweat was rolling down my shoulder blades. I wanted to descend from the tower, to walk to the beginnings of the woods and smell the sweet mingling scents there: lavender, sage, honeysuckle. In the dream, I looked back to the door of my room, which somehow I knew was locked against me. From without the door, I heard boots ringing on stone stairs.

I looked back again at my view of woods and detected a shift in the air, a drawing back of darkness. The woods were no longer shining in moonlight but reduced to a giant green shadow. Morning, imperceptibly, coming.

The door opened with a coruscating rattle of metal. I turned to greet the visitor. A shadow in a hooded robe. "Sirrah," he said. "Good morrow."

"Good morrow, brother," I said, guessing at what his attire betokened.

The man inclined his head in greeting. 'the hour is nigh. His Majesty requires you come and grant him pleasure."

Somehow I knew what this meant, as if it were a familiar utterance. I put a hand in my nightshirt to stroke my member into action, nodded once, and followed him, toward something I knew as my certain doom.

In the morning light I realised what I had dreamt about: the age of the woods, the sheer length of time men and women had looked at it from inside their civilised dwellings and loved it for its wildness and secrecy. And at the other end of history, here we were, letting it go to hell for the sake of a chemistry block. Well, someone should make a stand. Just to tell the history with a clean conscience.

I found one of those websites where things are laid out for you, and I set up a petition in about half an hour. I emailed it without hesitating, then went to shower.

By the time I was dressed and checking my email, the petition had gone three times around the campus and I was getting approached by local radio.

All day, people smiled at me in corridors, told me to fight the good fight. Graeme bought me a coffee, squeaked half a word of support, and ran away. I had tons of emails, a petition full of names. And yet, by the evening, I had a feeling of futility. The will was there, but nobody wanted to go up against Boxer. It would be like going up against a forklift truck.

Among the messages, one from Matt simply said: *Was that you?*

I told him: *I had to do something.*

He replied almost immediately: *You think breaking into the site will help your case?*

*What? I never advocated that!* I'd said nothing about chaining ourselves to the trees themselves. Though it'd be brilliant, I wouldn't dare.

*Someone broke into the site last night*, Matt replies. *Boxer just called me. Now you're saying it wasn't you?*

*I meant the petition. Why would I break into the woods? At night?*

*Because you're a romantic ;-) Didn't know about petition.*

*Romantic*ist, I replied, wondering if I should be reading more into his choice of words. I began squeezing my dick through my jeans; clicked onto the staff intranet to look at the staff profile of "Dr Matthew Marrien," where his photo shows him lazing, cocksure, against the wall of the library.

*Just seen petition*, he replied. *Hope you know what you're doing.*

It was late. I came *that* close to emailing him my report, the one I was going to read him and everybody at the meeting. My fantasy, in free verse, of the sacred grove in the heart of the woods and the man who rides there at night to take advantage of it.

Instead I went to bed, too exhausted by the events of the day to even picture us together and indulge in a nice long wank fantasy.

Fuck, I don't want to be distracted with these sorts of thoughts. Not today of all days, not now. I need to fight. I need to put my case.

"I have the final result of the petition here," I announce, my voice shaking a little. "I've made copies for everyone. Perhaps, Professor Boxer, you might present a copy to the vice-chancellor when you next—"

"I hate to interrupt a colleague," says Boxer, "but the grown-ups are talking at the moment. Perhaps you could spare the embarrassment of the group by circulating these bits of paper in your own time. Or perhaps you'll arrange a night of improv theatre with the drama students?"

I'm breathless, trying to summon my energies. Before it happens, I catch Matt's eye again. He really does look embarrassed.

"We must forgive the Romanticists amongst us, eh?" he says, and the room dissolves into polite laughter. Any words I was going to summon are suddenly lost. I can't believe I ever thought he was flirting with me.

I was so wrapped up in my fantasy, I even dreamed of Matt that night. It was the same medieval castle. I solemnly followed the man of the cloth. In the dream I knew to whom I was being led, the one who owned my body.

Down to the lowest depths of the castle. Down where the air was limited, I gulped for breath, wiped a drip of pre-come off my hard cock onto my nightshirt.

Into the deepest chamber. Flaming torches on the walls. A mattress laid on the ground; draped on the filth, a regal silken bed-sheet. Across the square of red silk, my eyes met the king's.

"Welcome," he said. "We appreciate your coming."

His eyes blazed like blue jewels, his hair and beard were salt-and-pepper, he was built like a bull.

"I could not refuse," I said truthfully. "You desire me to recite for you, my lord? To tell the old bardic tales for which you procured me? To spin the beautiful ancient poems of Greek heroes and Greek love?"

His handsome face melted into a smile. "I desire..." he said, musingly. "I desire that you perform."

I sighed. "Indeed, my lord." I shrugged off my nightshirt and stood there, heart beating, dick leaking. "Where do I begin, my lord?"

The king turned aside for a moment, and another stepped out of the shadows. A man in an open robe, of finest quality, but naught more. A man with a beautiful broad chest, a handsome look and a shy one.

"Marrien will be your lord today," King Peter said. "His pleasure will be the subject your performance and the object of my entertainment."

And as I knelt before the virgin knight, and felt his hard cockhead graze my tongue, I woke with a start.

And organised a poetry night!

Well, I thought, I still had that report. That poem. That work. I felt a renewal of energy and strength. At the gym I watched from afar as Matt lifted massive weights I could hardly bare to look at. I stood there, thin as I was, and thought: You have a strength, Rob. Your strength is in your power to hold an audience. So use it.

It was well-attended, too. Beatrix brought everyone from her department, of course, and there was beer, and biscuits shaped like acorns. There was a smaller but still rather vocal consortium from the chemistry department, saying, "Not in our name!" They were led by a tall bloke I didn't quite recognise, till he came up to me afterwards, beer in hand, big grin.

"Good stuff, mate!" I recognised a vague hesitation in his voice.

"Graeme?" I shook the proffered hand. A stronger grip than I'd remembered. "Thanks for coming. You're looking, uh..."

He looked down shyly at himself. "Say it."

"I don't know what to say," I told him. "You look more alive, somehow."

"It's the excitement of the fight," he said. "Knowing we have to do something, *now*." He knocked back his beer with a swig. There was a strange aggression about him. "I love your poem. It made my heart fucking swell."

I didn't know how to reply to this. I'd never had praise like this before. I'm much more used to people taking Matt's level of interest, that is, not much at all. And there was something that didn't quite add up about Graeme. It wasn't just that he'd perked up a bit. He looked *bigger* somehow. "Hope it raises the profile of the woods. They're so important," I gabbled.

"And beautiful," he said. "And strong. Stronger than Boxer."

I looked around the poetry evening, the biscuits and beer, and tried to believe it. It wasn't just that I didn't dare hope. I knew, deep down, there was nothing I'd experienced in my life so far that was as strong as Professor Peter Boxer's will, let alone *stronger*.

Look at him now, in his element. He's so secure in being the king of the heap, the leader of the pack, the big alpha male with the big swinging dick, he doesn't even enjoy it. And meanwhile, the green and gold delight of the woods, the ancient magic at its heart, are about to be knocked flat.

As I think this, the meeting room door bangs open and a cold breeze lifts glossy brochures and statistics off our desks. A new man walks into the meeting, crossing behind me to take his seat at Boxer's elbow, the place I was too cringing to take. He unzips his pencil case, opens a file. The chair squeaks under his weight as he gets comfy.

He's not been at any of the previous meetings, this muscularly outsized man in a long white lab coat. For a second, I tell myself it's Matt, but of course, Matt's sitting across from me, a small frown on his handsome face. Another member of the Chemistry faculty, then, come to tell us exactly where they're going to put their precious laboratories.

"Sorry I'm late," he says, his voice deep and resonant.

Matt is looking at him curiously. "Graeme?" he says.

"Matt?" The newcomer—I just can't believe it's the man I know as Graeme—sounds half apologetic, half ironic. "I haven't missed the conclusion of the meeting?"

Boxer looks off his stride, for possibly for the first time in forty-five years. "Not quite. I'm just circulating the projected plans for—for *your* new chemistry block, Dr Bryant."

"You still fancy the idea of that, huh?" And he laughs softly. Not in a creepy way, but as if we were talking about a holiday that Boxer was planning.

"Well," says Boxer, "it's not just me who feels that way."

"Oh, so it was democratically decided to destroy the area of natural woodland known as Oakhill Woods," says Graeme, toying with a pencil. "I see."

"Fortunately we don't have to employ democratic process at every level of our developmental procedure," Boxer says, at last scenting confrontation. "We have a satisfactory system of delegated decision-making."

"That rather sounds to me," says Graeme lazily, "like an admission of some sort. An admission that this decision was taken against, or at least outside of, the will of the greater university body. And therefore the admission that such a decision had to be kept from the university body, to protect it. An admission that you are running scared."

"The project is being formally announced later today—"

"Oh, but we both know that means nothing," says Graeme. "All sorts of things can interrupt an operation like this."

"Is that a fact?" Boxer says with a strange look of arousal.

"It's a promise," says Graeme. "You might be prepared to lock horns, *Boxer*. You like to have a quick spar, don't you? But you shouldn't pick a fight without asking whether your opponent is stronger than you."

Without any effort, Graeme snaps his pencil in two.

Boxer is smiling now. You can tell he's being led by lust and doesn't know how to behave. He forces the smile away. "You would like us to reconsider the proposal?"

"I think you'll have to," says Graeme. "I won't stand for anything else. It's not just me, of course. But would it matter to you if it was?"

I can't believe it. Graeme's making Professor Boxer his bitch, and not only that, he's commenting on it in the very meeting. Everyone is looking at Boxer to see what he'll say, apart from Matt who can't stop looking at his old colleague, the man who used to be a weed and has suddenly become a motherfucking oak.

"It's not just Dr Bryant," says Beatrix suddenly. "You know it's not.

We've got a petition list as long as your arm—longer in fact. As long as one of Dr Bryant's arms! And all we've been waiting for is someone who has balls big enough to make a stand."

We're all suddenly imagining Graeme's balls.

Boxer looks at all of us in turn, considering what to say. Finally he just shrugs. "Nice of you to let me know" is all he can say.

Afterwards, everyone heads victoriously down the pub. Beatrix is buying. Even Matt is going along with them, presumably to drown his sorrows but also, if possible, to rebuild some bridges with his colleagues. The announcement has been called off provisionally. The archaeological dig will continue.

Graeme and I, of course, go straight to the woods. He snaps the padlock on the gates and we plunge in: the trees bare and budding with green, the earth glinting with green shoots, the air filled with the scent of life returning.

Well, "straight" isn't quite the way we go.

He presses me roughly against the bark of an ancient tree, the power in his outsized limbs almost lifting me off my feet. His tongue is in my mouth, swirling and lapping as if I was delicious. He squeezes one of his mighty hands under my cardigan and clutches my left nipple. It's almost painful: I swoon slightly, and my glasses jolt onto the dirty ground.

He stoops to pick them up. "I've got to calm myself," he says, running his hand through a Byronic wave of black hair.

"Not for long, I promise," I tell him. "Give me some answers, though. Like, what the fuck has happened to you? You look like Captain America!"

"Over the last few months I've been steadily growing," he tells me. "It doesn't seem to stop. I just get bigger and bigger and—" He demonstrates by raising his arms to flex biceps. The white cotton lab-coat bursts open under the pressure, clothes hanging in tatters on his massively masculine frame. "It's all because of the Robin Hood plant."

"The what?"

"You remember. You spoke about it in the first meeting I went to. When I was normal-sized. You said it had never been identified before, and that there was a legend of Robin Hood coming here, gaining the strength of ten." He glances down, shyly. "I decided to investigate, synthesise a serum. Ever since I've been putting on muscle. It's not about working out—I had to stop going to the gym because fellows just stare."

"But how did you get hold of the flower thing, with the place fenced off?" I asked him. "You didn't—"

"I scaled the fence, the very first night. I was so full of new strength, new life. It's almost too much for me." He looks over his shoulder, then begins tearing away his clothes. His enlarged body is wonderfully hirsute, every limb dark with sweat-matted hair. "That's why I brought you here, Rob. It's like I'm a sunflower and it's the end of my season. I have to release my seed."

I can't catch my breath. "You mean you need to—"

"I have to fuck, Rob," the giant who used to be smaller than me explains. "Right now. Can you take me?" With a crack, he tears open his trousers at the fly. I'm amazed to see that everything is in proportion.

"Fucking hell," I splutter. "I really don't know. You might just have to get fucked instead."

"Let's get started," he says, lying back in the roots of the oak, beckoning me on. His dick seems to enlarge as I watch, or maybe he's just getting hard. "God, I want you, Rob. I've always wanted you."

As we fuck, the taste of Graeme filling my mouth, the smell of him filling my nostrils, the weight of him pressing me down, the strength of him lifting me up, I find myself floating away into another dimension, a dream of life and pleasure.

Boxer, in the king's guise, stands over me and Matt as we grapple on the mattress. Boxer's wanking a fat, purple cock and shouting instructions. Matt has me on my back, my ankles in his hands, as he fucks me slowly and nervously, the shy maiden arsefucker. His pectorals bounce as he thrusts.

The man of God stands looking on. Matt slowly warms to his theme, hips bucking in faster strokes, a look of satisfaction on his face, and Boxer's fist pumps harder.

"My lord," says the hooded man, "Does this performance please you?"

"I love it," says Boxer, licking his lips. "Harder, Marrien, harder! Imagine you're me!"

"I am satisfied," says the hooded man. "The diversion is a success. As we speak, the working people of the village are pouring through your open gates, emptying your castle of your worldly possessions. Revolution is at hand, comrade, while you indulge yourself in this pleasure of the flesh."

"I'm coming," Matt yells.

"I'm coming," I whisper in Graeme's ear.

"They're coming?" Boxer is drunk on sex, distracted by Matt and myself. "They're coming—into *my* castle?"

"Relax! Enjoy yourself with these honest pleasures of the flesh," urges the hooded man. He pulls back the hood, revealing the face of Graeme. "They are the treasure that endures, and they are best enjoyed in commonality, like song, stories and the woodland."

"That's it," gasps Graeme, waking me from my dream, and filling my mouth with hot, savoury seed.

As the shadows pool around us we embrace. Dirty, worn out, victorious and glowing with lust, we cling to one another. Night begins to fall.

"But wait," I tell him. "How exactly *did* you come?"

"With pleasure," he said. "You want a repeat performance?"

"No, I mean, *yes*—b-but," I say, "when you *first* came to the wood. How on earth did you get over the fence? And avoid Secu-Up? You didn't have these super-powers then. How did you get the plant in the first place?"

Graeme tickles my beard. "Do I have to tell you? I came here because of you, Rob. I loved you as soon as I saw you. I didn't care about the Woods when I first came. I just wanted to do something for you. Climbing a chain-link fence and running away from security guards was nothing. I already had the strength of ten."

"But now—you love the woods too, right?"

He grins at me. "Both of you. I belong to you, and to the woods." As our lips meet, he whispers: "And I feel I have done for a thousand years..."

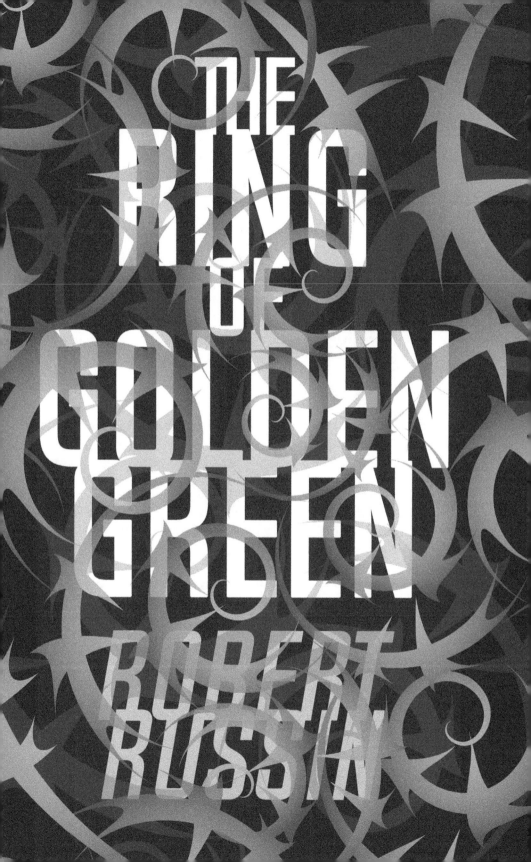

# THE RING OF GOLDEN GREEN

### ROBERT RUSSIN

*For K.*

THE FLICKER OF THE FLAME is the only thing they fear. If they are able to fear. Some days, I think it's just a series of tendril twitches—fire is bad, recoil. Blood is good, proceed. Other times, they do seem to have a cold sentience, one only concerned with relentless self preservation. They have no hearts. As far as I can tell. I'm not a fucking botanist.

They wait at the edge of the dwindling fire's light. They are patient. They could wait forever. Wait for me to get tired, get careless, get sick, get old. All of these things are happening. The rustling of leaves on a dead wind, in a dead world.

But it's *not* a dead world. Their fecundity would be impressive if viewed from orbit above the smothering cloud of their glowing golden pollen that clogs the air and my head. They'll win one day. One day soon. To think, for a few hundred years, we were worried about the fate of forests. So soon after we started playing with our toy engines, we nearly wiped them out. Should we really be surprised that they learned to fight back?

*We* were the flickering flame, so sure of our constancy, deliberately ignoring our own fragility. We were nothing. Are nothing. Will be nothing. Soon.

The roots rot, the roots consume, the roots devour our soft bits then our hard bits and grind us into bone dust. Even a child could see blades of grass poking from the concrete, the roots of trees splitting it from beneath the surface, and realize that the roots always win in the end. Back when there *was* concrete. The roots will do this to all the less tangible parts of our world that we thought were immortal and eternal. Google. Beethoven, Shakespeare. Pyramids. Swallowed by the roots, swallowed by the leaves. If anyone else ever finds this little rock in space, they will find a silent gold and green planet. All traces of us will be gone, and God help the ones that come next. Please keep going. Mars might have water underground. Enceladus, Europa, Titan. Venus is warm, I hear.

I still mark the days since you've been gone. Not since the world went to shit—the two of you *were* my world; I didn't care what happened outside. Let it burn, I said. Not since our green friends began to appear, either, although that wasn't too long before.

*Day 1000.*

NOTHING MUCH HAPPENED TODAY. I would have liked to commemorate the date. Attempt to mill some flour to make a small cake for myself. I miss sweets. But the thought is exhausting. I can't waste fire, I can't waste my own energy, so I do nothing, letting the moment live silently and die in the ruins of my heart in the ruins of the world. Without you I don't feel much like celebrating anyway.

I used to wear contact lenses. I had stockpiled as many cases as I could. My last pair gave out a few days ago, brittle and flaked away like bits of my hair and skin. I sort of prefer it this way. The less I see, the better. They've had me surrounded for a thousand days. An ominous, silent circle of death in the distance now faded to a ring of golden green. The circle draws tighter. I know that I'll lose myself to it one day soon, drowned in a sea of golden green.

Bentley barks and I wake, confused. He's barking furiously. The flames have gone low, almost dead. It's a warm summer night. That's okay. I go back to sleep.

No—not that world anymore—his howling reminds me. I try to stand but my legs won't move. I'm dreaming.

Bentley nips my arm and finally I'm awake and feel vines wrapped around my ankle. Alert, angry, terrified, I start to hack away at them with the machete I keep next to me, the one you made fun of me for buying a few years ago, the one you wouldn't let me bring into the house or near our son.

Something lashes out and whips across my chest. It's silent, it's dark, I'm half blind and something is drinking my blood. Bentley furiously tears at some of the vines but makes little difference. A thick root grasps me, piercing, sucking.

I grab for the dwindling bottle of emergency lighter fluid and accidentally pour too much on the fire. Fuck. I'll regret that later. I grab a burning branch and wave it at them. Silence. I *feel* the fury in the air, or am I imagining that, projecting my own emotions onto things that have none? Vines withdraw into the dark. I thrust forward and I see how densely close the circle has drawn. Flaming torch in hand, machete in the other, I could almost pass for a hero from the old adventure stories if I wasn't so drawn and gaunt, half starved.

I take down a few, the rest start to withdraw, and I don't have the energy to follow. Not sure if I killed anything. I gather up the hacked off bits and pieces and walk back, aware of them on the outskirts of vision, waiting. Patient. Silent, as always.

There's a fleshy pulp inside the vines. Tastes awful, but is non-toxic, or, at least, hasn't killed me yet. Seems to provide some protein. The rest I can burn.

None of this will save me.

But it's enough to keep the fire going.

I'm furious that I've wasted so much fuel, cranky from my bleeding lacerations, and willing myself to not panic about how close they were this time. I'm too densely surrounded now to make another run into the dead town. Whatever I have left, that's it. I definitely don't know how to *make* lighter fluid—hell, I don't even really know what lighter fluid *is*. It's something I bought in plastic bottles. I miss the days where I could have gone to Wikipedia and looked that up in two seconds and impressed you with my factoids. Bentley is next to the fire, looking at me. If he could roll his eyes, he would. Oh well, it's done, I might as well enjoy it. I decide to celebrate the thousandth day after all and make one of my little oat cakes.

A thousand days. Here's to a thousand more—I can't tell if this seems like a promise or a threat. Is anyone else out there counting? I long ago lost track of the months. The weather is warmer now. It's felt like late August for about a year. They changed the fucking *weather*.

I wake from what I wish had been a dreamless sleep. My heart is pounding. I'll let whatever memories lingered from the dark die in the dawn's first light.

*1001 days.*

I MARK IT ON THE side of the old house, I say my prayers at the two graves, the big one first, then the little. Bentley is a smart dog, but I am sad that even he can't be trained to dig a third grave and put me in it. I will try to die as close to this spot as possible.

Many days I dream of burying myself alive and wonder about the logistics of that, if it is even possible. Poe would know. I used to read "The Raven" to our son before bed because he liked the rhythm of the words. I never told you that. I don't think you'd have approved. I'm sorry.

The fire is still going strong from the night—damn my carelessness—and I start to walk my shrinking perimeter. I gave up long ago—day two hundred something, I think—on maintaining a fence around the whole property. It was useless to keep them out, and I needed things to burn. Behind the house, it's forest. Regular trees. I let that go first. Only once did one come from there. After that, I didn't care. I try my best to keep something of a half circle at the front of the property. I'd say I'm down to about a half acre now, from what started as maybe five or six. The old house, my work shed, the garden, the peach trees, the campsite.

The graves.

I check the plants—the good plants, the ones in the garden. The ones that keep me alive. I wonder if it looks, to *them*, as if I've kept these plants captive and enslaved. I wonder if they pity their broken domesticated kin. Somehow I don't think of them as being capable of pity.

Bentley barks and points to a broken piece of garden fence. It takes me a minute to realize what he's pointing at. Where was my mind? *You* used to be the dreamer, I was the pragmatist. Now it feels like I miss you so much that I might be turning into you, while Bentley takes my role—stern, protective, vaguely disapproving.

Hopefully better at protecting than I was.

This is probably brain death. Malnourishment. For breakfast I eat a tomato and a peach. Luckily, the water is still good. I chose this spot well. I thought I did a good thing for us here. I thought we would grow old here together in relative comfort. I thought our son would have *his* children here, running around and making fun of their two old grandfathers in a world where no one thought of that as strange. A new, gentler world.

Ha.

Two graves. One big, one small. Half of my heart buried in each one. My heartless body still somehow upright, pushing itself along, alone with a sad and frustrated corgi.

Bentley is wrong. The garden fence will have to go next. I'm not sure there's anything left to get into the garden anyway. I haven't seen any small animals. I'm running out of things to burn.

Our son's rocking horse squeaks on cue. When it's not weighted down and the wind blows, it makes that horrible sound. There's nothing more miserable than the squeak of that damn horse...Ra-Ra, he named it. I built it for him when he was two. Too young for it, really. Wait, you said. It's too dangerous.

Ha.

The blurry sight of that ring of golden green inching forward to devour me—the sight of my inevitable death—is easier to take than the sight of that damn horse, but I've stared it down for a thousand days and I will not burn it. Just like I will not eat Bentley.

I'm not the pragmatist you thought I was. I've been boiled down to something softer and stupider, useless marrow-mush now that I have nothing to protect. Bentley? He'd be fine without me. Corgis are small and tough. He'll survive.

Killer plants. It's ridiculous. It's something out of the B-movies you wouldn't let our son watch. It's impossible, but less impossible than how the world goes on without you both. A world where the plants went bad and turned against us still somehow makes more sense than a world where you both left me alone. A world where I wasn't able to save you. Where, my God, I wasn't able to save *him*. For all I know, I dreamed this entire nightmare world in my head—a clumsy metaphor to cope with the sheer impossibility of a life without you.

But no. I see the pinprick welts on my legs. I feel my body eating itself. I see the world gone green and gold and silent. I see the fire dying.

I will join you both soon. If there is a you to join. And a place to join you. I never believed there was. But starvation, end times, desperation breed religious mania, and now I believe there will be. Sometimes I think I see your faces in the fire.

Fire. The cities burned first. Ever the pessimist, I saw this coming, and I got us out. Ridiculous, you said. Trees were safer than people, I said.

Ha.

Two men with a baby moving into the country—what would people think? Always a concern of yours. To your credit, once upon a time that *was* all we had to fear. Before things turned. I told you there would come a time when those sorts of distinctions wouldn't matter—the new world would be tough, with little of the comfort and luxury you were used to. But with the cities gone and the world destroyed, arbitrary distinctions would blur, and we would all help each other survive.

Then the plants began to move.

I don't know what caused it. Were they like certain kinds of seeds that need a forest fire to germinate? Hard seed pods burst open in the smoking ashes of our dead civilization? Was it something in the radiation, the nuclear winds that turned our coasts to obsidian glass? No more beach vacations for us. Dormant spores from another world, traveling silently, endlessly through the black of space, looking for a fertile ground? All of this seems like the stuff of bad science fiction. All I know is that it was terrible timing. The days were gone where we could lock ourselves away, certain that someone—the government, the military, *someone*—would take care of the problem for us. All of those things were gone. There was just us, the flames, and the stars. And those were the happiest days of my life.

We didn't have much, but we had everything we needed. I gave us a good life here. I hope you think so too, wherever you are. I hope you remember that you loved me. Despite my failure to protect you, I hope you still love me. At least a little.

Ra-Ra squeaks in the wind and slams me back to what I'm forced to call reality. There are things to do, to keep the body alive, to keep the fire going.

The house is mostly gutted. I sleep outside and avoid it as much as I can. I do still go down to the basement to feed my other pet. Bentley won't go down there with me. He stands guard outside. This is my next chore.

I keep it there, in a small pot, starved of sunlight and earth and room to grow. When it buds, I pinch them off to stunt its growth. Sometimes I let them grow a little bigger, just to delay my pleasure in hacking it to bits or burning it alive. Why should it get to see its seed grow into new life? It robbed me of that same chance. Sometimes I feel bad for it. Rarely. Almost never. Sometimes I think part of him lives on, some of his blood in the veins of the leaves...but no.

Burn the fucker.

It survives. Like me.

Two new buds have appeared since yesterday. I rip them off, unzip my tattered jeans and piss all over it, wanting to drown it in the acrid stink. I don't know if they can feel pain. I hope they do.

I still do.

It's just the same goddamn silence, even as I rip off pieces of it. I sometimes expect it to cry out "Feed me, Seymour!" but no, just the silence. It stays silent as I burn and eat its babies. I suck out their insides, as it did to my son.

They taste like flowers. Bitter, terrible, and they stink when they burn, reluctant even in death to add anything but suffering to my existence. Even their damn flowers are poison. The pollen clouds were the first wave. That alone killed half the people in town with violent allergic reactions. The two of you actually suffered less than I did from this. I love when I get to burn pieces of this fucker.

Keeping this thing alive in here isn't purely an act of sadism. I've been able to study it to some degree. As I said, I knew nothing about plants. In all my book hoarding that you always nagged me about, I managed to amass about six hundred Stephen King paperbacks but not a single book about botany or biology. John Wyndham is the closest I have. But even he had more hope than I do. He would've written in a last minute rescue by now. I'm long past the point in the story where the lone helicopter appears to offer a glimmer of hope.

From what I can tell, they have several ways of extracting the nutrients they need for growth, though they seem able to survive indefinitely without any discernible means of sustenance if denied. Their locomotive ability seems to develop later, in healthier, larger plants. The juvenile plants are rooted in the ground, with flailing, twitching vines lashing at the air for whatever they can grab. The vines seem almost like tentacles, studded with little stinging suckers to pierce and paralyze and draw the body and blood into them.

On the mature plants, the roots are the primary means of locomotion, able to unearth themselves and roll the thing forward. The vines grab and slice and the blood seems to activate something deeper in the roots that causes them to grab tight and suck, drawing you in as the upper leaves unfurl, revealing something like an artichoke before enveloping and digesting.

Not the most pleasant way to go.

Outside in my work shed, I jot down a few notes with the last of the good pens you gave me for the last birthday I celebrated. I feel like the post-apocalyptic equivalent of a nineteenth-century British duchess. Notes about the plants, about the garden. Quite a bit about those damn oat cakes. What the dog does. Even the apocalypse can be mundane when you no longer give a shit about anything. And yet, bizarrely, the urge to fill the blank page still remains after everything else has left. The last part of me that hasn't died. Ink is fading, as am I. Somehow the thought of this pen dying feels like losing you all over again. But still I scrawl, with a desperate, fevered need to fill the blank space. Even I don't understand why I do this. With him gone, maybe these pages are the last way for me to leave any bit of myself behind. I'll write in blood when the pen dies.

Bentley is at my feet. I bend down and pet him, my mind still on this. He misses the way you did it, I'm sure. You were always better at corgi-stroking than I was. But there's work to do still, the fire to feed, water to draw, tomatoes to pick, and I've sat for long enough. I drag myself to my feet, wondering how Bentley still has the energy to jump around and push me forward.

Now I see why Bentley was so agitated. Two mid-sized plants, about my height, have crept through a break in the fence and are feeling the air with flailing vine fingers. Bentley tears at the rolling roots, drawing their attention as I hack off what I think of as their heads—a dense bulbous grouping of leaves that sort of looks like a moldy Brussels sprout. One thing I love about my little corgi—he doesn't yelp or cry out when he gets lashed. He takes the pain silently. There's no sound more pitiful than a crying corgi. I'm grateful for this.

I throw hacked-up bits of acanthine spikes into the fire after I extract the meat, and rub some aloe vera—what I've come to think of as the *good* plants, traitors to their nastier kin—on our bloody cuts. Bentley rolls onto his stomach with his legs up in the air and his mouth goes slack and stupid and I rub his belly. He gets to act like a dog again, and I savor the moment.

*1012 days.*

THE WORLD IS BLURRY AND for the millionth time I'm furious with myself for having been careless with my eyeglasses. This world without my contact lenses looks like a fuzzy flashback sequence in a terrible old sitcom.

Ha.

I realize, with what feels like a punch in the stomach, that my son has been dead for more days than he was alive. I look back at the house, I see him there, grinning atop the damn rocking horse. I loved when he used it because his weight was the only thing that silenced the damn squeak. But I don't love what I see right now. He's there, grinning at me. The skin rotted and pulled back from his tiny head, he's a baby reaper, maybe the last thing a child sees before a child dies. Maybe all the infants that died in cribs see a tiny reaper in a black diaper with a rattle-sized scythe.

I think about digging for you and curling up next to you, but I remember again that there's nothing down there. Nothing solid. Nothing I can touch. In a way that's harder.

Blurry sitcom flashbacks indeed.

Flashbacks. The creaking of the rocking horse in the whispering wind. Your scream, behind the house. Stay there, I told him. Be a good boy. Stay on Ra-Ra. The stupidest decision of my life, I ran to you. Like I always ran to you. Too late. You were enveloped in the vines, in the leaves. I remember the one that took you, I could see it clearly then, I still had my eyes. It had a huge purple flower on it. I remember that being the last thing I saw before my life was over—a beautiful sight to end a beautiful life.

I started to run at it, and then I heard that sound. That horrible sound. The squeaking of the riderless rocking horse. No.

Panicked, terrified, unthinking, the loss of you still impossible, I ran back to the front of the house. It was on him, the vines were wrapped around him.

He wasn't crying.

I hacked it to bits, screaming, tear stained, blood stained, blind. His small body already growing cold in my arms. Of you, all that was left was a hand. One ringless hand. Of the thing that ate you, a single flower petal left behind as it fled back into the woods. Of the thing that ate my little boy, a root. A small root, still twitching, a sprout at the end, a new life from the death of my son.

The hand I planted in a vase. I ate the soft bits off; any way I could get your fat fingers inside of me again. The root I planted in the basement. Some days I nurture it, wondering if any of his blood lives on in it still. Others, I burn it for fun, hoping that it feels the flame.

That's when I started counting the days.

*1016 Days.*

DAMN IT. THIS PEN IS dying. This was supposed to be a chronicle of the end of the world, in case anyone ever found it, in case you came back to read it. I thought these pages might survive, if nothing else. Do they eat paper? Would that be cannibalism for them? Somehow I don't think they care. I don't care about the end of the world. The end of my family—*that* was the end of the world for me. The rest of it. The fires, the vines, the silence, none of that matters. I'm dying.

Why do I keep the fire going? Who am I making these notes for, with no one left to read them? Why do I do this? Why do I do any of it? Oh, for you, I guess. You're the only reason I ever did anything of value. Every single word I've ever written, every single step I take when I want to lie down and die, all of it is for you. I'm still hoping it's all been a mistake— that the pieces of you both that are beneath my broken blistered feet belong to someone else. That you and he went to town, that you got stuck behind the ring of trees, that you're on your way home, that you'll be here any minute, bursting from the ring of golden green.

Why do I keep the fire going? For my own failure to keep our family alive and together. For the impossibly remote chance you're both coming back to me. There's only one small body in the ground. All I found was a hand. It could be anyone's hand. Your perfect nails, but no ring on those fingers. You never took that ring off. I'd know those fat fingers of yours anywhere. These looked skinny. It was someone else's hand. Maybe you got away. I'm keeping all of this going in case you ever come home. I haven't burned your clothes—they're neatly folded in the drawer exactly as you left them. You'll see that I waited. You'll see I kept the fire burning, a light in the dark to guide you back home to me. Any day now you'll both burst out of the sea of golden green. The wind blows, leaves rustle. If I can just keep it going, you'll see it. You'll come home.

They've crept past where I grow the oats. No more oat cakes for me after these last three are gone. I was running out of sugar anyway, and getting too tired to grind that flour. No big loss. They're closing in, but it's okay. Less space to keep clear, less energy wasted. The fire is still going. So am I.

And any day now I'll see you coming. Bursting through a ring of golden green.

*1018 days.*

I HAD TO USE A little bit of lighter fluid today. The fire almost died. They had pushed past where I keep some of the kindling. I didn't feel like I had the arm strength to cut them back. I have enough left to fill a shot glass, maybe not even a full shot. A shot poured by a Hell's Kitchen bartender, back when being overcharged for a shitty drink was my biggest concern. God, I miss alcohol. The only thing I miss almost as much as I miss you. I've tried experimenting with various methods of fermentation, but nothing seems to work. I'm tempted to drink the last of this fuel as a shot.

I tried making a drink out of *them*. It tasted worse than the time we tried to eat cocaine, in the early days when we were both dealing with our allergies from their damn pollen and couldn't snort it.

Earlier today I accidentally caught the cuff of my disgusting pants in the fire, and now they're almost comically reduced to a pair of denim cutoff shorts. I look more like I'm getting ready to walk in a 1980s Pride parade than I do like I'm holding off an ongoing killer mutant attack during the apocalypse.

Pants. One of the things I never thought much about, before. You chose, bought, washed, and folded my clothes. I have no idea how to make a pair of pants, and now I have none. I don't have any fucking *pants* left. Somehow this feels like crossing a line. Unacceptable, you'd say. You'd order me a new pair immediately. I wish I knew how to do things like weave a pair of pants from their leaf fibers or something. The thought of it appeals to me—draped in the skins of my enemies.

I'm reacting strangely to this. The loss of this last pair of pants is the first real loss I've felt for one thousand and eighteen days. I write the word "pants" on the cover of this notebook, feeling for a moment that this is significant, and then forgetting why.

*1021 days.*

I'VE RETREATED INTO THE HOUSE. I don't care anymore. I've moved the huge stone circle of fire that I've kept going for a thousand and twenty-one days and built a smaller one in front of the back door to the kitchen. *Your* kitchen. Where you wouldn't let me wear my boots or use your good plates. What were you saving them for? How I'd give anything to hear your disapproving voice, your golden green eyes rolling in your head like this golden green earth rolls silently through space. Shoes off at the door. Watch my language in front of the baby. Lights and darks separated in the laundry. These are the things that kept me grounded. Without them, without you, without him, what's left?

My teeth are in bad shape. I've broken every mirror, but I know how I must look. Starved, crazed, ranting about the dead—like Jesus.

The kitchen is a mess. I realize now that this is why you haven't come home. You *can't* come home to this. I'm sorry that I got mud on your floors. I'm so sorry. I'll make it right. I begin to scrub.

*1024 days.*

MY FINGERNAILS—THOSE THAT REMAIN—are caked with blood and mud. You would be *furious* with me if you saw me sitting at your table in such a state, carrying our son into dinner with both of us such a mess. I felt around in closets I hadn't opened in years and found some candles—I love you for being so organized. The fire outside is dead. I light the candles from its last flicker and bring the fire inside. You should be home from town any minute, and I want to have everything ready for you. The three of us will have a nice candlelit dinner together. The bones of a stranger's severed hand stick straight up from the vase I use as a centerpiece. I wait for them to start tapping on the table, impatient for your arrival.

Our son is quiet today. He misses you too. He sits there, motionless; I think back on happier times, of him pushing Cheerios around with his tiny hands. The Cheerios fade to tiny rings of golden green.

Something is wrong with Bentley—he doesn't seem to want to come near us. He's whimpering in the corner. We might have to take him to the vet next week. He's looking at me strangely. I tried to calm him down and he backed away from me. Still can't stroke a corgi like you could.

The good plates tonight. It's a special occasion. It feels like you've been gone so long. Traffic must be terrible today. Are there still cars? I can't remember. Every minute we're apart feels like a thousand days.

The sun is low. Your windows are clean again, and now there's beautiful golden green sunlight pouring in. I think the window is covered by a screen of ivy. I hope you won't ask me to cut it back too much—it's a beautiful effect. It makes the house look rustic, I think. Things grow so fast in the country. It's up to you, of course.

Quiet. The flickering of the flames, the whimpering of a sick corgi, a tapping on the window. Tap, tap, tap. Maybe I *will* have to cut back some of those vines after all.

Our last three oat cakes on your best china. Not our best meal, but we'll make it work. We always did.

I don't know how long I wait. Our son is still quiet, still asleep. I'll let him nap so he can be up with us later. Maybe we can all snuggle together on the couch and watch a movie if you don't get too mad about me letting him stay up past his bedtime. He feels thin, though. His color seems off. Maybe you'll need to take him to the doctor when I take Bentley to the vet.

I start to scribble a note about this, and the pen dies. Damn it. I love these pens. What a great gift, the last gift you gave me before...before?

It's dark now, and I light a few more candles from the last flame I carried in from the fire outside. There's still a tapping on the window.

Bentley is going out of his mind.

I open your perfectly organized cabinet and find the last of your zolpidem. They taste so bitter. I give him two, and let him outside. He scratches and yelps at the door, and then he doesn't.

The kitchen door creaks open. Slowly, so slowly, you creep into the kitchen. You must be tired. Your color looks a bit green. But you're home. You brought me flowers? I love you so much.

Thank you for the flowers, please come sit with me. I pull out your chair for you.

Why do the purple flowers make my stomach twist? Allergies, maybe. Doesn't matter. What a thoughtful gift. Thank you so much. They're beautiful.

God, how I missed you.

Come, sit and have a glass of wine with me.

I love you, I love our little boy, I love the three of us together as a family again having a family dinner by candlelight. There's tapping on the window and then the window shatters. You'll be mad about that later but I'll fix it for you, it's okay for now. You're here, and you even brought me flowers!

The ivy really does grow fast in the country—I think it's coming through the window. I'm covered in ivy. Bentley is up and barking like crazy—I'll let him inside in a minute. I see your hand, your beautiful big hand, your beautiful thick fingers with your wedding ring, that little ring of golden green, still securely in place. I knew you'd never take it off. I knew you'd never lose it. Your ring shines gold and green on the hand I've kissed in my dreams every night. The window is gone. The wind blows in. The candles flicker. I'm wrapped in your arms. I never fear the dark when I'm deep inside of you. And at last, at *last*, I lose myself in those beautiful eyes, your eyes that glow a golden green.

The flames flicker. And then they don't.

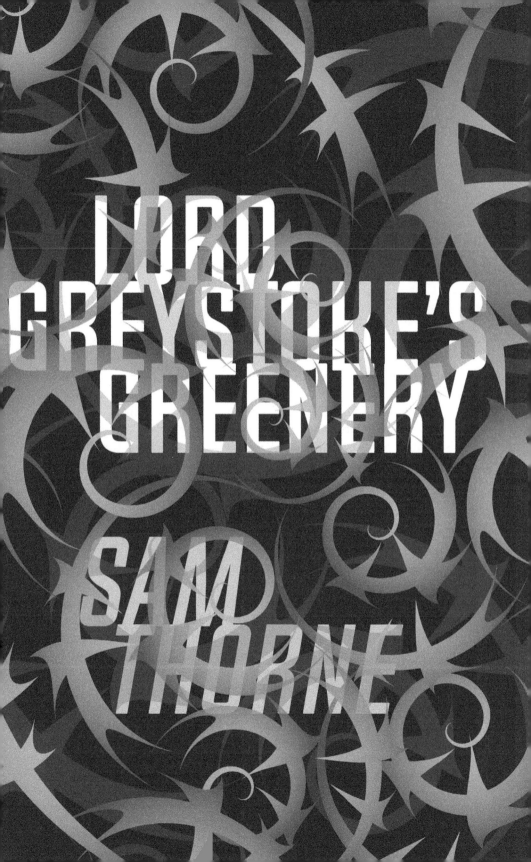

"I'll be back from the hall by four." Jeremiah poked Arthur's chest with a hairy ginger forefinger. "Get the ape dressed, and keep him out of the ruddy conservatory, d'ye hear? I've got a couple of chaps from the Royal Society coming to inspect those plants and I want them in as fine fettle as the viscount himself. Those plants are worth as much as he is."

Jeremiah's voice faded into background garbling as Arthur saw Viscount Greystoke—the "ape"—make his way from the first-floor balcony to the hallway by the simple expedient of flinging himself over the bannister rail onto the plush carpet. Arthur flinched as the sun-darkened man landed heavily on knuckles and the balls of his feet, just a couple of feet away, but Greystoke appeared entirely unharmed as he straightened, flicking dark hair back over his shoulders. Arthur peered up at him with a nervous smile, and was rewarded with a non-hostile grunt.

At least Greystoke had undergarments on today. Perhaps today would be a luckier day than most.

But then, Arthur's luck tended toward the bittersweet, like the pneumonia which had nearly carried him off last year, but which had also prevented him from being fit to board the *Titanic*. He ought not complain, but he'd spent his inheritance on those blasted tickets. And he'd never heard of any other man in his twenties getting pneumonia.

"Feldman!" Jeremiah snapped his fingers under Arthur's nose.

"Y-yessir."

"Repeat your orders!"

"D-dress his lordship, and keep him out of the conservatory." Arthur mustered every ounce of courage he had and cleared his throat. "Though, if I may be so bold as to observe, your nephew—ah, his lordship—appears m-more familiar with these plants than—"

"He is *not* to go near them." Jeremiah marched a few paces towards the door, then turned back, almost stepping on Miller. Ignoring the driver's muffled swearing, Jeremiah fixed Arthur with a glare of contempt. "Do your job, lad. Last chance."

Jeremiah swept out to the Daimler. In a rare show of compassion, Miller, usually a rough sort of fellow, clapped Arthur on the shoulder. "Good luck playing valet. I feel a proper shit leaving you alone with the bugger, but don't be scared, right? If he pins you down and sniffs you, knee him in the nuts."

As Miller followed Jeremiah out to the car, Arthur went to collect the day's pile of fresh clothes from the table in the hallway. He must not, on any account, allow his mind to drift to thoughts of being pinned down by Greystoke, or Tarzan, as he dubbed himself. Arthur's coordination was poor enough without the additional distraction of an aching encumbrance in his drawers. In his waking hours he concealed his feelings effectively, but his nighttimes were a hectic release of desire. And thanks to Miller, he'd probably wake tomorrow morning in a blazing, sticky sweat, squeezing himself after dreams of being pressed supine upon a bed and intimately examined.

Alas, other than his first undignified introduction to Tarzan, when he'd been tipped upside down and briskly checked for sharp sticks, he'd remained sadly unmolested.

As soon as the front door banged shut, Tarzan padded barefoot into the conservatory and lost himself yet again among the foliage. Arthur followed, feeling a pang for the man as he stroked the plants. They seemed to give him solace in this alien place. How strange life must seem for Tarzan, cooped up in between the narrow walls of this anonymous townhouse, with talkative manservants who spoke another tongue.

Tarzan had been brought home to England with good intentions. Jeremiah had found his brother's hut in the trees and his nephew delirious with fever upon the floor boards after an infection had set in to some recent wound. The facial resemblance between Lord John Greystoke and the feral man with the hog's pelt for loin-clothing had been undeniable. Tarzan had healed on the boat trip back to England but could not adjust to his new environment.

Arthur waited at the doorway of the conservatory with the bundle of clothes, unwilling to move until Tarzan had registered his presence in the sunroom.

Tarzan cradled the yellow bud of one of the new plants. His uncommon gentleness relieved Arthur's anxiety regarding the welfare of the valuable vegetation. The bundle of clothing tucked forgotten beneath his arm, Arthur watched Tarzan stroke and sniff the bud. The plant was pretty enough: an explosion of long, slender stems whose nectar-loaded flowers made the buds hang low across the table. But Tarzan's strong, lightly-veined hands drew Arthur's attention; Tarzan's forefinger tapped the sticky, central cone with a delicacy that matched his leonine grace. The man's physique dwarfed that of Britain's finest Olympians, yet his simple slide across a room would make a ballerina foam at the mouth with envy.

Tarzan's dark grey eyes peered between two fat, lengthy stems of a particularly rude-looking plant, and then away again. His face dipped beneath his curtain of hair, which remained long, if no longer tangled. Tarzan had permitted Arthur to wash and brush it, and to show him how to shave. He had discouraged the barber hired to cut it by waving an antique cutlass under the poor man's nose. It had been difficult to hire another barber.

A fragile trust had slowly built between Tarzan and Arthur. He hadn't yet been successful in dressing or civilising the feral lord, but his initial fear of the man had completely gone. No, Arthur's fear was reserved for the collection of impossibly vicious flora which Jeremiah Greystoke had brought back from Africa. They kept threatening to shrivel up and die, and Arthur didn't know what he was doing wrong, or what he should be doing to sustain them more successfully. If even one of the specimens failed to make a first, healthy impression upon Jeremiah's Royal Society colleagues, there would be hell to pay.

Since none of the plants had, as yet, acquired official names, Arthur and Miller had come up with monikers of their own. The one with the yellow flowers—that Tarzan was still toying with—was the "smooching plant." This plant had the annoying habit of flooding their ears with wet nectar whenever they bent to water the aloes. The petals seemed to move themselves through some peristaltic force. The sensation might be pleasant if it didn't come as such a shock each time. Then there was the Bastard (Miller's name) or whiplash plant (Arthur's), which had an extraordinary manner of drawing perhaps a full two or three pints just poured into the soil up into its flimsy leaves until they swelled and straightened in a rush. The leaves turned from thin, thistly, spidery things to fat, thistly deadly things, snapping out and up like ready hoses.

He'd been watering the whiplash plant a few weeks ago when a self-filling frond caught Miller between the legs and felled him as sharply as a donkey's hoof to the crown jewels. After many hours of prickle-removal and intense nursing, Miller was finally able to rasp, in the manner of one uttering final words, "Got me right in the crack, that did," before succumbing to another prolonged faint.

Lastly there were the red-pole plants (a mutually agreed name), but the less said about those, the better. Arthur couldn't even look at them without imagining Tarzan's own nights in the wild, and the manner in which he might have learnt about the zones of human pleasure with no other human to guide him.

Arthur gave himself a mental slap as his gaze fell on the clock in the conservatory. He'd been staring like a moonling for some twenty minutes already. Tremors began in his wrist and hip and he limped forward, trying not to let his anxiety, or the physical manifestations of it, affect him too severely. "Good morning, your lordship."

Tarzan snarled and turned his back on him.

"Tarzan?"

The man slunk to the far side of the sunroom, still growling. Unemployment loomed. Arthur sighed, knowing he had to play his only ace—the Grovel. He'd researched tribe leadership of the great apes. If Tarzan had survived some twenty-four years in the wild, he must have been a leader of some standing. Arthur appealed to his mercy as a penitent ape might prostrate himself before a group leader, dropping to his knees on the teal and white tiles, pushing the clothing to one side. He bent over onto his forearms, pressing his face to the floor.

Bare feet approached, stopping at his head. Tarzan ran his palm across the back of Arthur's neck and scalp, his touch light.

Arthur didn't move his head, but peered up into the dark grey eyes. Tarzan's expression was beautifully human—a mingling of confusion and concern. The same expression on Miller's face would've been ruined by "What are you doing down there, you daft sod?" Sometimes silence could be a wonderful thing.

Arthur cleared his throat. "Now, here's the thing, sir. I'm not a popular servant. I limp—badly—my hands shake, I drop expensive things. That's why I've been demoted from the hall to run this little house, which you dislike so intensely. I think we'd both prefer living at Greystoke Hall with its twenty rooms and huge garden, but we get on all right together, don't we?" Arthur sighed at Tarzan's blinking. "I'm sorry. I wish we spoke the same language. Anyway, if you don't get your togs on, I won't be around much longer."

"Nnnnrh?"

"It's true, I'm afraid." Arthur sat slowly, not wanting to make sudden movements that would dissuade Tarzan from continuing his hair-ruffling. His voice failed as he ran into difficulties, having to wipe his eyes with the back of his hand. "I don't want to go. Quite apart from being destitute, I'll miss you. So would you please put your damned clothes on?"

Tarzan's brows raised in astonishment at this outburst, and at the mad twitch in Arthur's arm that made his hand vibrate against the floor. Arthur looked away in mortification, freshly reminded of the threat of his father's disease. Tarzan gave a soft growl, gripping his trembling hand.

Arthur had perhaps a second to wonder whether that growl was of annoyance or concern when he was hauled to his feet by an almighty grip under his arms. He was caught in a crushing bear-hug, his face rammed against Tarzan's bare collarbone, then placed carefully back on his feet. In a further flash of movement, Tarzan snatched fists of material at Arthur's thighs and detrousered him.

"No," Arthur protested, "This is all the wrong way rou—oh, for heaven's sake."

Tarzan pushed the jacket off the back of his shoulders and yanked it from his arms. His shirt was ripped down the front, the buttons becoming dangerous flying things, then went the same way as the jacket. Arthur didn't even bother to protest as his vest top was whipped up the length of his torso and over his head. He just raised his arms to make it easier. Not wanting to be incapacitated by a trip hazard, he removed his shoes with heels and toes, then stepped out of the trousers.

All the begging had achieved was a compassionate response. Pleasant and unexpected, yes, but not commensurate with his goal of getting the man into his clothes, as instructed. Arthur put his stern face on, hoping this would countermand the unimpressive sight of his fairly slender body, bruise-spotted from his various stumbles.

"Very well, you've seen me now. Can we get dressed *together*? Perhaps in the lounge?"

"Nrrr." Tarzan looked him up and down, making him feel even more naked than he was already.

Arthur sighed, reclaiming his vest from the floor. "This is a perfectly harmless garment. Not even a sleeve to ruin your arm's day. It slips over your head like so—"

Tarzan snatched the garment and flung it across the conservatory, then turned to snap off one of the aloe leaves.

Arthur's heart slammed against his ribs. This was plant sacrilege, for which he'd be financially or terminally punished. "No, no, no...*please* don't do that. Don't—"

"Still."

Arthur felt a warm hand on his bare shoulder, pinning him to the spot, and a vast palm ran over the sore strip along the bottom of his ribs where he'd stumbled into the side-cabinet in the kitchen. He gasped at the initial tenderness of pressure upon a bruise, then released a soft moan that embarrassed him as the warmth at his side gave way to a cooling tingle that almost entirely numbed the spot. When the pleasure fog passed, his mind registered Tarzan's single word.

"Still?"

"Still." Tarzan grunted a confirmation, tightening his shoulder grip.

"You can speak?"

"C'nspik."

"Heavens."

It was perhaps not so much speaking as repeating, Arthur considered, but clearly the man had been taking in a lot more of what was going on around him than he could convey. Arthur was mortified at not having given him more credit, but his moment of self-flagellation was disrupted by the heat of Tarzan's palm pressing down his belly to the hem of his underwear. He shut his eyes, feeling his throat tighten. He must *not* think about how much he longed to feel that hand between his legs.

"Y-yes, that's splendid. Thank you. Let's, um..." Arthur slipped from Tarzan's iron shoulder-grip and shot him a hopeful smile. "Shall we attempt this dressing lark again, please? Perhaps just with the shirt?"

Tarzan's only answer was to whip him round by the shoulders so he was facing away. A low snarl tickled into his ear as a light fingertip traced the outline of a particularly tender spot where he'd crashed into the Welsh dresser at the weekend, after his foot had given way. He found himself whipped round to face Tarzan again, who fixed him with a glare of enquiry and mimed the experience of a savage battle.

"No, no...nothing like that. I've not been thrown about. I'm just... not quite steady on my feet—wh-what are you doing?"

Arthur stared in horror as Tarzan strode over to one of the rude plants with the long, red poles and squeezed the stem roughly with both hands, pulping upwards. Arthur could see the finger-dents in the greenery and felt his life draining away before his eyes. Not only was he entirely failing to get Tarzan into his clothes, he was allowing the man to destroy Jeremiah's collection.

"Please be careful!"

Tarzan ignored him, now squeezing the red pole flower itself. It didn't seem to suffer too badly from Tarzan's grip, though it dripped with goo as Tarzan pulled his hand away. Arthur was once again turned round and felt the slick stickiness applied to his bare upper back. The effect was astonishing. He was aware of a raging heat seeping through him which seemed to warm, but not burn. It relaxed the muscles there, almost as much as the soft roll of the finger pads running beneath his shoulder blade and up and down his spine. The shoulder had been locked so long that the release of the pain there was a sort of ecstasy. Responding only to the growing pleasure, he tilted his head all the way back and moaned up to the ceiling. The heat ran down his spine and between his legs. His erection grew so rapidly, he was left feeling dizzy.

*Get a grip, man. You need this job, do you not?*

*I do.*

*Then why do you not stop this?*

Arthur's resentful side rebelled. *You stop it, then.*

His pious side seemed to have nothing further to offer the inward conversation but the sound of a garden gate slamming had an electric effect upon him. He broke free from Tarzan's grip and sprinted about the conservatory, gathering his clothing. After that first squeal, there was nothing. No banging upon the door, or calls through the letterbox. Arthur allowed himself to relax, feeling bad about Tarzan's expression of hurt resentment. His vast would-be nurse was now pouring a full bucket of water into the pot of the Bastard plant. A dish had been added, Arthur noted, no doubt to catch the fluid that the soil could not hold while the plant began its refuelling exercise. Well, at least he'd learnt something about the amount of fluid the plant truly needed.

Tarzan caught his eye and waved him away.

"I'm sorry to yank away from you like that, but I thought we had a visitor. Can't be seen undressed. It's not the done thing."

"Nrrr." Tarzan waved more vigourously still, now pointing into the hallway.

Lost, Arthur floundered for a solution to the problem of fulfilling his duties. He was ready to resume the Grovel when a searing, puncturing pain filled his loins like lava and he pitched down on his knees, and then sideways. He gripped himself through his drawers, appalled by the agony in his groin and feeling truly faint. The Bastard plant had struck again. Before the sprawl of white and grey stars completely eroded his vision, he could've sworn he saw Tarzan roll his eyes and flick his hands up in exasperation.

LIFE RETURNED IN INCREMENTS. ARTHUR'S brain presented him with an inventory of sensations in descending order of proportion. Overwhelming all, initially, was the bone-deep tenderness in his dick. He tried raising a hand to grasp the extent and means of the damage, but a firm grasp around his shoulders dissuaded him. His memory woke and he recalled a harsh blow to his groin, and Tarzan's annoyance. Arthur groaned. He thought Tarzan had been shooing him away, but he'd been trying to warn him about the imminent unravelling of the Bastard Plant.

*Stupid. Stupid, stupid, stupid.*

Picking up speed, his brain informed him that he was partially sitting, leaning side-on against Tarzan. He felt a strong pulse against his left cheek and a hot arm around him, holding him in place. Cool air caressed Arthur from head to toe, and there must be some sort of blanket or cloth beneath him, because he couldn't feel the cold tiles. Finally, he became aware of a cool, moist, caressing sensation between his legs, and along the length of his cock.

*You're naked.*

He snapped his eyes open and tried raising his head but a firm tap on his forehead oppressed him.

"I'm naked. In a glass house!"

Tarzan tapped him again, his lips set in a firm line.

Arthur could at least be grateful for the high fences around the poky garden behind the conservatory, and the knowledge that the rear windows of the nearest house were quite some way off. It was a sunny day, too. Hopefully reflections would be his friend. He did his best to rest, but couldn't let go his anxiety to be dressed—and have Tarzan dressed—long before Jeremiah got home. He also needed to somehow disguise Tarzan's abuse of Jeremiah's vital plants.

Tarzan drew his finger down the line of hair running from his belly button to the thatch at his groin, almost as if he were marvelling at its softness. Or perhaps its sparseness. Arthur had sandy hair, blond at the temples and nape, but that on his body was a few shades lighter. He lay still as he was inspected, Tarzan using his hand as a comparison tool to note their differences in size, pallor and muscularity. These were many, but Tarzan appeared to like what he saw. He developed a fondness for the ridge that ran under Arthur's pectorals, and the neat line that ran down his middle, separating trim but unremarkable muscles.

A cool touch at his arse made him jolt and he was pinned by the vast arm round his shoulders as Tarzan reached a lower leg between his own, pulling them further apart. The wandering hand moved down to his balls, cupping them lightly.

*Good god, he's holding your balls.*

*I know. He's somewhat casual about it, though. Just trying to get them out of the way so that odd nectar can work. Don't worry, I shan't read too much into it.*

Arthur's inner cynic rolled his eyes. *We both know it's rather too late for that.*

That distant feeling of being caressed between the legs became a real, intense thing. It was like being licked through a layer of something cool and liquid. The same light sensation played over the tip of his cock, which nudged from its foreskin in a series of timid, intrigued little throbs. The swelling hurt—one part of him on the underside felt deeply bruised as if punctured—but alongside the ache was the delicious, dubious pleasure of the wet nuzzling sensation.

A glance at the floor showed a pot containing a nasty, bloodied barb. He looked away, not wanting to think about Tarzan having to pluck that out of him. The smooching and rude plants must have anaesthetic properties; after being assaulted by the Bastard Plant, Miller had been out cold for hours. He, however, seemed to be recovering rapidly.

He released a long sigh, postponing the moment when he'd be forced to think about what was happening to him. He was being molested by greenery, and he was mysteriously happy about it. The cool nectar reminded him of what came from the smooch plant, but he didn't remember it having such long stems, or the little buds being so...lively. It was almost as if the need for heat moved petals. There was plenty of heat between his legs.

The light tickle at his arse became a press and he gasped as the central cone of the little yellow flowers entered, teasing him, no more. His legs seemed to spread of their own accord. He found the strength to push up from his heels and lift his hips an inch or so, craving deeper, broader, harder penetration. He knew that his face and chest had flushed red and he bit his lip to suppress a groan as his cock surged all the more forcefully to erection. It hurt like the blazes—and little wonder, given the viciousness of the barb that been pulled from it—but not quite enough to counteract his arousal. If anything, the pain enhanced his tumescence.

Tarzan looked amused now. Amused, but glad, glowing with a strange sort of pride in the pleasure the little flowers brought.

Arthur wondered how Tarzan had come to know about the hedonistic and healing properties of this plant. He pictured the man staggering into a bushel of them after some hectic fight with a vicious creature and dropping on his back to rest. Perhaps he'd lain there awhile with no notions to do anything but sleep, but soon found himself panting up to the canopies of the sky as the flowers sought out the heat of his body, suckling round his cock, balls, nipples and neck.

And what of those pole plants with their fat, hard flowers?

How had Tarzan come to the conclusion that squeezing them would release that nectar which had made such short work of the intolerable stiffness of the muscles?

He pictured Tarzan's mighty arms spread across a rocky escarpment of some sort—perhaps the side of a cave—his fingers digging into the rock as he lowered himself onto the head of one of those plants. He looked delicious, every muscle standing out in sharp relief as he raised and lowered himself on the balls of his feet, head tipped all the way back, his guttural cries of pleasure rising to the roof of a forest otherwise bare of humanity.

Arthur's hand had moved to his cock without his direction or consent. He winced at his first impulsive squeeze, but the little yellow flowers had wrought their miracle. His cock, usually a neat, functional pipe, throbbed and swelled as it had never done before. A pressure and nudge against the side of his upper chest announced the emergence of Tarzan's own erection.

The ape man's face now gleamed with more than casual interest in his new friend's body. His hand closed over Arthur's, and Arthur gasped at the extra pressure as they stroked up and down in tandem, the bigger hand fully in charge. The soreness was almost too much. Arthur slipped his own hand away and Tarzan continued to stroke, eyes wide with fascination and enjoyment.

Between the suckling of the persistent yellow plants, his captivity at Tarzan's hands and the increasing need to be filled hard and fast, Arthur surrendered to his lust, emitting a ceaseless stream of open-mouthed moans.

Abruptly Tarzan scrambled out from beneath him, putting him back on the floor. Arthur's head snapped up from the blanket beneath him and he watched in dismay as Tarzan sprinted across the tiles. The fear that he'd upset the big man in some way gave way to cold terror as Tarzan yanked one of the red poles from its pot and scrabbled back over to him, ripping the green covering of the stem away to show a woody core, like bamboo.

As Tarzan knelt between his legs and his plans for the pole-plant became clear, Arthur's cock pulsed and puddled its hot, clear fluid into the shallow basin of his navel. Tarzan parted Arthur's legs further, then stroked the red head of the plant once again, making it glisten. The flower was perhaps seven inches from stem to tip, Tarzan's fingers just barely overlapping his thumb as he clutched around its width.

Arthur was seized by the worry that the flower could break off inside him, but Tarzan seemed to sense his anxiety. He used it for a moment as a stroking tool. Arthur lay absolutely still as Tarzan held the very end of the stalk and brushed the cool, faintly abrasive tip of the "flower" from one nipple to the other and back again. It seemed that the flower was little more than an explosion of soft, colourful fibres from the woody stem itself. As Arthur gradually relaxed, Tarzan removed the flower from his torso and placed the tip of it lightly against the pulsing bud of his arse.

It was without warning that Tarzan pushed the flower deep inside and Arthur released a howl that echoed around the conservatory, gripping the blanket in both fists as he was taken swiftly and deeply by the slick plant. He panted, barely able to wrap his mind around the fact of his penetration. But then the heat of the nectar made its presence known, tingling against that special spot inside him, sinking into every muscle. He cried out again and again with the pleasure of it, even as the intruding stalk remained still, save for a slight twisting of Tarzan's wrist from one side to the other. Arthur wished his arms and ankles could be bound, so he'd be held defenceless as the plant was slammed in and out of him, stretching him at the entrance, delighting him with its bruising presence deep within.

Tarzan read his mind, pumping slowly at first but picking up momentum, seemingly driven by Arthur's helpless moans as he was taken with force. Between the resumed suckling of the yellow buds at his most intimate parts, his powerful ravishment and the beauty of the man making him a slave to his own senses, Arthur grew delirious. Pain twined with pleasure, jerking him to a peak, and just as he feared he might swoon before reaching completion, Tarzan covered Arthur's puny body with his mighty one, resting a hand on the ground by Arthur's head, then latched his mouth against a point low on his neck.

The suction on that point combined with a harsh press of the stem deep within, sending the orgasm crashing through his whole body, bouncing him against the ground, making his chest and belly too tiny a platform for the hot liquid that burst from his cock. He seemed to spurt and spurt as if he hadn't been touched for a decade, and all the while Tarzan chewed at that delicate, bruised spot, prolonging the pleasure, sensitising the skin. Marking him.

It was some considerable time before he was capable of movement and he was still limp as the flower was drawn from his body. He could not yet speak. He followed Tarzan's progress around the room as the savage lord made some rudimentary attempts to clear up their area of congress. With some astonishment, he watched Tarzan take the flower and casually repot it alongside the other buds. Laughter rippled softly from him and a little energy returned. He pressed himself up upright and glanced at the clock. He still had an hour to get Tarzan dressed.

Though exhausted, he felt more limber as he pulled his undergarments back on, and then his trousers. To hope for those plants to cure for whatever ailed him was an insanity, but he had observed their power as a palliative. The knowledge that he might get relief from the twitches, muscle failure and stiffness gave him a levity of heart he hadn't felt for a year or so. He might even summon the courage to finally see a physician and either confirm or deny his suspicion that he was developing the Parkinson's disease that had taken his father. Anything seemed manageable with the pain-shattering promise of those plants, and Tarzan's companionship.

He caught the big man's smiling eyes and pointed at the plants. "I hardly dare ask how you know about the healing powers of those things."

In his first ever burst of anything approaching conversation, Tarzan performed a magnificent pantomime of gestures through which Arthur surmised that he'd dropped from trees into a pit, and been attacked by a vicious creature of uncertain identity. He'd been left in a shocking state.

"Sabor," Tarzan explained mournfully, doing an excellent tiger impression and indicating the claw marks that ran across his back.

"Tiger?"

Tarzan nodded vigourously, happy at being understood. "Tiy-ger."

Arthur gave Tarzan's bare shoulder a sympathetic pat. "I know this move's been hard for you, but some things are good. You'll be amazed at how few tigers you'll find in Wandsworth."

"Few...tigers?" Tarzan gave a smile that could've been seen across the channel on a clear day.

Arthur was moved to laughter by Tarzan's expression of delighted relief. "Right. Now, I—we—need to get dressed." Leaving nothing to chance, he enacted a pantomime of his own, clearly depicting their respective fates if Jeremiah were to return to find Tarzan padding around in a continued state of semi-dress.

The sound of the key in the lock froze Arthur's blood in his veins. He met Tarzan's eyes in a panic. "Oh...hell."

"Bugger," Tarzan offered, perfectly imitating Miller.

No amount of emergency dressing could get Arthur in any state to be seen as Jeremiah led another fellow down the hall and into the conservatory. Already a ruddy-faced man, Jeremiah went almost purple to see his manservant in a state of undress as well as his feral charge, who was standing in the very place he wasn't supposed to be—the conservatory. Jeremiah raised a hand shaking with rage and pointed it into Arthur's face.

"You...are finished."

Arthur didn't have time to answer and didn't know what he'd say in his defence if he did. The gentleman behind Jeremiah pushed past with an expression of rapt wonder and strode straight into the conservatory, kneeling by the yellow-budded flower on the ground.

"I say. I've heard talk of these, but thought it was just that. Talk. I've heard of the nectar from these being used to help in the treatment of gout."

"It's good for bruises," Arthur said, looking down as Jeremiah shot a fulminating glare at him.

Their visitor, who seemed oblivious to both the tense atmosphere and his state of undress, darted a friendly smile up at him. "Good to know. Thank you." He stood, offering his hand. "I'm Doctor Porter. Botanist, not medic." He turned to Tarzan. "And this would be the prodigal Lord Greystoke?"

Tarzan frowned as his hand was seized and pumped up and down, but let it happen, doing little more than shooting a glance of confusion at Arthur.

"You still seem to be here," Jeremiah observed, putting extra loathing into his stare. "What in God's name were you doing? How dare you strut about unclad?"

Misery welled in Arthur's chest. He was inclined not to answer, given that he'd already been dismissed, but saw a potential ally in Doctor Porter, who was peering at Jeremiah in shocked surprise. Arthur tried putting a little conviction into his voice. "I was trying to teach him how to dress. By example."

"Hasn't worked, has it? You're a poor excuse for a teacher of civilisation. Bally man won't even speak." Jeremiah stared at the carnage of the snapped aloe plant. "And what the blazes happened here?"

Porter chuckled. "Oh, never mind that. It'll re-grow. You're meant to snap the leaves. It's how one removes the sap. Might I take the plants away now, Jerry?"

"Mmm? Yes. Yes of course."

Porter bent to pick up the red-pole plant, beaming in satisfaction. "My Jane will love this one."

Tarzan had been hanging back but now leapt forward, snatching at the pot. He yanked out the flower that still had the green coating over the stem and handed it to Porter, putting the pot behind him.

"Oh, a cutting? Yes...um. Well. I can work with that, absolutely. And might I take a cutting of the yellow one, too?"

Tarzan understood the hand gestures if not all the words, and tugged a few of the yellow stems from their pot, shoving them into a smaller, empty container. By way of softening his aggressive stance, he handed over the Bastard Plant in its entirety, a pleasant smile lighting up his face. Arthur would've laughed if he wasn't so miserable about his dismissal. He straightened his shirt, doing the buttons, but not before Jeremiah noted the bite.

"What in God's name is that?"

"I'm dismissed, sir, so I reserve the right to not tell you." He barely raised a flicker of a smile for Tarzan and trudged off to the front door. "Please ask Miller if he'll deliver my possessions to my mother's address."

He'd taken no more than three paces before a giant arm wrapped him round the waist, bringing him to a halt.

Arthur patted the huge forearm. "I've been told to go, Tarzan."

"Friend."

"Fired," Jeremiah corrected.

Tarzan whipped round to face his uncle, his torso broadening and vibrating with the growl that passed through it. He pointed to the plants, and then to Jeremiah and Porter. "Yours."

Jeremiah stared. "You spoke!"

"I say, that's marvellous," Porter announced.

Tarzan hauled Arthur in front of him, the forearm clamped across his shoulders. "Mine."

"The lad's clearly good for him," Porter said. "Marvellous civilising influence."

Tarzan snatched Arthur's jacket and tried to get it on. His display of willing impressed, even if the jacket's fit did not. Jeremiah gave consent to Arthur's continued employment by not arguing. As he and Porter carried the various plant specimens out to the Daimler, delighting Miller by removing the Bastard from the property, Tarzan sloped back to the conservatory, pulling Arthur with him.

Arthur sighed as Tarzan broke off another aloe leaf and squeezed the sap straight into his mouth. "It's going to be a sod of a job keeping you out of this room, isn't it?"

"Sod...room," Tarzan agreed.

"*Please* don't repeat that first word."

"Bed...room?"

Grinning, Arthur swept an arm towards the stairs. "That's a much better word."

# THE CROP OF CONTRIBUTORS

M. Arbon lives and writes in Toronto. They are a regular contributor to the online gay fiction webzine *Shousetsu Bang\*Bang* under the name Hyakunichisou 13.

Evey Brett lives among prickly plants like saguaro cacti, ocotillo and the vicious jumping cholla in the desert of Southern Arizona thanks to her Lipizzan mare, Carrma, who wanted a human to look after her during her retirement. Evey's had numerous erotica publications with Lethe Press in anthologies such as *Threesome* and with Cleis Press in *Best Gay Erotica of the Year 2016 & 2017*. You can find more of her work at eveybrett.wordpress.com

L.A. Fields is the author of The Disorder Series, the short story collection *Countrycide*, the Lambda Award finalist *My Dear Watson*, and *Homo Superiors*, a modern retelling of Chicago's Leopold and Loeb crime.

Keith Glaeske is a medievalist and collector of speculative fiction living in Washington, DC. His articles about medieval literature have been published in *Medieval Perspectives, Traditio, Ériu,* and *SELIM: Journal of the Spanish Society for Medieval English Language and Literature.* He regularly reviews books for *Chelsea Station Magazine, Lambda Literary Review,* and *Out in Print.*

John Linwood Grant lives in Yorkshire with a pack of lurchers and a beard. He may also have a family. He writes a range of supernatural, horror and speculative tales, some of which are actually published. You can find him every week on his website which celebrates weird fiction and weird art, greydogtales.com, often with his dogs.

Lawrence Jackson has written *Misadventure in Space and Time* (a sort of madcap queer spin on the work of H.G. Wells) and *Muscle Worshippers* (intended as an erotic gay take on *Rosemary's Baby*). His short fiction has appeared in such anthologies as *Threesome* and *Geeky Boys, Freaky Boys.*

PHILLIP JOY is currently a PhD student in gay men's health. He lives in Nova Scotia with his partner and two world-travelling teddy bears named Wallace and Sizzle. "Yellow Buttons in a Glass Forest" is his first published story.

SPENCER KRELL has had a passion for writing his entire life, with a preferred genre of historical fiction (though he also enjoys erotica). No matter the genre, he strives to write unique pieces which transgress boundaries and reader expectations. When he's not writing, he enjoys reading a wide array of novels, watching Netflix, and attending drag shows. The Greenhouse is his first published piece of erotic fiction. He hopes to sell more in the foreseeable future. If you wish to contact him, you can find him on Twitter @spencerkrell.

C.B. LEWIS is a Scottish writer who will happily write anything once, just to see whether it can be done. She has been telling stories since childhood and writing since she learned her letters. Her first novel was published in 2015 and she is currently ears deep in the middle of writing the third, fourth and fifth novels of a five-part time-travel series.

DALE CAMERON LOWRY lives in the Upper Midwest with a partner and three cats, one of whom enjoys eating dish towels, quilts, and wool socks. It's up to you to guess whether the fabric eater is one of the cats or the partner. When not busy mending items destroyed by the aforementioned fabric eater, Dale enjoys gardening, listening to podcasts, studying botany, getting annoyed at Duolingo, and reading fairy tales. You can find more of Dale's speculative and paranormal erotica at dalecameronlowry.com.

A native New Yorker, JAMES PENHA has lived for the past quarter-century in Indonesia. Nominated for Pushcart Prizes in fiction and poetry, his LGBT speculative story "Leaves," also set in Indonesia, was a finalist for the Saints and Sinners Short Fiction Contest and so appears in the *Saint & Sinners Literary Festival 2017* anthology. His essay "It's Been a Long Time Coming" was featured in *The New York Times* "Modern Love" column in April 2016. Penha edits *TheNewVerse.News*, an online journal of current-events poetry. On Twitter he can be found: @JamesPenha

ROBERT RUSSIN daydreams about having a garden and a family with a man who vanished. Stories like this sprout from that scorched earth. He lives in the Bronx.

SAM THORNE is an editor, ghost-writer and semi-successful feller of trees from West Sussex, England. After years of enjoying everyone else's steamy stories—albeit with red pen in hand—Sam was finally bullied into overcoming writer's stage fright by a bossy friend last year. Favourite hobbies other than writing include cooking and unfair-rules football.

CONNIE WILKINS began with Marion Zimmer Bradley's *Fantasy Magazine*, Bruce Coville's anthologies for kids, *Strange Horizons,* and various similar publications. Then she was seduced by the erotic side of the force, publishing scores of erotic stories as her alter-ego Sacchi Green and editing fifteen anthologies, including two Lambda Literary Award winners. Now and then she gets to cross genres, editing *Time Well Bent: Queer Alternative Histories* and co-editing *Heiresses of Russ 2012: The Year's Best Lesbian Speculative Fiction* with Steve Berman, both for Lethe Press. She also writes the occasional erotic sf/f for Circlet Press, and has edited most recently, for Cleis Press, *Witches, Princesses, and Women at Arms: Lesbian Fairy Tale Erotica.* Connie lives in western Massachusetts, retreats whenever possible to the mountains of New Hampshire, and makes regular forays into the more-or-less real world for readings in NYC, Boston, Provincetown, and anywhere else she can get to without too much effort. Online she's at sacchi-green.blogspot.com and on Facebook.

# ABOUT THE EDITOR

Steve Berman has edited more books of queer speculative fiction than anyone alive or dead. Berman spent most of his adult life in New Jersey, which happens to be the Garden State.

9 781590 213063